DEATH IN S

By

Bernie Steadman

First published in 2015 by Bloodhound Books

Re-printed 2018 by Bloodhound Books

Print ISBN 978-1-912604-35-7

For Stuart

Chapter 1

Date: Sunday 23rd April Time: 01:47 East Devon

The driver flicks off the headlights, killing the puddle of light. He puts the vehicle into neutral and lets it coast to a stop at the kerb.

Two men get out of the vehicle, leaving their doors open, and move to the rear, pressing their hands against the cold metal of the rear doors as they twist the handles. A girl lies curled amongst the detritus in the back of the vehicle, her white skin reflecting the silver sliver of a spring moon. The taller man picks her up, cradling her head, and follows the smaller figure through the trampled green netting into the stand of bent and beaten pine trees.

He places the girl carefully behind a fallen log and the other man covers her with a leafy branch he tears from a tree.

Back at the vehicle, the smaller man notices the girl's shoe, a flat, black ballerina slipper lying in the mud on the side of the road. He retrieves it, folds it in half and thrusts it into his hoodie pocket. 'She'll be safe there for a little while,' he whispers. The other man does not reply, but wipes sweat from his face with the bottom of his tee shirt.

Starting the engine, they creep forward, only switching on the headlights as they turn onto the main road.

Hours later, a shaft of early sunlight like the beam of a lazy torch searches the patch of pine trees. It passes over golden highlights in a curl of dark hair half-buried in a nest of needles and cones. A bird sings in the still of the morning. A black-eyed magpie sidles over and makes a tentative stab at the onyx and silver ring on the girl's finger. Her face turned into the bed of pine needles, the girl lies on her side under the broken branch, as if simply asleep.

'Gi's a fag, then, Parker.' Lee Bateson leapt onto Parker's back and grappled him to the ground, pummelling at his head.

Joey Parker squirmed out from underneath in a tangle of skinny legs and arms. 'Gerroff me. I haven't got any smokes, so...' He swung an arm back and grabbed Bateson by the tie, throttling him while the other boy floundered, gasping and wriggling to get free.

'Leave it out, lads,' said a voice from the other side of the barbed wire fence.

Parker dropped Bateson and scuttled over to stand next to the bigger boy.

'Just messin', Ryan. Got any fags?'

'Might 'ave. Come on.'

Ryan Carr disappeared amongst the conifers of a small, dense wood fenced off at the top of the school field. The others dumped their bags and slipped after him through the broken fence, casting furtive glances towards the school buildings.

Joey Parker checked his phone as he followed. Not eight-thirty yet, just about time to cadge a smoke and get to registration before they were missed.

Carr waited by the clearing, kicking a dead crow with his boot. He fiddled about in his blazer pocket and fished out two cigarettes, passing one to Bateson and keeping one for himself. He slid a lighter from his sock and lit them.

Bateson shared a complicit smirk with Carr, who puffed in quiet contentment, then wandered off to sit on the fallen log dominating the small clearing. Carr went to sit, but stopped mid-movement, cigarette hanging from his bottom lip. He stared at a curl of hair peeking out from the side of the log.

Bateson trotted over.

'What is it? Let me see,' he said, words trailing a haze of smoke. He pushed past Carr and handed his cigarette to a grateful Parker. He moved closer, and flashed a look back at the other boys, eyes wide, as a he saw a magpie behind the log picking at something on the ground, its black beak stabbing. Bateson's eyes narrowed to a single focus no more than six feet away. It was a ripped and shredded finger, and near it, the remains of an eye, hanging by who knew what, to a dark, empty socket.

Bateson stared, mesmerised by the whiteness of bone protruding from the bloodiness of flesh and the pinkness of the string attaching eyeball to socket and the shining silver ring the magpie was attempting to steal.

Closer now, Carr leapt backwards startling the magpie into a defiant caw as it flapped for the sky.

Dread gripped Lee Bateson. It was obvious now what would be under the branch. He knew. But he couldn't stop himself. He had to look.

Behind him, Parker threw up the Weetabix he had consumed not an hour before.

'No, it can't be...' Lee Bateson dragged the branch away, exposing the still and silent form of Carly Braithwaite.

Detective Inspector Dan Hellier hurtled across Topsham Road, ignoring the red traffic lights, and ducked down Trew's Weir Reach to the echo of an angry lorry's horn. The new bike was living up to the hype. He grinned and stood into the pedals, powering the bike up to speed, hitting 25mph as he took a sharp right followed by an equally sharp left across Trew's Weir Bridge and onto the cycle path. Morning air crisp in his nostrils, he breathed deeply, relishing the peace of this stretch of river. Trees were springing green after a long winter, and the River Exe, wide and shallow at this point, rolled along beside him. Swallows, newly returned and hungry, raced with him past the apartments and waterfront houses of Exeter's quayside, looking for insects.

Thighs pumping, Dan pushed himself for the last few hundred metres and slewed to a halt outside his apartment building, heart working hard. He tapped his stopwatch. It read nine thirty-two a.m. Thirty-four minutes to do the circular route. Better than yesterday morning. He climbed off the bike and let it rest against a bench. Gulping air, he wiped his face with his jersey and stared into the green water, transported for a moment back to childhood summers when he and his skinny, pale friends would play and swim in the river all day. He looked around, as if he could see them still, but that all felt like a very long time ago. Things had moved on. There were only strangers there now.

Dan shook off the start of a sombre mood and stretched out his shoulders and legs. He had a nice flat in a great part of Exeter, what on earth was he getting miserable about? The café on the opposite side of the river had been baking. He could smell croissants across the water and hear his stomach rumbling in appreciation. He turned away from the water and looked up at his flat, situated on the corner with its own balcony overlooking the bustle of the quayside pubs and restaurants. It was good. He'd have been lost in the countryside after so many years in London's noise and craziness. It wasn't the spacious Victorian flat he had owned in London, true, but it suited his needs. His single needs.

His phone vibrated against his back. Dan unhooked his helmet, dangled it from the handlebars, and took the phone from the back pocket of his cycling jersey. Dammit, Sally Ellis. He thumbed the slide across; 'It's my day off.' He walked the bike towards the doorway to the flats, steadying his breathing.

'Sir? Is that you?'

'Yes, Sally, it's me, hoping this is really important.'

'Oh, I don't think you'll be disappointed. Chief Superintendent Oliver's asking for you. A body's been found.'

Dan stopped mid-walk.

'Suspicious?'

'Oh, yes. Young girl, in the woods at the back of a school playing field. Kids found the body. Scene is being secured now. DCI Gould is on his way and you're to head straight over there. I'll text you the details.'

Dan flushed, bending forward to catch his breath. Gasbag Gould, of all people.

'Is he going to be leading on the case, Sal?'

'Don't *think* so, but you'd better talk to the boss. She's waiting for your call.'

Dan raised his head and stared back towards the weir in the distance. Ducks and swans squabbled for bread to the delight of a screaming toddler. Runners and cyclists sped past, enjoying the spring morning. He breathed out. First case in charge, if he was in charge.

'Are you breathing heavily down the phone at me, sir? Sort of panting?'

'Only in your dreams, Sergeant Ellis.'

Sally laughed. 'There was I thinking you were harbouring lustful thoughts.'

'You're way out of my league, Sal,' he chuckled. 'Tell the Superintendent I'm on my way. And now get off my phone - I need a quick shower first. I don't think she'd be impressed if I turned up in Lycra.'

'Now, there's an image I'll have to inwardly digest,' she replied, and rang off.

Dan locked his bike in the hallway, and took the stairs to his apartment two at a time, excitement and nerves vying with the hunger in his empty stomach.

Twenty minutes later, Dan was splayed flat on his front with his left arm wedged under the bed up to the shoulder. He was sure he'd kicked his shoe under there the night before. His phone rang. He rolled onto his back, squeezed the phone out of his trouser pocket and looked at the screen, Superintendent Oliver. He scrambled to his feet.

'Ma'am?'

'DI Hellier, where are you?'

'At home, Ma'am. I'm almost ready…'

'Save it, I know it's your day off, but I need you. Get your notebook.' She waited.

Dan reached over to the other side of the bed and grabbed notebook and pen.

'Got it, Ma'am.'

Two slices of toast popped up and their warm scent wafted through from the kitchen. His stomach rumbled again.

'Right, so far we know the victim is a teenage girl. No obvious cause of death on first look, so it's not murder until the pathologist arrives and confirms either way. The PC first on the scene has made a preliminary ID. Seems she knew the girl.' She hesitated and he could hear her pen tapping the paper, 'Deceased is a Carly Braithwaite, age sixteen. Just bringing up her address. I'll text it to you.'

'It's OK, Ma'am, Sergeant Ellis has sent over the details already, and I know the way to St Andrew's.'

What he really wanted to know was where he stood in relation to Ian Gould, but he couldn't think of a way to phrase it without sounding whiny. 'Ma'am?'

'What?'

Here goes nothing, he thought. 'Is DCI Gould leading? Because I thought the next major case was mine, but if he's already at the scene…' He drifted to a halt. Whiny, definitely.

'Oh, got you. No, Inspector, that's the whole point of me getting you in on your day off and bringing you up-to-date. This will be your first lead.'

His heart did a sideways lurch. Leading the case, and with a possible murder to solve. Christmas come early!

'But before you get all gushy and start imagining your face on the evening news,' she continued, 'DCI Gould will be with you all the way. Acting as your senior support and sharing the load. Especially as the silly pillock has messed up the rosters in your unit and let two Sergeants and a DC go on leave in the same week.'

Right, so Dan was 'in charge' but he'd have Gould breathing down his neck the whole time. Great.

'I have got Sergeant Ellis, Ma'am, and a couple of good lower ranks. With all due respect, I don't think I need to be supervised. Except by you, of course.'

He stumbled to a halt and listened to the change in her breathing, and the speed of her pen tapping.

'With all 'due respect', Inspector, this is DCI Gould's last shout before he retires. You'll work with him and enable him to slope off in three weeks feeling good about himself, or I'll make your life such a misery you'll be begging for yet another transfer and your fledgling career will go right down the toilet. Is that enough 'respect' for you?'

Dan sank onto the bed, face burning.

'Yes, Ma'am. Sorry. Just wondering.'

'I'll bet you were.' Her tone changed. Back to business. 'Everything you do comes straight to me, Inspector, no keeping stuff to yourself and giving me nasty surprises. Let's keep this one clean and tidy. Right, I think that's all for now, you know the ropes. Off you pop, then. Back here for five o'clock briefing.' She didn't say goodbye.

Dan stared at the phone for a second. Tough but fair, they said at the Station. Well, straightforward, that was certain.

Frustrated, he pulled the bed away from the wall and finally located his shoe. The toast cooled to inedible leathery cardboard in the toaster as he slammed the front door behind him.

Chapter 2

Date: Monday 24th April Time: 10:07 St Andrew's Academy, Exeter

By seven minutes past ten, Detective Chief Inspector Ian Gould was resting his bulk against the reception desk at St Andrew's Academy and chatting to the receptionist. He sighed when he heard the siren blasting away as Hellier arrived with a scream of tyres into the car park.

Dan switched off the siren, jumped out of his Audi and surveyed the school frontage. Situated on the eastern edge of the city outskirts, five miles from the centre, this was practically a country school. Low rise and low key at the entrance, he could see evidence of new building further on the site. He thought it probably took its catchment from a mix of farms, the large estates at Whipton and the villages of East Devon. Almost a thousand students, and over a hundred staff, Sally had said; a successful school. This could be a mess if it's murder. He corrected himself; the death of a child was always a mess, wherever it occurred. He locked the car door and made his way into the reception area.

'Alright?' Gould said, eyeing Dan's damp hair and red face.

'Cycling,' Dan replied. He signed in and smiled at the receptionist as she let them through the double doors into the corridor.

Gould pursed his lips. 'The boss says you're leading on this case. You know I'm retiring in a few weeks?'

Dan glanced across at him, unable to gauge the DCI's mood.

'Yeah, that's what she said.'

Gould stopped in the mid-lesson quiet of the corridor and regarded his hands. 'I know you all think I'm past it and it's time I was put out to grass. Maybe I am. But you will show me respect on this case, DI Hellier. I am still your senior officer.' He stared Dan down. 'And you, you're just a smart-arsed kid up from London, really, aren't you? Got it all to prove.' He placed his forefinger in the centre of Dan's chest. 'Everything you do goes through me.' Jab. 'No sneaking to the boss behind my back.' Jab. 'We're a team.' Jab. 'OK?'

Dan swallowed the flash of heat that being poked in the chest had ignited. He wanted this job, needed it.

'Got it, sir,' he said in as neutral a tone as he could manage.

Gould studied him. 'Right. So don't mess up.' He offered half a smile. 'You'd better follow me then. The crime scene's a quarter-hour walk away.'

Dan followed him through the building and out onto the play area. He'd recovered a little since the earlier phone call with Superintendent Oliver. Once it became clear that he would be working with Gould whatever he felt about it, he'd backed down swiftly. The alternative was a transfer - another transfer, he corrected himself.

Oliver had also told him that everything he did had to go through her. What was it they said about a man serving two masters? He sighed, his earlier excitement at leading the case waning into resignation. He was the newbie, with everything to prove, no matter what he had achieved in London.

Gould tramped along for a few moments, grumbling. He hurried to match Dan's stride, puffing and wheezing. 'I don't suppose anyone would care if I ended up with a heart attack.'

In the distance, Dan could see black and yellow tape and two figures in uniform at the far end of the large playing field. 'Probably should have shut the school,' he offered.

'Yeah, it's happening. Buses will be arriving back from their depots within the hour. Teachers are doing lessons as normal and will send the classes out one at a time. Better control that way. The headteacher would prefer it to stay open, of course.'

A young police constable, who identified herself as Lizzie Singh came down the field to meet them. She gave her report as they walked towards the wood. 'I got the call just before eight forty-five this morning. The deceased was discovered by three boys who had nipped up to the wood for a cigarette, like they do most days. When I arrived, I got the older of the three, a Ryan Carr, to lead me back to the body. I then called it in and began to secure the scene.' She stopped walking before they reached the wooded area and looked at her superior officers.

Gould made an expansive gesture towards Dan and stepped back.

Singh nodded and turned to Dan. 'I knew Carly, sir,' she said. 'I was able to identify the body. She was a member of our Youth Matters group. She won "Exeter's Got Talent" at Christmas.'

'What's that? Local talent show?'

Singh snorted. 'Bit more than that. The winner gets a recording session and the last two have gone on to get a contract. It's quite well-thought of in the music industry.'

'So she was that good?'

'Yes, she was a good kid all round, really. Bit loud, bit opinionated, but a fantastic singer.' She grimaced, close to tears. 'It's so sad, a young girl dead when she had so much to live for.' She sniffed and blew her nose on a tissue. 'Sorry. I've asked the school nurse to sit with the younger sister, Jenna, until her dad comes to collect her. He's a builder so he's got to get back from Newton Abbot. There's no mother at home, apparently. Mr Braithwaite has brought the girls up.'

'Does Jenna know what's happened to her sister?' asked Dan.

'No, only that we have news, and she's to wait until her father arrives. She told me that Carly didn't go home last night.'

'Right, good summary, PC Singh,' said Dan. 'I don't want to break the news to the family in school. Could you ask Mr Braithwaite to drive Jenna home and tell him we'll be round to talk to them as soon as possible?'

'Yes, sir, of course.'

Lizzie led them over a broken barbed wire fence towards a clearing where the forensics team had set up shop. 'It's not great in the woods, sir,' she said. 'Someone's been shooting crows and there are half a dozen dead ones on the ground. The maggots have been busy. The floor is mainly pine needles so no footprints to speak of. There's loads of rubbish everywhere, too. Typical kids' mess - fag ends, tobacco pouches, sandwich wrappers. Forensics are all over it, and the pathologist is waiting for you.'

Gould winked at her. 'Good job, Lizzie.'

Dan stared at the DCI. He'd winked at a female PC. What century did he come from? He'd never get away with that in the Met. He shook his head as PC Singh handed them their protective clothing.

Gould complained through the entire process of getting into the protective suit, irritating Dan, who had got into his suit with ease. He felt obliged to wait for Gould to make yet another attempt to close the zip before they could head into the crime scene.

They followed the designated path through the trees, pulling on latex gloves. Doctor Campbell Fox, the pathologist, was sitting on a log, writing up his notes. 'Aha! It's the cavalry at last. I was ready to lie down next to the wee lassie myself.' He stopped and did an obvious double take. 'Ian Gould! I thought you'd retired to Budleigh Salterton or another one of God's waiting rooms.'

Gould laughed and shook Fox's hand. 'It's been way too long Cam, you old bear. Still fly-fishing? Still not managed to catch yourself a wife?'

Dan ignored them and studied the clearing and the position of the tent that protected the body. He wouldn't approach until the pathologist gave him the nod, so he was trying to work out how the girl might have arrived at the wood. It was a nightmare of a crime scene, as PC Singh had said. He picked out a path through to the school playing fields, and one that seemed to lead to a narrow lane that ran alongside the school grounds. It was unlikely she would have entered via the school, too public. They were bound to have CCTV on the main gates, though, so he could check.

The DCI and his mate were still standing there joking with a dead girl lying just a couple of feet away. Dan shook his head for the second time that day. He wanted to shout at Gould, *Get your priorities right, man*, but common sense compressed his lips into a flat line. He ignored their banter until he heard his name.

'This is Detective Inspector Hellier,' said Gould, 'Dan Hellier. He's leading on this case – his first and my last. Dan, this is Dr Campbell Fox, the best, well, probably the only, leading pathologist to come out of the Gorbals. He is the expert. Be glad we've got him.'

Dan turned, took in the vast girth, height and beard for the first time, and felt a bit overwhelmed. Standing at just less than six feet, Dan felt short compared to this giant.

'Pleasure to meet you, sir.' He put out a hand and felt it disappear into the moist softness of Fox's latex-covered paw. Together they ducked under the flap of the tent and Dan experienced the familiar feeling of cold, of quiet stillness that being in the presence of death always brought. Even Gould was quiet.

Fox turned the girl onto her back. Dan knelt and studied her face, close enough to see each eyelash on the good eye, far enough away to ignore the gaping darkness where her other eye should have been. She had dark hair and pale skin, just like him. She was slender, and tall, just like him. She could be his sister.

He breathed rapidly through his nose. It had been the substance of his nightmares for years, that one day he would be called to a crime scene and it would be Alison lying there, white and silent instead of this girl. Although, in Alison's case, the cause of death would be only too easy to read in the mad dance of tracks that would, by now, be pocking every available vein in her body. He shook the thoughts of his sister away. Not now.

Dan pulled back a lock of hair from Carly Braithwaite's face. There was so little damage, it was hard to see how she had died. Would it have been better for everybody if Alison had died, he thought, early on in her chosen career of addict, thief and prostitute, before she'd become welded into the life? He and his parents could have grieved then, and shared good memories. As it was, the only time they heard from her was when she was begging for money, or had broken into the house and taken it.

He often wondered if it was the regular police visits when he was a boy, bringing Alison home drunk, or high on who knew what, the tension and relief mingling with his mother's tears, and the calmness and kindness of the officers, that had made him want to join up and become a police officer.

Gould winked at Fox from his position outside the tent. 'Straight to work, eh? Nice to see them keen when they're young and green.'

Fox laughed briefly. 'Well, gentlemen, you already know who she is. All the personal stuff can be read in my report at your leisure. No obvious cause of death, but there are faint marks on her neck and face which may indicate asphyxiation.'

Fox bent a knee and used Dan's shoulder to steady himself as he knelt next to the body. With some delicacy and precision, he pulled back the top of Carly Braithwaite's hoody to expose her white neck.

'I draw your attention to the faint bruise marks on the front of the neck. Such marks may indicate pressure from a forearm, perhaps. She wasn't strangled in the way you would understand such a term, with fingers round the throat. No ligature used.' He pulled up the sleeve of her t-shirt. 'There are bruises on the upper arms, consistent with being held around the biceps. The eye appears to have been dislodged by a crow or magpie post-mortem. I don't think it relates to her death. She was fully clothed except for one shoe, and there is no bag, phone, purse or anything else personal in the immediate area.'

Dan noticed that Fox lost his strong Glaswegian accent when he was in professional mode. Seven years at medical school in Edinburgh would do that to a man. He'd lost his own Devon burr after three years with the Met. It didn't do to give people too much ammunition.

'Any idea what time she might have died?'

Fox pushed himself up and sat on the log to gather his notes. 'Rigor Mortis has set in, so at least twelve hours ago, but I'll know more when we get her back to the hospital. She has got some pooling of the blood suggesting she was either carried here and dumped, or moved within the copse to hide her. That's what forensics are doing now, trying to work out if she was brought here post-mortem, and if so, how.'

Dan stood up and stepped back outside to join Gould.

'D'you know what I hated most about working Vice?' he asked.

'I didn't know you had,' said Gould.

'It was finding girls like this. I could cope with the whores and the druggies, but young kids found like this, in the wrong place, at the wrong time…makes me angry.'

Gould sighed, 'Yeah, and this one doesn't even look used, does she? No needle marks, no smell of alcohol.'

'No obvious cause of death, added Dan. 'Obvious result, though.' He stared off into the trees.

'You alright?'

Dan shrugged. 'Yeah, sorry, thinking about something else.' Thinking about my stupid, disaster of a sister. But he couldn't say that, not to this stranger. Gould had been around so long he'd probably arrested her on more than one occasion, and Dan didn't want to be associated with her through work. Not yet, anyway.

Fox struggled to his feet and tore off his gloves. 'Too soon to tell what time she died, but I can say that there are signs of some kind of altercation. Now, if ye'll back away nicely, boys, I'll get the lassie back to my nice cool hospital and we can find out what else she wants to tell us.' He finished stuffing his papers into his bag. 'I'll see you tomorrow. Post-mortem will begin at ten a.m.'

He nodded at the waiting undertakers, who zipped Carly Braithwaite into a bag and lifted her onto a stretcher, ready for the long walk across the field to the waiting black van.

'She must have been killed somewhere else,' said Dan, eyeing the debris around their feet. 'Forensics aren't going to find anything useful amongst all this rubbish, and there's no sign of a bag or a coat or anything, just an old school scarf that could be hers.' They watched as the scarf was bundled into a bag and labelled.

Dan poked an empty tobacco pouch with his toe. 'If you killed her elsewhere, why bring her to this copse? It's hardly a safe place to dump a body with a thousand kids on site. Anybody could have come up here.'

'Maybe that's what the murderer wanted, for the body to be found,' offered Gould.

'Hmm, maybe. Or maybe he had to stash her somewhere quickly and was planning to come back tonight and move her, but three snot-nosed kids discovered her first?'

They watched the forensic team tracing a third possible route through the trees to the quiet road beyond. One of them turned and gave them a thumbs up, indicating fresh tyre marks on the soft mud at the side of the road.

'Guess we were right about her being brought here,' said Dan. 'I'll bet you a tenner she was killed Saturday or Sunday and moved here in the dark.'

Gould thought about the bet for a moment. 'Nah, easy money for you.'

Dan shrugged. 'Fair enough. It'll be good if they can isolate the tyre prints, it may help to identify the vehicle that brought her here.'

'And a set of footprints would be handy. At least we've got an idea when she died now.' Gould looked up at Dan from under bushy eyebrows, 'and it looks like you've got your first murder case, Hellier.'

Dan fought the treacherous worm of excitement in his belly. First case, first murder, all his. He almost rubbed his hands together.

'We've got a lot of people to talk to, and there's no point hanging round here. If I go over and see the family once they're home, will you supervise the school interviews?'

'Sure,' replied Gould, unzipping the front of his protective suit with an audible sigh, and stuffing his hands into the pockets of his jacket. His earlier antagonism appeared to have been softened by the encounter with Fox. 'I'm quite looking forward to interviewing someone on a murder case for the first time in four years. Nice to be let out of the office.'

'Right. I'll get Sally Ellis to meet me at the Braithwaite house, sir. She can act as family liaison for the next few days.'

'Good idea. By the way, you can call me Ian,' he said, 'as we'll be working together.'

Dan smiled, one small battle won.

'I won't mess up, you know, Ian. We'll get to the bottom of this and you can bow out in a blaze of glory.'

Gould snorted. 'Right, I'll look forward to that, then.'

They walked back to the small broken gate at the edge of the wood and handed their used coveralls, overshoes and gloves to the PC on guard duty.

'Another slog down the bloody field,' Gould grumbled. 'Come and meet the headteacher on your way out. He needs a bit of reassurance that we're not turning his school into an episode of "Midsomer Murders".'

Chapter 3

Date: Monday 24th April Time:11:37 Alan and Jenna Braithwaite's home

Alan Braithwaite, father of Carly, sat in the worn armchair by the fire-place, staring at the empty grate and clutching the photocopy of Carly's white face that the woman police officer had passed to him. Jenna, his younger daughter, was squashed next to him. She held his hand and cried, letting the tears run down her face and soak into her school shirt.

Dan looked across at Sergeant Ellis. She had folded her hands in her lap and was looking at the floor, projecting calm and waiting for him to start. So far, they'd had to force Mr Braithwaite to even let them over the threshold and into the living room. Braithwaite had the look of an angry man, a man used to thinking with his fists.

'Mr Braithwaite, we have good reason to believe that the girl we found this morning is your daughter, Carly. I know this isn't a very good image.' Dan paused, 'So I'll need you to go down to the hospital later today to make the formal identification of the body for us.'

'Body?' Braithwaite stared at Dan, his face quivering, 'Who the hell are you to come into my house like you own the place?' His voice rose, thick with distress, 'That "body" you're talking about is my daughter, and she's a good girl, not some little tart who had it coming to her.' He clutched at his hair, shaking off his daughter's hand.

Dan watched the flush rise from Braithwaite's chest, rush up his throat and into his face and heard his breathing flatten into a rapid rattle of phlegm at the back of his throat. He had no time to react before, with a roar, Braithwaite raised his fists and lurched for him. He grabbed Dan's jacket in his left hand and lifted him off the chair so that their faces were level, foreheads touching.

Red anger flooded through Dan. There was no way, bereaved or not, that he was going to let this character threaten him. He brought his arms up under Braithwaite's and forced them apart, breaking the taller man's hold. Before Braithwaite got his balance back, Dan placed an open palm on the centre of his chest.

'Just sit down, now, sir,' he growled, struggling to control his anger. He pushed Braithwaite backwards slowly, towards his chair. 'Just take a seat, please.'

'Dad!' Jenna leapt up behind her father and tugged at his arm, forcing her way in between the two men. Her voice was shrill with fear, 'Dad, you don't want to do this. Stop it. Stop!'

Braithwaite tried to shove her out of the way, but the act of pushing his daughter and her yelp of shock brought him back into the room. He lowered his fist and stared at it. He looked dazed.

Jenna spun round to glare at Dan. 'Can't you just leave us alone? My sister's just died. Can't you see what you're doing?' She swivelled once more and pushed her father back into his chair, and perched next to him, pink spots of anger gilding her cheeks.

Dan let go of the breath he'd been holding. In his most truthful moments, he'd admit to hating having to deal with grieving parents. They were unpredictable and even the most docile of them could get angry... and this one was not docile. He glanced over towards Sally. She stared back at him wide-eyed and slid her baton back into her bag.

'I really didn't mean to cause offence, Mr Braithwaite,' he began, 'I apologise if I upset you. What I meant to say was, please would you go down to the hospital with Detective Sergeant Ellis later this afternoon? She'll transport you there and back.'

Ellis nodded faint approval.

Braithwaite sank back into the chair, bewilderment blurring his sharp features.

'Was she…was she murdered?' he mumbled through hands clasped over his mouth.

'We don't know that yet.' Dan lowered the tone of his voice, and the pace of his speech. 'That's what we need to find out. When we get Carly to the hospital, our pathologist will find that out, and then we'll let you know as soon as possible.'

Sally Ellis cleared her throat, indicating to Dan that she would take over.

'Jenna, love, will you put the kettle on and make us all a nice cup of tea?' The girl left her father's side with obvious reluctance and headed for the kitchen. Sally turned in her seat, 'Mr Braithwaite, we do need to know when you last saw Carly.'

Braithwaite was quiet for a few seconds, gathering his thoughts, chest still heaving.

'Yesterday afternoon, about four o'clock. She was going to that studio place to record some of her songs after tea.'

'Studio?' Dan asked.

'Illusion Studios. Bloke called Jed Abrams runs it. It's on Sidwell Street in town.' A dawning realisation twisted his face into a snarl and he sat up, hands forming into fists again. 'If he touched her… if it was him…' His voice was harsh, choked with emotions he could not have put a name to.

'Then we will catch him and prosecute him, sir,' interrupted Dan, voice as firm as he dared. The last thing he needed was some vigilante nutcase running around Exeter avenging the death of his daughter on any bloke who happened to know her. Alan Braithwaite was tall and wiry, and a lifetime of working in the building trade had made him hard and muscular. Dan wasn't sure who'd come off best in a fight with the guy, but he wouldn't put money on it being him.

Sally continued her gentle questioning. 'Did Carly have a good voice, Mr Braithwaite?'

Her soft West Country vowels and calm delivery settled Braithwaite. Dan watched his chest relax as he began to speak.

'She's a bloody good singer, would give that Adele a run for her money. That's why she got the recording session, won a singing competition last month.' He looked away, close to tears again.

Jenna came back from the kitchen with four mugs of tea. 'I put milk and sugar in all of them, Miss, 'cos I didn't know what you took.'

Dan noticed the girl had given her face a scrub and gained more control than her father had yet managed.

Ellis smiled at her. 'Why don't you call me Sally? I'll be here with you for the next few days.' She made a space for the girl on the sofa. Jenna handed out the tea, and sat next to the police officer, staring down at the milky drink.

Dan sank back into the sofa and let Sally get on with asking the questions. He was annoyed with himself. He knew how to deal with the bereaved. He'd been trained. He'd done it before. Why couldn't he engage brain before speaking? He didn't want to look like a total pillock in front of his Sergeant, and yet she handled this angry man like an expert and Dan had just made him worse. Tutting to himself, he slugged down a mouthful of sweet tea and yanked his thoughts back.

'Did Carly have a boyfriend, or close friends we could talk to?' Sally asked.

'No.' Braithwaite was emphatic. 'She's only just sixteen, and she was going to concentrate on her music, not mess about with lads, wasting her time.'

Jenna peered from under the fringe of fair hair framing her face. 'She was sort of going out with Jamie May from school, Dad.' She looked at Sally. 'He's been here for tea and to have band practices. He liked Carly a lot.'

Braithwaite stared hard at her, black eyes blazing again. She blinked tears away.

'It's true, Dad.' She looked round at Sally for reassurance.

Dan couldn't work out if her father was angry with Jenna for giving information to the police, or whether he was mentally adding Jamie May to his list of suspects.

'Do you like him, too?' asked Sally.

'No, not much.' The girl was still eyeing her father.

Dan mentally added Jamie May to his own list of suspects. So many women were killed by someone they knew, and so few by strangers.

'Tell us about yesterday, sir,' said Sally. 'What was Carly like during the day? Was she excited? Did she seem worried by anything? And what time did you take her to the studio?'

'She was fine. Normal.' He shrugged. 'Excited, yeah. Spent about two hours deciding what to wear. I didn't take her to the studio, though. She said she make her own way there with that Jamie lad.'

'So Jamie went with her?'

He hesitated, 'I didn't actually see him arrive here. I went to the pub at about four o'clock to watch the match. Didn't get back until late.' His eyes filled again and he swiped at his face with the back of his hand.

Dan watched Jenna. 'Jenna, did you notice anything different about your sister at the weekend? Did she mention meeting anyone new recently?'

'No,' she shook her head. 'But she probably wouldn't tell me anyway. We didn't get on all that well. I mean, I loved her, she's my sister, but we weren't really close, like some sisters are.' A tear dripped off the end of her nose.

'How would Carly have got into town from here? Which bus would she catch?'

Jenna looked at her father, who answered, 'She probably walked to save the bus fare, that's what she usually did if it wasn't raining. I don't know, I'm not her jailer, she just went, alright?'

Dan pressed him, 'But what about coming home? Did you check on her when you got back?'

His voice rose again. 'No, I didn't. I bloody didn't, alright? Her bedroom door was closed and I thought she was already in bed. So was Jenna. Her door was closed, too. So what are you trying to say? I was drunk? Yeah, well maybe I was. I'd had a few.' He squeezed his eyes to stop the tears and held onto one fist with the other. 'But I did not hurt my daughter. I did *not* hurt her.'

Jenna held onto his arm with both hands as if she could prevent another explosion through sheer willpower.

Dan recognised the warning signs. He stood and made his way towards the door. Sally would stay there for the rest of the day, to support the family, gather more information about friends or enemies, and have a good look at Carly's room. Someone from the forensic team would be over to examine the family car and the bedroom during the day too, if they could move it along at the crime scene.

He closed the front door quietly behind him, and tapped his car key against his lip. Dan couldn't make up his mind about Alan Braithwaite. Was he really so naïve that he thought a sixteen-year-old girl wasn't interested in boys, or was he hiding a darker set of feelings altogether for his daughter? And what would make those feelings spill over into murder?

Chapter 4

Date: Monday 24th April Time: 10:57 Jamie May, St Andrew's Academy

Jamie focused on the small figures he could see at the far end of the school field. Shock etched lines onto his smooth face as he tried to hold back tears. He pressed his forehead against the cool classroom window.

Claire Quick watched him from the front of the classroom. The Head had broken the news to each class in turn, and told them that they would be sent home. Until then, he expected that they would honour Carly's memory and be quiet and respectful. Jamie had let Claire get away with talking about Romeo, Juliet and Tudor attitudes towards love for ten whole minutes without making a single smart, rude or sexist comment. She didn't flatter herself that her control of this particular class of sixteen-year-olds had improved that much from her previous lesson. He was far more distressed than the other upset kids in the class. He'd had a real crush on Carly.

She checked the clock for the third time. They should have been called out for their buses ten minutes ago. The class was supposed to be attempting to write an essay, but the rhythmic thumping of Jamie's head against the window-pane made that impossible. Most of the kids were staring at the question paper or doodling and whispering amongst themselves. A couple of the girls were crying and holding hands. She wasn't planning on telling them off.

Claire shuddered at the thought of that poor girl lying at the top of the field. It was unreal. It was every teacher's nightmare - that no matter how much they tried, no matter what precautions they took, the kids in their care weren't safe.

The Head had delivered the news at an emergency staff meeting, which had interrupted the first lessons of the day, but that couldn't be helped. There had been tears and shocked disbelief. Whatever the police said about not jumping to conclusions, most of the staff knew it was Carly Braithwaite. They'd only needed to talk to the three lads who'd found her to discover her name.

I suppose they have to speak to Mr Braithwaite before they release the name, thought Claire, and good luck with that. Mr Braithwaite was banned from the premises for threatening to wallop the receptionist, Marcia. On the other hand, quite a few people had wanted to do that to Marcia Penrose.

The Head's plan had been to recall the school buses, carry on with as normal a day as possible and let the students go, one class at a time. Carly's friends and key staff would be interviewed before they went home. Claire felt her own tears prickle and she swallowed hard. She had to keep a lid on her emotions, at least while she was in the classroom. The kids were relying on her to provide a bit of normality. And what on earth would happen when the press got going?

Jamie stirred by the window. A couple of men in coveralls were wheeling a stretcher across the field to the waiting ambulance. The outline of a slight figure could be seen in the bag. Jamie stood up, pushing his chair back as if he was about to run after them.

'Jamie,' Claire called, 'leave it. They won't let you go with her.'

The other students stared at him, mute sympathy on their tear-streaked faces. He banged his forehead back onto the window-pane, his hands clenched into fists, and watched the stretcher until it was out of sight.

A messenger finally arrived at the door and passed Claire a note. She spoke to the class. 'Look, I know how hard this will be for us all, but let the police find out what actually happened. Don't start the Facebook rumours as soon as you get home. Those of you in my tutor group need to go to the meeting room and talk to the police before you go. The rest of you, take care. I'll see you soon.'

Claire sighed, relief mingling with dread as the class left. She touched a marked essay that Carly had completed the week before, her first grade A, and realised the girl would never know about it now. There was a police officer in the meeting room waiting to interview her. Claire could feel tears waiting to overwhelm her.

Jamie's boots sank into the red mud of the ploughed field that ran alongside the school grounds. He sidled round the edge of the field towards the old caravan in which the farmer stored feed and fertiliser. The door was locked, so he flopped down onto the small patch of concrete on which it stood, letting his back rest against the mottled plastic side panel. He opened his guitar case, moved aside history and maths books and found his tobacco pouch and Rizlas hidden under the body of the Fender copy guitar.

Jamie's chest heaved. He battled the emotions down and rolled a cigarette, sucking the tears down with the nicotine. He ripped off his school tie and, in a practised movement, rolled his blazer small enough to squash into the case alongside the neck of the guitar and swapped it for a rolled-up grey hoodie he kept there. He couldn't go back into school. There was no way he was talking to the police.

He smoked the roll-up down to a damp end and flicked it into the mud. He rose, a slim figure in grey hoodie, white shirt and black jeans, hefted his guitar case over his shoulder and set off to walk to the only place he could think of where he knew he could hide out.

Chapter 5

Date: Monday 24th April Time:11:03 DCI Ian Gould, St Andrew's Academy

The Head teacher had allocated two adjoining offices at the front of the school to the police team. One had a phone and both could be used for interviews. Ian Gould was pleased with the arrangement as it meant they could come and go as they liked without having to run the gauntlet of the nosy old bag on reception. She'd already been in three times to see if they wanted more coffee, or needed to know where the facilities were. Eyes on stalks. However, he'd been in the job long enough to know that old-timers tended to know all the gossip, so he kept his patience and gracefully accepted yet another cup of weak coffee.

The other member of the interview team, DC Sam Knowles, had set up a computer in the corner and was linking in to the main police computer. He was a good lad, steady and not stupid, a bonus in Ian's book. These flashy young characters like Dan Hellier came down here after the bright lights of the big city and thought it was all about making a name for yourself, solving the big crime.

Well, he sighed, maybe it was like that for him, once. It wasn't so many years ago that he and Julie Oliver had been going for the same promotions. He wasn't quite sure when she had got away from him, but she had, and how. Her star was burning brightly now, while his had dimmed. Gone out, in truth. He shrugged, no point getting bitter and twisted, Ian lad, he thought, only a few weeks to go.

He was just wondering if he could get that sparky Lizzie Singh seconded to the murder team so she could give them the benefit of her local knowledge, when there was a knock on the door and the young English teacher, Claire Quick, arrived. Ian leapt to his feet, met her at the door and invited her in.

She looked nervous.

'You alright? No need to worry, we just need to ask a few questions about Carly in school. Won't take long.'

Claire offered a tentative smile. 'I've never been interviewed by the police before. I have this stupid idea that you can see directly into my mind and will know all the bad things I've done.' She sat upright on the edge of the plastic chair.

Gould laughed, 'I think you're mixing us up with voodoo, love. And I doubt you've done anything all that bad - or is there something terrible you want to talk to me about?'

He watched her settle back into the chair, with a shake of her head and a faint smile. What on earth did people think policing was actually about? Mind-reading?

Collecting personal details took only a couple of minutes, it was the fact that Claire had been Carly's form tutor for four years that interested Gould.

'Describe Carly to me, Miss Quick. Anything you think that might help us to understand what kind of person she was. Friends, boyfriends, any arguments or disagreements with them recently? That kind of thing.'

Claire thought for a moment. 'Carly was complicated. Eleven years old when her mother left her and her sister. She was new to secondary school, already developing the hard shell of cheek and sarcasm she used to protect herself. It took me three years to break through and build a successful relationship with her and that was because of her singing.' She took a breath. 'In a nutshell, she was brittle, easily offended, loud, shy, difficult, helpful, rude, vulnerable, funny, sad, talented, moody...' She stopped. Gould was trying to get it all down in his notepad. 'You could just write "typical teenager",' she said.

Gould chuckled. 'I get the picture. What about her friends then?'

'Hmm… Carly found it hard to maintain friendships with other girls. She wanted to be the centre of attention all the time, which would annoy them. When she found her singing voice a couple of years ago it made it worse because she got so much praise. It did make her much nicer for the staff, though, as it gave her a purpose other than disrupting lessons.' Claire paused and played with a strand of wavy, blond hair. 'I certainly don't think she annoyed anyone enough for them to have killed her. Surely this was a mugging gone wrong or something? It can't have been anyone at school, can it?'

She looked at Gould for confirmation, but he kept his face calm, impassive. He'd seen too much over the years to offer false comfort, however attractive the plaintiff. 'Anything else?'

'I was giving her extra English lessons to help get her grades up so she could stay on and do A levels. That would be quite an achievement for someone from Carly's background.'

Gould interrupted, 'What other subjects was she good at?'

'Well, obviously Music, she would have taken that at A level as part of a Performing Arts course, and probably Art and History. She was in every school production, usually singing the lead role. There wasn't a scientific bone in that girl's body, though.' She put a hand to her mouth. 'God, what an insensitive thing to say.' Claire's eyes filled with tears, which she tried to cover by foraging for a tissue in her bag. She wiped her eyes and blew her nose. 'Sorry. But how can she be dead? It's so wrong, I can hardly believe it.'

'Wrong, it is, you're right, there. Let's see if we can find out who was responsible, eh?'

'Yes, of course. Sorry.' She sniffed. 'I suppose her best friend was Jamie May, also in Year 11. I teach him English.'

'Is it likely that he saw her yesterday?'

Claire nodded. 'Could have. She was very excited about the recording session last night. They may well have met up for a rehearsal. I don't know if he was supposed to be going along to the recording or not. Perhaps her Dad took her?' She hesitated and looked at Gould. 'Jamie was madly in love with Carly, Chief Inspector. He's devastated. You will be gentle with him, won't you?'

'I'll need to see him today, but I won't make it worse for him, I promise. I assume he'll be waiting with the rest of the class?'

She shook her head. 'I'll check on them, but I saw him heading off across the field when the buses arrived. I think he's gone. You might be better off seeing him at home, later. It was the stretcher coming down the field that did it.'

'Yes, it wasn't good timing. We thought the students had all gone by then. Thank you, Miss Quick. You've been very helpful.' Gould saw Claire Quick out of the room and beckoned in a subdued Lee Bateson.

'Sit down, lad.' Gould said, and flopped back down onto his own chair, waiting until the boy had seated himself. 'No need to be frightened. You're not in any trouble with me. I just need to know, in your own words, what happened this morning.'

Bateson shrugged and stuffed his hands into his pockets. 'We was playin' a game in the woods, and she was just there, beside the log where we always sit.'

Gould nodded. 'Good so far. What did you see first when you got to the clearing?'

'Nothin'. It was Ryan who saw Carly's hair. I went in for a better look and saw…' He faltered.

'Go on, it's OK.' Gould smiled in encouragement.

'It was 'orrible, sir. Her finger was all bloody and a crow was eatin' it and tryin' to get her ring off. Her eyeball was just hangin' there, on her face. Tim Parker was sick all over his shoes. Gross.'

Gould saw Bateson's eyes shine as he re-lived the moment. *Blood-thirsty little sod. He'll dine out on this story for weeks.*

'How did you know it was Carly?'

Bateson looked up at Gould as if he was stupid. 'Everyone knows her. And her sister's in my tutor group.'

'Did you notice anything strange about the area? Anything different from usual?'

'You mean apart from Carly lyin' there?'

'Yes, apart from that.' You're asking for a smack, smart alec, thought Gould.

'Well, the branch that was covering her wasn't there last Friday, but…' he thought for a moment and shook his head. 'No, it was like it always is.'

'Is that all?'

'Yeah.' Bateson nodded to emphasise that he had finished and looked over his shoulder at the door until Gould let him loose.

The interviews with the other two boys followed a similar track without, Gould was pleased to note, the same fascination with blood and gore shown by young Master Bateson. As he and Hellier had suspected, the place where the body was found would tell them little about when, how or why the girl had been killed. It was just a dumping ground.

Gould sighed and checked his watch. Half an hour should cover the rest of them. It had taken him twenty minutes to get Marcia Penrose out of the door after her interview, and he'd only managed it by taking her elbow and propelling her into the corridor. Not a classic exercise in positive community policing, but at no point during that time, or in the corridor after the interview as she walked back to reception, did she stop talking. She was indeed a mine of information, but most of it was gossip, and the only bit that helped with the case was her report of the altercation with Alan Braithwaite. Braithwaite was apparently 'aggressive, vicious and argumentative, just like his daughter,' and she 'wasn't surprised at anything that little madam got up to.'

He gazed at the roast beef and mustard sandwich sitting on the little table near the door and practised self-control. One more to do. Gould glanced at the list, Miles Westlake, Music teacher.

He heard footsteps outside the room but they disappeared into the Gents' toilet opposite before he could get to the door. He could hear the unmistakeable retch and hurl of someone throwing up, flushing the toilet, sluicing the sink, and, he assumed, washing his face.

Gould held the door open and waited for Westlake to come out. He could hear Sam Knowles next door interviewing one of Carly's friends and struggling to get her to stop giggling. Her friends didn't seem unduly upset at her death, but that was girls for you. The door to the Gents' opened across the narrow corridor and a tall, slim figure with a mane of gold curls came out, scraping back damp hair from his face. Gould saw anguish in the red-rimmed eyes.

'Mr Westlake?' Miles Westlake nodded and took a seat in the small office, winding one leg around the other and clasping both arms across his thin chest. Gould wondered how long this guy had been in teaching, he didn't look a day over twenty. 'How long have you taught at this school?'

'Three years in September.'

'So, that would make you about what, twenty-four? Did you come into teaching straight from University?'

Westlake shrugged. 'No, Inspector, I tried to be a pop star first, like many a teacher, so I'm twenty-six. But I love teaching now, it's a great job.' He dropped his eyes to the table-top.

Gould could see the tension in his arms, his face. Westlake was hugging himself to stop himself from shaking. 'How well did you know Carly Braithwaite, Mr Westlake?'

'Pretty well.' Westlake let the breath he had been holding go in a quiet sigh. 'She was a talented girl with a fantastic voice and real determination. I wasn't surprised when she won the Exeter singing competition. It was just a matter of time until she got her break.' He gulped air and let out another shuddering sigh.

'If you don't mind me saying so, you seem very upset. More upset than the other teachers I have spoken to this morning.' Westlake's eyes were full to the brim with tears again. Talk about the highly-strung artistic type. Gould could feel dislike setting his lips into a thin line.

'I'm sorry,' said Westlake, 'I'm not usually like this. It's not just what has happened to Carly. Things haven't been going too well for me and this is sort of the last straw.' Westlake made an attempt to smile. 'I guess I feel things too deeply. Bit pathetic, I know.'

'When did you last see Carly?'

Westlake gave the briefest hesitation. 'She and Jamie May came by my place on Saturday and we had a last practice in the afternoon before her session on the Sunday.'

'Is it normal for school students to visit teachers' houses, sir?' Gould couldn't imagine ever having wanted to set foot in a teacher's house. Marie Claire, the French teaching assistant's house, however, now that would have been a very different matter.

Westlake hesitated again. 'My wife didn't mind as it was for such an important reason. But you're right, it's not normally what happens. We were finished for about three-thirty and then they both left.'

'So you didn't see Carly on Sunday before she went to the studio?'

'No, I thought her Dad was going to take her. I was waiting in the music room this morning to hear how it had gone.' His eyes filled up again. Gould bit back feelings of distaste. He couldn't see this one as a murderer, he probably needed his wife to get the spiders out of the bath for him.

'Ok, Mr Westlake, thanks very much. I may have to speak to you again, but that's it for now.'

They both breathed a sigh of relief.

The lunch bell rang as Westlake left the office and Gould took it as permission to fall upon his sandwich. When Sam Knowles entered the room a few minutes later, Gould was wiping the crumbs from his chin and pointing at the kettle.

Chapter 6

Monday 24th April Time:13:12 Illusion Recording Studio

Dan drove slowly into the centre of Exeter, negotiating the Monday morning shoppers and avoiding speeding where he knew cameras lurked. He left his beloved Audi in the multi-storey car park behind the John Lewis store, and walked round onto Sidwell Street. He checked out his reflection in the glass as he walked, sucked in his stomach and pushed his shoulders back. He spent so much time over a computer these days he was developing a hunchback.

The open doors of the store were tempting. A nice display of squashy sofas distracted him. He'd got virtually no furniture in his flat yet. Four weeks in and he'd been working practically every day. How could he entertain friends, even just have someone round for a drink, when he only had one chair? He just needed a couple of days browsing and he reckoned he could do all the furnishing in one go.

Sidwell Street had once been the centre of Exeter's shopping district, but it was fast deteriorating into the cheap end of town. He scanned the peeling shop signs, looking for the recording studio as he walked. He wondered if, now he was a DI, he could delegate furniture purchase to a member of the team. Someone with good taste. He thought about his colleagues. Unlikely. Or, he could do what his mum had suggested; find a room display in John Lewis that he liked and buy the whole thing. He could do it for the bedroom and kitchen, too. Great idea, mum. Just might be lacking the thousands needed to pay for it, until the settlement on his flat in London came through, of course. That would cover everything, wouldn't it? He hoped.

Dan hadn't exactly been in the mood for entertaining since he'd returned from London, tail between his legs, grateful that he got a transfer rather than a demotion straight down the ranks. He'd been so stupid to let himself get caught out like that. It wouldn't happen again.

Things had started to go wrong with Sarah when he talked about getting married and having kids, about settling down and moving out of London. Sarah had stared at him like he was a stranger. She moved out two weeks later, after some horrible late-night discussions that always ended in tears, most of them his.

That part he got. She really didn't want kids, and it was a deal-breaker. Fair enough. He just couldn't believe that she would choose that ugly loser over him, and only wait a couple of weeks before falling into his open arms. The familiar flush began in his chest, bloomed over his throat and into his face. That ugly, rich, loser smirking and raising his glass to him in the pub with his arm around Sarah, like he owned her. Tosser deserved it. Every punch and kick. He unclenched his fists and realised he'd stopped walking and was looking at his reflection in a shop window. Looking but not seeing.

Dan shook his head and crossed the road. Sarah wouldn't even talk to him now, so no point in going over it again and again. He just felt like a massive hole had been cut into the place where all his security had been. The tosser had decided not to press charges, which had made Dan even angrier, although he knew that was irrational. He walked further towards the old Odeon, checking side streets and wondering if he'd missed it altogether.

He'd been shocked to see how few possessions he had to show for the five years they had spent together. It had only taken one trip in a Transit van for him and his dad to wipe out the previous ten years of his life in London. Or at least that's what it felt like. In reality he hadn't stopped missing Sarah and worrying about his decision to take the transfer back to Devon for a single minute. Had he just been a stubborn fool, hankering after an impossible life? He knew the answer. In those middle-of-the-night honesty sessions where he lay awake on one side of a bed too big, he admitted to himself that he did want a life like he had imagined, with marriage and kids and a dog. That was who he was. So Sarah of the long legs and clever brain was not the girl for him, and he had to get over it. He scrubbed his hands through dark hair and walked more briskly.

He still couldn't understand how they could have been so far apart when he'd thought they were so happy together. But that was the way it was. His mum had said the usual clichés about 'better to find out now than later', 'going through a divorce was worse', etc. Dan didn't know about that. He couldn't see that a marriage certificate added more weight to the feeling of loss he experienced pretty much all the time.

Two weeks back with his parents in the Exeter suburbs, however, had been enough to convince him to take his small flat on the quayside, and he was growing to love living near the water.

He trotted past more shop fronts, noticing the gradual decline from glass and steel to badly painted wood and hand-painted signs. Students occupied much of this part of town; there were bars, cheap takeaways, laundrettes and open-late mini-supermarkets.

The Illusion Recording Studio was located in the basement of a spacious, two-storey music shop. Dan approached via a small alleyway, where a Mini in Racing Green and a rusty white Transit van were squashed nose to tail. He squeezed past the van. Did Carly Braithwaite actually get here on Sunday and did she leave again?

Pulling open the external steel security door, Dan found himself in a small lobby facing a locked glass door. He looked into the security camera and pressed the buzzer. After a brief conversation with a Welsh accent, he was buzzed through.

Illusion Studios was far more impressive than the dingy entrance had led him to expect. Once through the glass door, Dan followed a carpeted stairway to the basement. The walls held well-lit pictures of semi-famous bands and singers who had recorded at Illusion as well as pictures of the owner, Jed Abrams, at parties with celebrities. They appeared to have been taken over a period of at least twenty years. Dan smirked at the ponytail. Abrams really didn't carry it off as well as Bono had, and hadn't had the sense to chop it off when he hit forty, either.

He entered through the lower door, experiencing a small thrill in the pit of his stomach. As a teenager he too had harboured dreams of being in a band and becoming famous. He and a group of lads from school had played in a band for a while, called rather embarrassingly, *'Kids eat Free'*, but they had split up when university beckoned and their parents made them choose a more reliable method of earning a living. But Dan still played guitar and would have loved to have the opportunity to record in a proper studio with the lads. Who knew where they might have ended up?

He looked around. The place was large with a roomy reception area furnished with two enormous in-trend, battered leather sofas and a slate coffee table holding music magazines.

'Can I help you?'

The Welsh accent belonged to a tiny woman with short, black, spiky hair and dramatic eyeliner. She seemed to be wearing several tee shirts of various colours and sleeve lengths, stripy leggings and Doc Marten boots. Fashion student earning a bit of extra cash, Dan guessed.

'Only you've taken five minutes to get down the stairs. Don't think anyone has actually looked at those photos for years. Is it someone in a photo you're looking for?'

'No,' said Dan, showing his warrant card. 'I need to speak to Jed Abrams. It's urgent.'

The girl took a step forward to read the card. She only came up to the middle of his chest.

'He's recording at the moment. I'm due to take them in a cuppa, though, so I can interrupt them then. What's it about?' she asked, heading for the compact kitchen behind her desk.

Dan hesitated. He wanted Abrams to hear the news first. He needed to judge Abram's reactions before he had a chance to work out a cover story, if he needed one. On the other hand, he had a few minutes now to gather some useful information. 'What's your name?' he asked, following her into the kitchen.

'Chas Lloyd', she replied, 'short for Chastity. Laugh and I'll never speak to you again. I'm the product of Welsh Presbyterian lay preachers.' She lifted one corner of her mouth up into half a smile, 'but my brother is called Ezekiel, so I guess I was lucky. Tea or coffee?'

Dan remembered he'd eaten nothing since the night before, and his stomach, betraying him utterly, rumbled loudly enough for Chas to hear it and smile.

'Biscuit?'

He smiled too, ice broken. 'I'll have coffee with milk, please. Ms Lloyd, did you know about the recording session won by Carly Braithwaite?'

'The schoolgirl? Yeah, course. Call me Chas, by the way, everyone does. Jed's been going on about this girl for ages, said she has a good voice and he's hoping to manage her once she leaves school.' She made air quotes as she spoke. 'He's always looking for the next big thing.' Turning, she measured coffee into four mugs and emptied half a packet of plain chocolate digestives onto a plate. 'He's just got one guy in there this afternoon,' she explained. 'Does most of his band work later in the day.'

'Did Mr Abrams say anything about the session with Carly on Sunday evening?'

She nodded. 'Yeah, he was furious, said she didn't turn up and he was hanging around for an hour waiting for her.'

'Were you here then?'

Chas shook her head. 'No, I'm usually off on a Sunday unless we've got a really busy day. He doesn't exactly like paying me overtime, so if he's just got one punter in, he manages by himself. Suits me. Pile of talentless losers, most of them. I'm only here to earn a bit of cash so I can go to design school next year.'

'Fashion?'

She laughed and looked down at her stripy leggings. 'Is it that obvious?'

'How do you get on with Mr Abrams? Is he a good boss to work for?' Dan saw a wariness enter her eyes, as if she'd suddenly remembered that he was a police officer.

'He's OK.' She turned away, filled the mugs with hot water, gave each one a vigorous stir, and re-arranged the biscuits on the plate. Classic displacement activity. He didn't push. He could speak to her again later.

Dan took his coffee and two biscuits and stood outside the long window, which looked into the studio control room. Inside, he could see the back of Jed Abrams' head and smiled at the hopeless ponytail. Abrams was twiddling knobs on a vast console as a lone guitarist sang and played. The player wasn't bad at all.

Chas opened the control room door, waited until the young singer finished his song and took in the coffee.

Dan watched Abrams turn around and stare as Chas gave him the message that a police officer was here to speak to him. He pressed his warrant card against the glass and smiled. He couldn't work out whether Abrams' expression was hostile or fearful. From the front his hair was scraped straight back into the ponytail, and was an unlikely shade of dark brown. Some help from the dye bottle there, I reckon, thought Dan. Here is a man fighting the inevitable onset of middle-age, and making it worse.

When Abrams stood and came towards the door, his belly stretched the waistband of his jeans around the tight ball of his stomach. Fighting but losing that battle too, thought Dan. There was something pathetic about a middle-aged man wearing a ponytail and skinny jeans to disguise a lifetime of no exercise and a rubbish diet. Abrams was pasty from working underground all the time and had the clammy handshake and puffy eyes of the habitual drinker.

Abrams withdrew his hand from Dan's and indicating one of the leather sofas in the reception area, said, 'Shall we go over here? Chas will replay the song for the punter, which should give us a few minutes uninterrupted. Can I ask what this is about?'

Dan decided on the direct approach, 'Mr Abrams, I'm investigating the unexplained death, in fact the murder of a young girl called Carly Braithwaite. Did you see her on Sunday?' He scrutinised the music producer's face carefully. He'd missed all his ex-girlfriend's non-verbal clues and look where that had got him.

Abrams' eyes widened and he swallowed noisily. 'Murder? Carly? I don't understand.' He took another long drink of coffee and wiped his mouth with the back of his hand. 'What's this got to do with me?' he asked, a Bristolian burr betraying his origins.

Not much of a show of spontaneous feeling for a fellow human being, thought Dan. He could really have done with Sally Ellis here to build the guy's trust and get him to spill all.

'Carly was supposed to come here on Sunday for a recording session, wasn't she? Did she arrive?'

Abrams stared at the table. 'Err, no, she didn't come. I was sat around like an idiot until eight-ish and then I left and went for a drink. I was well mad, I can tell you, wasting my time like that. I could have had a paying customer in for that slot.'

Hellier felt himself take offence at the man's tone. 'A young girl is dead, Mr Abrams. I'm not really interested in what *you* could have had.'

Abrams looked down at the table again. A finger crept to his mouth and he chewed on a hangnail, but he asked no questions about the death of the girl at all. Dan couldn't work out why the guy made him feel so uneasy, apart from his lack of reaction to the news that the girl he should have been recording was dead. He pushed on.

'Did anyone see you leave at eight o'clock?'

Abrams' eyes slid sideways to where Chas was chatting to the guitar player.

'No point looking at Ms Lloyd for an alibi, she's already told me she had yesterday off. What pub did you go to?'

It was the word alibi that seemed to galvanise him. He sat upright. 'Look, am I a suspect in this murder, or what? I've told you what I know. Why should I have to have an alibi? I'm not being accused of this, mate, whatever you think.' He stood and put his hands in his pockets. 'Excuse me. I have to get back to work now. See yourself out.'

'Just one more question, sir,' said Dan. 'I just need to know where you went for a drink last night and then I'll leave you alone. I appreciate your co-operation and I'm sure you want to help our enquiry into this dreadful crime.'

Dan relaxed back into the sofa and dunked a biscuit into his coffee, throwing the soggy mass into his mouth before it fell. Abrams sank back down onto the sofa. Dan watched emotions flicker across Abrams' face as he tried to decide what to say.

'I didn't say I went to a pub, I went home and had a drink there,' Abrams offered.

Dan nodded. 'Right, I see. Anyone see you coming home? Talk to anyone on the way? Anyone at home I could check with?' Dan waited, but got the same nail-chewing lack of response.

'Are you sure you wouldn't rather just tell me where you were?' He could see the muscles twitch in Abrams' face as his brain churned, trawling for a suitable answer. Dan felt a small lurch in his stomach that this might be the murderer sitting right in front of him.

'Don't worry sir,' he said finally, fed up of waiting for Abrams to spit out an alibi, 'we all forget things in the heat of the moment. Just jot down your contact details on my pad for me and I'll be on my way. Here's my card so you can ring me if you remember anything useful.'

Abrams took the pen and wrote down the details. His hand shook, but Dan couldn't work out if that was because he had something to hide or because he needed a drink.

Abrams avoided shaking Dan's hand and scuttled back into the studio.

Chas Lloyd came out. She raised an eyebrow at Dan. 'Do you want to tell me what that was all about?' she asked. 'I haven't seen him looking that worried since his ex-wife's lawyer came round.'

Dan took a few moments to explain about the girl's death and where she had been found. Chas was both shocked and sympathetic and wanted to talk more, but Dan needed to get her back to talking about her boss. There had been something there when she said he was 'OK' to work for.

'Would you say that Mr Abrams was capable of hurting a young girl, Chas?'

'What? And killing her and dumping her body?' She laughed a quick, chopped off snort. 'I don't think so, Inspector. Don't get me wrong, he's not above trying to get his end away with any female who enters his pathetic little world, but you can sort him out with a sharp tongue and swift left hook. All these ex-rock stars are the same, huge egos. Hit 'em where it hurts, criticise 'em, they crumple. To be honest, though, I don't *really* know. How can you be sure of what anyone would do if the circumstances were right?' She shook her head. 'I just don't think Jed's capable of actually killing someone. He's a bit of a plonker, really.' She peered up at him and twinkled a smile.

Dan smiled back. 'Thanks, Chas, you've been really helpful.' He pulled a card from his wallet and gave it to her. 'Call me if you think of anything else that may be relevant.'

'I will. Bye, then. Oh…'

Dan turned back.

'Are your eyes grey or purple?' she grinned at him.

Dan gave her a level look and headed for the stairs.

'Just asking,' she called after him.

Chapter 7

Date: Monday 24th April Time: 17:07 Miles Westlake's home

Although the students had been sent home, the Head had negotiated that staff could work in the main building for the rest of that day, as long as they didn't go near the field. After lunch, Claire Quick checked on the last of the tutor group waiting to be interviewed and realised that Jamie wasn't coming back to school that day. When she checked the signing-out book she saw that Miles Westlake had signed out sick at 1.13 p.m., and that Jamie had indeed just disappeared. His name was not in the book.

Claire asked Marcia Penrose to contact Jamie's mum to explain what had happened and arrange for him to give his interview at home.

Then she tried to raise Miles on her mobile. She was worried about him. He'd looked terrible in the staff briefing that morning, and he was never the most robust of people. It was one of the reasons they had split up, that he was too soft, with all his emotions on the outside. She'd been delighted when he fell for her old friend Sophie, and they seemed happy together.

There was no answer on his mobile. She considered ringing Sophie who she assumed would be at home with the baby, but thought better of it. Miles would need to tell Sophie what had happened to Carly in his own way. She had to think hard to remember that last time they'd all been out together as friends. Claire had been seeing the trainee doctor - a relationship doomed to fail under the weight of his working hours - and they'd all gone for a curry and a drink in town. She realised it had been back before Emily was born. Months ago. Some friend she was.

She slung her laptop bag over her shoulder and headed for the staffroom. She would call round to see Miles after school.

Claire parked outside the Victorian terrace. Although it was gone five o'clock, and time for people to be arriving home, it was quiet at this end of the street. Miles's car was parked outside, but the curtains were pulled roughly across, and she was surprised to see how dilapidated the place looked. She supposed having a baby changed your priorities. She banged on the door but no one answered.

Claire bent down and put her mouth to the letterbox. 'Miles, Sophie?' she yelled. 'It's Claire. Can I come in? I just want to see how you are. I won't stay long, promise.' She could hear music coming from the living room, like heavy metal played low, and what sounded like an argument, again low but furious in tone. Both noises stopped abruptly. She tried again: 'Miles, please, I just want to make sure you're OK. Is Sophie there? Can I speak to her?' A germ of unease ate at her stomach.

She stood back as she heard footsteps coming down the hallway. Miles opened the door but leant against the door-frame, blocking her path into the house. Claire's uneasy feeling grew.

'Aren't you going to let me in? I only want to talk to you about today.'

With reluctance he backed off and opened the door wide enough for Claire to follow him down the hall and into the kitchen. Soft music was playing in the sitting room again, but the door was closed.

'Claire,' Miles began, but he stopped when he saw the expression on her face.

'Look at the state of this place!' she cried, horrified at the mess in the kitchen. It looked like he had spent weeks living on takeaways, and she was amazed at the quantity of bottles and cans left on every surface, and the sink piled high with dirty dishes.

'Where's Sophie, Miles? Where's Emily?'

Westlake didn't answer. He collapsed against the sink and sobbed, shoulders heaving. Claire let him carry on for a few minutes, trying to take in the chaos in the once pristine kitchen. Then she opened every drawer until she found a clean tea towel and passed it to him.

'You'd better dry your eyes and tell me what's happening. Shall we go and sit down in the other room?'

The look of alarm on his face alerted her that there was something wrong. She turned, strode down to the sitting room and pushed open the door. Jamie May was sitting there, smoking what looked like a joint and drinking beer from a can.

Jamie shot to his feet when he saw his English teacher. He dropped the joint into the can and sputtered, 'Miss, what are you doing here?'

Claire stared at him. Things were not making sense. She struggled to keep her shock under control. If pushed, she would have agreed that she screeched her next point.

'What am I doing here? I don't have to answer to you, Jamie May! But I definitely want to know what *you're* doing in a teacher's house, drinking beer and smoking weed. I've been worried sick about you all day. Your mum's probably been on to the police saying you haven't gone home by now. Everyone will be looking for you. Carly's dead, for goodness' sake. Anything could have happened to you.' Her voice cracked as she released some of the distress she had been holding onto since early that morning. She leaned back against the door, hands on hips. 'I'm waiting.'

Jamie shifted on his feet and thrust his hands into the pockets of his trousers, threatening to bring them down. She could see tears forming at the sides of his eyes, but he rubbed them away on his sleeve.

'I just came to see sir, to see how he is,' he tried, but the look on Claire's face stopped him mid-sentence.

'And he just happened to have drugs and beer in the house so you could have a little party? How convenient.' Sarcasm was probably not going to get her very far but she was so angry, and it was easier to be angry with a kid she taught, than to confront the colleague who was now pushing at the door behind her and trying to get into the room. She couldn't begin to understand what had been going on here, but it felt bad, very bad.

'Claire,' Miles shouted through the door, 'let me in. I can explain.'

Jamie backed away to sit in the chair by the window. He leant down and and turned off the music and sat, hunching his shoulders in a parody of a naughty child expecting a slap round the head. Claire moved over to stand with her back to the fireplace. She could not have explained why, but it felt better to be facing out into the room from a position where nobody else could spring any more surprises on her.

Miles came in. He slumped onto the sofa looking up at her with what she could only describe as the expression of a beaten dog, ever hopeful of mercy but ever anticipating further pain.

'Sophie has left me,' Miles said.

'What? What do you mean, left you? When did she leave? Why? And why didn't you tell anyone?'

'Six weeks ago.' He shrugged scrawny shoulders. 'We haven't been getting along too well since the baby came, and she said she wanted time to herself, so she's at her mum's with Emily.'

Claire stared at him, eyes narrowed in disbelief. 'And it's only taken you six weeks on your own to totally destroy the house? I don't think so.' Claire could feel her hands forming into fists. What had he done to make Sophie leave, and how did it tie in with Carly and Jamie? She suddenly felt scared. Scared for her friend and scared about what Miles might have done. 'I don't know what's going on here, but you better tell me the truth, Miles, or I'm going to the police.'

Jamie launched himself off the chair fists raised towards Claire. 'No police! No police!'

Frightened, Claire put her hands up to protect her face, but he stopped moving as quickly as he had started, dropped his arms and ran from the room. Seconds later she heard the front door bang. She turned in confusion to Miles. 'What the hell is going on? You'd better tell me.'

Miles sat numb, staring at the carpet. 'Party,' he said, 'on Saturday night. Haven't cleaned up yet.'

'Right, so who came to this party, then? I don't recall anyone from school mentioning it.'

'Not school friends; other friends. I have got other friends, you know.'

He was rallying a bit, but not enough. She was convinced she knew exactly who these other "friends" were, and it was making her feel sick. 'Was this party for kids from school, Miles? For Carly?'

He looked up at her again, beseeching, but she stared back, a coldness gripping her heart. The idiot had ruined his marriage and it looked like he had done the same for his career. 'You may as well tell me the rest, I've guessed most of it already.'

He coughed out the words. 'It was Carly's idea. She persuaded me to hold a party here as a celebration for the recording session. For the band and their mates. It just got a bit out of hand and I wasn't up to cleaning up on Sunday. Hangover.'

'So, you had a bunch of sixteen-year-olds in your house on Saturday night for a party, and you are drinking with them, and the next day one of them is killed? Bloody hell, Miles, no wonder you're in a state.' She sank down next to him on the sofa. The adrenaline leaving her body had made her muscles weak and her knees wobbled.

More questions crowded into her head. 'What did DCI Gould have to say about all this? Why aren't you a suspect? Why aren't you already in custody, or giving evidence, or whatever it is?'

Westlake's eyes shifted from hers.

'You didn't tell him, did you?' She shook her head. 'I can't take in what's happening.' She clasped both hands to her mouth but she couldn't stop the words pushing out. 'What didn't you tell him, Miles?'

Miles rocked his head from side to side and backed away from her into the corner of the sofa. 'He doesn't have to know, does he, Claire? It won't have been any of her friends and it certainly wasn't me that killed her.' He paused. 'I... I loved her.'

Claire recoiled to the other end of the sofa, sickened. But still she had to ask. 'She was a child…' She tried to get him to look at her, tugged at his arm, but he pulled away. 'Please tell me nothing actually happened between you and her, Miles. Tell me that?'

His eyes filled up again and still he didn't answer.

'You are unbelievable,' Claire said, anger giving her voice a rare, thick vitriol. 'I don't know who you are anymore, but you are a monster, Miles Westlake, a monster.'

'What are you going to do?' he asked, and looked past her as he heard the sitting room door softly open behind her.

But Claire couldn't answer. Jamie lurched in and smashed her hard across the back of her head with an empty vodka bottle. The bottle fell to the ground. He looked at Westlake, his gaunt, red-eyed face a reflection of the teacher's.

Miles bent down to catch Claire as she slid from the sofa. The shock made his voice shrill, 'What the hell have you done, Jamie?'

On the sofa, Claire's eyelids fluttered as she struggled to remain conscious. The back of her skull hurt like hell, and the pain was intense, like someone had stuck a needle in her head.

'I had to do something,' the boy replied.

Through one eye, Claire saw violent spasms shake his body. 'You were going to tell her about Carly. I told Carly we should never have come here, but everybody always did exactly what she wanted, even you. Oh yeah, I know what you did. You're sick in the head and I'm gonna see you go down for this.'

'Shut up, Jamie,' Miles yelled, 'just shut up. I can't listen to you anymore. Look at what you've done, you stupid little shit. You've hurt a teacher. How can we keep this quiet? Get out, get out now.'

Jamie didn't move from the doorway. 'I'm not going anywhere, mate. Neither's she and neither are you, if you know what's good for you. Who d'you think the police are gonna believe? Me, or a pervert?'

'But we can't just keep her here, you idiot.'

'I've got a few things to do, then you can do what you like, and so can she.' Jamie squared up to Westlake. 'Just for tonight. That's all. We'll just keep her here for tonight, alright?'

Westlake lifted Claire's legs onto the cushions and pushed past Jamie to get out of the room, but Claire realised he was trapped in this hell he had created, and so was she.

Her heart began to hammer. Had Jamie really hit her over the head? Why? She guessed she must have been getting close to what had happened at the weekend. Could these two have murdered Carly? And if they did, what did that mean for her? A few seconds later, she lost the battle to stay conscious and swam down into blackness.

Chapter 8

Date: Monday 24th April Time:17:09 DI Dan Hellier, Exeter Road Police Station

Dan sat in the Major Incident Room adjoining the main office. He twirled a piece of paper in his hands. He had eaten a cold pasty and drunk a cup of stewed coffee at his desk while attempting to draw a Mind Map onto several large pieces of paper he had stuck together. Jotting down everything he knew, he was trying but failing to make useful connections. It was ridiculous. So early into the investigation, he only had a small amount of information. But he wanted to be able to say they had made some progress by the end of the first day. Performance anxiety, he thought.

The day before, he had finally plucked up courage to ask Colin White, the desk sergeant, to check the records for Alison Hellier, AKA Annie Porter, A.k.a. Allie Smith. A.k.a. total nightmare. He had been able to push her back into the dark recesses while he'd been living in London, but now he felt obliged to find out how she was. He couldn't cope with the mute expectation in his mother's eyes, either. She assumed it was easy to find out anything he wanted to know. It was. He just didn't want to do it. Colin had placed a folded sheet of paper on the desk an hour ago, and he hadn't looked at it yet.

He unfurled the sheet. A list of arrests, cautions, short sentences, and then, at the bottom, eighteen months for dealing. He checked the dates. She'd been inside for three months and hadn't contacted mum and dad once. His lip curled in disgust. The temptation to throw the sheet away was huge. He knew that as soon as he told them where she was, they'd be off in the car to Bristol on another mercy mission that was doomed to failure. He couldn't bear the defeated look in his Dad's eyes as they set out to rescue her again. She was so downright selfish that she took whatever they gave her as her right. She'd actually said to him once that she might as well have what was hers now rather than wait until after they were dead. Unbelievable. He tore the page into tiny shreds, threw it into his bin and stared across the office at his newly formed team.

Known throughout the station as the Flowerpot Men, Sergeants Bill Larcombe and Mark 'Ben' Bennett were catching up with their notes and adding to the incident board on the rear wall. As Crime Scene Manager, Bill had already begun to add crime scene photos to the wall and was organising the office into a viable working space. Ben was collating the evidence and would handle house-to-house interviews, phone calls and witnesses. They had given him a polite nod when Oliver had assigned them, but he knew they were Ian Gould's men, through and through.

So far, the whiteboard showed pictures of Carly Braithwaite taken at the crime scene and a map of the local area with her house and the school picked out in red. The forensic team had passed on prints of the morning's close scrutiny of the copse floor, but they were messy because of the state of the ground. It was hard to pick out any particular footprints. Even the bruising to the girl was faint on the photos.

Dan looked at the clock and wondered when he would find out what Ian had learned at the school. He had a feeling the old bugger would be typing his notes up at his desk next door rather than committing them to computer memory so everyone could read them. He shook his head, the guy just made more work for people. Sally should be back from the Braithwaite's soon, so they could have a quick de-brief before going home. He looked at the slim results of two hours thinking and sighed. Who on earth would want this girl dead, and more importantly, why?

The rest of the team arrived within minutes, carrying coffee and notebooks. They sat round the big rectangular table in the middle of the room, chatting and laughing amongst themselves. Once again, Dan was all too aware that he was the new boy who needed to make an impression on his first case. He cleared his throat, leant against the edge of the table and waited for the chat to die down. Before he managed a word, the door opened and Superintendent Oliver walked in. She also had coffee, but Dan had a feeling that hers had been freshly brewed by the efficient Stella rather than dispensed by ancient machine. Her arrival stopped the conversation faster than his throat clearing had.

'Carry on, Detective Inspector,' she said. 'I just want to listen in so I can tell the press where we're up to. They're hovering in the meeting room like flies round a carcass.'

Dan's face fell. He'd wanted to do the press interviews.

Oliver hadn't finished, 'As this is your first case, I thought it would be better to have the voice of experience in front of the TV cameras. I will expect you to be by my side, of course,' she added, sending a brief smile in his direction. 'I'll lend you some powder for your forehead. Awfully bright under all those lights.'

A snigger sneaked out from the direction of Ian Gould who had wandered in and sat beside the Flowerpot Men. The three of them were giggling into their mugs.

Oliver glared at them, 'It's like school in here sometimes.'

Dan cleared his throat again. He would have to have a word with the naughty side of the table later. He didn't want Gould taking a disruptive role just because he was de-mob happy.

Dan indicated the Mind Map, a visual representation of the case which looked like a spider with too many legs, with Carly's name at the middle. 'I have added a string, or spider leg, for all the people we know saw Carly over the weekend. I've added the places we know she visited in the last couple of days before she died, but I need you people to fill in the gaps.' He nodded to Bill Larcombe, who rose and stood by the board, pen poised. Dan turned to Gould first. 'DCI Gould?'

Gould looked at his notebook. 'I interviewed Claire Quick, the girl's form tutor, who seems to have known her well. She also said that Carly could be difficult but that she couldn't think of anyone who would want to harm her. I mentioned Jamie May, the boyfriend, but she seemed convinced that he wouldn't harm her, as he was, and I quote, "madly in love with Carly".

'The boys who found the body had little to report other than their shock at finding her. They are regulars up in the wood but didn't notice anything unusual. I have their written statements here.

'I then interviewed the school receptionist, Marcia Penrose, who was keen to tell me that Carly Braithwaite was quite a rude and difficult girl. Mr Braithwaite had threatened Mrs Penrose in the past. Apparently she refused to let Carly go home when she felt ill. In Mrs Penrose's opinion, the girl just wanted the afternoon off school. Allegedly, Alan Braithwaite made threats to punch her in the face and the headteacher had to intervene to get him off the premises. He has been banned ever since. He could be a person of interest.

'Lastly, I saw the Music teacher, Miles Westlake. He was a mess, breaking down all the time and blubbering.' He made air quote gestures, 'He's the "sensitive" type. He saw Carly and Jamie on Saturday afternoon for a couple of hours to rehearse the songs for the next day's recording session, but let them go by three-thirty pm. He says he was waiting in the school on Monday morning to hear how it had gone. Don't think he's the murdering type.'

Ian closed his book and sat back, shaking his head at the whiteboard. Bill was adding his notes to the messy diagram on the board. 'I don't get this spider diagram stuff. Prefer columns myself.'

As Dan continued to look at him, he added, '*What?*'

'Weren't you supposed to interview Jamie May, the boyfriend?'

'Yeah, but he didn't stay behind with the others like he was supposed to. I called round to his house on the way here - rough old street - but there was no-one home. Thought I could get Sam to see him tomorrow morning.'

Oliver raised her eyebrows, indicating for him to continue.

'Look, he's just another kid. Kids don't kill other kids unless they're in some sort of gang, and there's no sign of anything like that here. Tomorrow will be fine to interview him. Chill a bit, guys.' He muttered into his mug of tea and drew a spiky spider on his notebook.

Dan rolled his eyes. It really was like school in here. He practised his best glare on the Flowerpot men who were nudging Gould and pulling faces at him.

'Concentrate, you two,' said Oliver, bringing instant silence.

Sally Ellis went next. 'Well, after spending the day with the Braithwaites, I feel I know them a little better now. I don't think that Alan Braithwaite killed his daughter unless, of course, the motive was jealousy, in which case, who knows what he may be capable of? He had an obsessive interest in her singing career and has kept copies of everything she's done since she was a small child.'

Sally passed pictures of Carly singing and receiving her Youth Matters award to 'Ben' Bennett to go on the board.

Bill Larcombe interrupted, 'He has a record for Drunk and Disorderly ten years ago and Actual Bodily Harm six years ago, for which he served a six month sentence. There has been no trouble with the police since then apart from the incident at school which was logged last November.'

'When did his wife leave him?' asked Dan.

Sally continued, 'Just before he came out of prison for the assault case, about five years ago. She apparently ran off with the guy he assaulted, leaving the two kids behind with his mother until he came out. She hasn't been back since. Not that he's bitter or anything.

'Carly's room was pretty tidy for a teenager. I didn't find her phone or shoe, but her bag was there on the bed. She obviously didn't take it with her when she left on Sunday. Kids are never parted from their phones, so we should make finding that a priority. Forensics will be in there tomorrow for a search.'

Bill wrote 'PHONE?' in large letters on the board.

'Jenna is my last person of interest. I think there is more to that girl than people see. She's only thirteen but she's the cook and the cleaner, and there are very few pictures of her around the place. She's like Cinderella. She seems to be in a permanent state of anxiety about her Dad's moods but she doesn't complain. Even when I used all my Devon charm to draw her out, she wouldn't have a word said against her sister or her Dad. I don't know how she's holding up.'

Bill scribbled furiously. Dan realised he hadn't quite got the point.

'Bill, just the main facts or opinions go on the map, like headlines, we've got the proper reports for the details, and I need a bit of space to add the forensic and post-mortem stuff when we get it.'

Bill stopped and glared at Bennett and Gould who were pulling "who's got told off by the boss?" faces at him.

'OK. Pictures are beginning to emerge, I think,' said Dan. 'I spoke to the character who runs the studios in town, Jed Abrams. He said he didn't see Carly at all on Sunday night, that he waited an hour and then went for a drink on his own. He couldn't remember where he'd had the drink at first, and then he remembered he had gone for a drink in his own home and that nobody had seen him at all.' He stopped for effect. As far as he was concerned it was the first proper lead any of them had got that day. 'He was not in a good way, lots of nervous tics and sweaty palms, so we'll bring him in tomorrow and interview him under caution, and give him this evening to stew a little. I have no idea what his motive for killing this girl could be, but we'll know more tomorrow.

'I also spoke to his assistant, Chas Lloyd, age 19 and a student on gap year. She left at six pm and said that Abrams usually did evening sessions on his own at weekends, to avoid paying overtime. In her opinion he is a bit of a letch, but she didn't think he had it in him to kill someone. But we all know how wrong members of the public can be. Bill, any chance we could fingerprint and photo both of them tomorrow?'

Larcombe sat up. 'Easy to do Abrams, he'll be here. Might take a day or two to get to the girl though. I'll see what we can do.' He made a note in his pad.

Dan looked over at Sam Knowles, but he shook his head, 'Sorry, sir, nothing to go on the board except gossip and vitriol.' Sam paused, then added, with a wistful sigh, 'I have a dream that one day I'll have a junior officer on my team who I can force to spend the whole day being giggled at and toyed with by sixteen year-old girls who think they are hilarious and irresistible.'

Dan tolerated the wolf whistles and hoots round the table. With his great height and extreme skinniness, Sam was nobody's idea of a sex symbol, including his own.

'They did know about Carly's relationship with Jamie May, and most of the girls were jealous of her, in a catty sort of way,' he continued. 'She was clearly Mr Westlake's favourite, too, and that made them even more jealous. Jamie's considered very cool at school, although a couple of boys said he has a nasty side when he's crossed. I've got the contact details of a couple of lads from his band if we need to ask for more.'

'So,' Dan said, 'what have we got so far? Why would someone want this girl dead? We need to find a motive. What did she see, or hear, or find out, or threaten to do that would cost her her life? Who was the last person to see her alive?' He paused. 'I think we look closely at Jed Abrams - he's hiding something.

'Sally, keep close to the family, I'm not convinced that Dad hasn't got something to do with it.

'And Ian, the boy is important, you should find him. It may be significant that he disappeared from school today.' He squeezed the tendons at the back of his neck – solid. Definite headache lurking there under the three paracetamols he'd swallowed. 'Did Carly get as far as the studio on Sunday night?

'Sam, go round the local shops on Sidwell Street and check their CCTV recordings for Sunday. There was a camera outside the studio door, start with that one.'

The young officer nodded.

'Also, what about this music teacher? It's not normal for teachers to have kids at their houses, is it?' He looked across at Gould who consulted his notes.

'The teacher said it was a one off because of the recording session. His wife said it was okay, so I assume she was there.'

Dan glared at his superior officer. 'So, in fact, they could have been there many times, couldn't they? And did his wife really agree to this rehearsal? Was she even there? Should Miles Westlake be in the frame, not Jed Abrams?' He let the thought slide around the room. 'Too much we don't know, and every hour takes us away from finding the killer.' Dan shut himself up. He knew he had a tendency to go on a bit and state the bleedin' obvious. They were all professionals and there was no need to over-egg the seriousness of the situation. He was just angry at Gould's assumptions. It was poor detective work.

'Right, post-mortem tomorrow morning at ten am. Ian, will you and Sam pick up Jed Abrams and bring him in round about ten-thirty? He can sit and sweat for a bit while I watch the PM. Can you both then go and talk to the boy, Jamie May, please? He is the girl's close friend and possibly the last person to see her. I really wanted to interview all the main suspects today.' He stopped himself having another go at Ian for not catching up with boy. It was only one more day.

Julie Oliver nodded to the team and suggested Dan joined her in her office straight after the meeting to plan a brief statement for the late news. The noise level in the room rose as she left. People shuffled papers and pushed back chairs.

'Night all,' shouted Dan. 'Take your own mugs back to the dishwasher and I'll see you at eight-thirty tomorrow, bright and breezy. Thanks for your efforts today.'

He saw Gould raise his eyebrows again at the Flowerpot Men, and mimic Dan's thanks in a little girl's voice. A wave of anger washed up his throat. Gripping the edge of the table, he put his burning face down and made busy with his paperwork. It was a small victory for him. Two years ago, he'd have been across the office floor shouting in their faces and providing entertainment for the whole team, as well as loss of face for him. They were just having a bit of fun at his expense. He'd done it himself, and this lot were much more gentle with him than the general banter in the sergeants' room at the Met had ever been. He gathered his stuff and headed for the Superintendent's office.

Oliver's office was spacious and furnished in beech. Probably laminate from Ikea, but still, it looked comfortable and modern, unlike the main office downstairs. Oliver pointed to a chair and shouted for coffee from the reliable Stella. Dan wondered if Stella ever went home, imagining her living in a cupboard under the stairs so she could be on hand to satisfy Oliver's every whim.

He looked past the Chief Super's shoulder to the Victorian rooftops of the University buildings opposite. Pigeons jostled and hooted on the ironwork as they settled in for the night. He ran his tongue over his teeth, folded his arms and settled back on the wooden chair to wait for her to finish reading the briefing notes from the meeting. He wondered who got invited to sit round the fancy table at the other end of the office.

Oliver bit down hard on the lid of the biro, her eyes following the secretary as she brought coffee and dropped a fat file onto the desk. She waited until they were alone.

'It was a total nightmare getting into the station this morning,' she said, cracking the silence. 'How do those vultures find out about people being killed at the exact same time as we do? It's not right. It stops us doing our job properly. We haven't even released the name yet but there were three of them hanging about hassling me. And I nearly trampled that silly mare from the Echo who wouldn't get out of my face. Someone must have leaked it. Must have…'

Dan moved to answer but she ploughed over him.

'I know we don't get many murders in Exeter, and before you say anything, I know that the body being found on a school's grounds is even more entertaining for the press than usual but...'

She placed her elbows on the desk and rested her chin in both hands, looking up over her glasses. 'Oh God,' she sighed, rubbing her temples. 'It's bound to attract the nationals, and the telly. Just what I don't need.'

Dan thought about the way she had spoken about Gould earlier in the day. He'd heard rumours about an affair between her and Gould once upon a time. He found that hard to credit. Oliver was lean and fit and attractive in a viperish sort of way. She was always neat with her brown bob and white shirts. Gould was bloated and balding and grunted when he got out of the chair. Unconsciously, Dan smoothed his hair down and pulled his stomach in.

'Anyway, enough of my worries. I'm afraid you'll be leading a somewhat smaller team because of people being off, but we've brought in people from the other teams. So don't worry, they're a good bunch.' She gave him a brief smile and said, 'Dan, you're keen, but you're very new to this level of responsibility. You're bound to make mistakes, to miss things, things that may be vital to the case. Don't get so carried away trying to catch the bad guys that you forget that your eyes and ears and your instinct are your best tools.

'We're not the Met. We don't see many guns or terrorist threats. Here, low-lives will give themselves away if you let them. Not as sophisticated as your average London crim. But develop some decent people skills and persuade them to talk to you, otherwise you'll get nowhere. Ian can do all these things – learn from him while you've got him.'

She paused and gulped down the last of her coffee, wrinkling her nose at the lukewarm bitterness. 'I know what you were going to say about Gould this morning. He's unreliable and a bit of a maverick, we all know that. But he was a good copper once, and I want him to leave on a high next month, not creep out with his tail between his legs. So you will work together. Got it?'

'Got it, Ma'am.'

'Right, let's prepare the statement for the Press and then we can all go home.'

Dan finished presenting the TV broadcast for the late evening news with Oliver and was on his way home by shortly after seven pm. He hoped that would keep the press off his back for a day or two.

It was a mild and clear evening, so he parked the Audi in his reserved space and wandered round to the quayside. He bought a bottle of lager from the Italian restaurant, which ran the length of the bottom floor of his apartment building, and took it outside.

He sat on a bench watching the rowing practice on the river. He wondered if that would be a good way to make friends as they seemed to be young and having fun. He wanted to get in touch with some of his old school and university friends, but it felt like too much time had gone by. People change so much. And, if he was being honest, he felt like a failure because his relationship with Sarah had fallen apart and he wasn't ready to talk about it to anybody yet. He wasn't ready to talk about Sarah or his sister. They were two scabs he would constantly pick at that were probably best left alone to mend.

He felt so alone. Funny how quickly you become used to waking up with a familiar warm body next to you. How quickly you fall into routines over breakfast or last thing at night. How you develop shared jokes and sayings picked up from people encountered and places visited. A relationship was a whole private language and landscape, the result of thousands of hours of commitment and compromise and love that he had thrown away when he had walked. And, at the moment, he still wasn't sure it had been worth it.

Watching the light change to purple dusk, he wondered if he should just get on the phone anyway and call a couple of old friends. What had he got to lose except a bit of face? He let his eyes wander to the river basin to his left. The swans that haunt the river harassing visitors for food were quiet, having settled onto their nests further up river. Sounds of laughter reached across the water from the pub.

On the bench under the soft lamplight, Dan understood that he had been living in a bubble of grief for the last two months, pretending to be a human being but not connecting with anyone, not making a commitment to anything. Here on the side of the river, in the kindly evening gloom, he could hear the sounds of birds settling, and bats swooping. He could also smell the tantalising garlic from The Veneziana's kitchen behind him. It was like watching his first 3D movie – everything seemed heightened. Maybe, after all, he was ready to move on and just needed to give himself permission do it.

He drank his beer feeling full of a nervous energy that had nowhere to go except out through the bottom of his tapping foot. He felt the urgency of the case and was frustrated at having so little information yet to go on. How could the others go home to their families and forget all about it until the next day?

He sighed and swallowed the last of his beer. No point fretting about things you can't change, as his mum would say. Something to eat would settle him down. His mum would say that, too. He realised he was hungry. Really hungry. The smell of the food cooking was overwhelming his taste buds, and he could feel saliva awakening his mouth. He needed a plate of pasta Puttanesca. Now.

As he turned to enter the restaurant he noticed someone trying to attract his attention from the water, waving at him with an oar. It took him a few moments to realise that it was Chas Lloyd, balancing in the front of a canoe and looking fetching in Lycra shorts and a performance tee shirt. Dan smiled and walked towards the water's edge. The team was getting out of the boat on the other side of the river.

'Wait there,' she shouted, 'I'll come over for a beer!' The evening might not be entirely lost, he thought.

Ian Gould and the flowerpot men peeled out of the Barn Owl at seven-thirty pm. The early-doors crowd had thinned and the evening throng was beginning to fill up the corner tables and order food from the menu. Ian waved the pair an extravagant farewell and wove his way towards his car. Blimey, three pints and he was wobbling like a virgin ice skater.

Ian hated the way pubs had changed. They were once proper men's places where you stood at the bar or perched on uncomfortable wooden stools and drank only beer, with a whisky chaser if it was pay day. Dark- brown stained places where you could smoke and eat pork scratchings and have a laugh about football and the stupidity of politicians before going home late to a congealed supper and an angry missus. He sighed. Simpler times.

He knew he'd been a pillock when he sorted out the holiday roster, but his mistake had led to the flowerpot men coming over to Team Two for the duration of the investigation, so it wasn't all bad. They were enjoying taking the piss out of young Hellier. Gently, though. Oliver wouldn't be happy if they went too far. Dan was the boss after all, ridiculous though that seemed. Policemen really were getting younger. He chuckled to himself as he patted each pocket. 'I'm becoming a right old sweat,' he told his elusive car keys.

Julie had been cool with him in front of Hellier. She'd been right, of course. Ian didn't want him putting two and two together and sensing any history that there might have been, even if their fling had been over for years. She still looked good though, and thinking about her still raised a bit of interest in the trouser area.

He shrugged off his jacket and threw it onto the seat, unimpressed with the sweaty aroma escaping his armpits. He squeezed behind the wheel and made his cautious way through the back streets to the small house overlooking the canal where he and Marilyn had lived for over thirty years. These days, it was a pleasure to go home. Laura was grown and expecting her first kid. He'd be a granddad in a couple of months. He chuckled. Who'd have thought?

He was going to sit down with Marilyn at the weekend and talk about retirement and what they were going to do with all this free time they would have. He'd put off thinking about it for long enough. Perhaps on Saturday they could get a Chinese takeaway and a bottle of red and he could broach the subject. He had a secret dread that she might suggest ball-room dancing, but other than that, he was open to offers.

Chapter 9

Date: Tuesday 25th April Time: 00:14 Illusion Studio

Jed Abrams rubbed his eyes, pressing his fingers into the sockets until he saw stars. The copying machines were working flat out, but he still had another hundred to complete before the bloody Latvian mafia arrived in the morning. And, he'd got a new film to shoot that he didn't want to do, what with the police sniffing around about Carly. He didn't dare cancel it though, he was far more scared of Irina Akis than of anybody in the British police force.

But Jed could feel the panic rising in his chest. That Inspector already thought the murder had something to do with him, and he didn't know what to do about that. What if he came back with a search warrant? No, it mustn't happen. He'd have to speak to Irina and get the stuff moved somewhere else until it all died down.

He reached for the vodka bottle and was, as usual, surprised to find it empty. Nowadays, he didn't feel better when he drank. In fact, the best he could hope for was that he passed out more often, sometimes losing whole days.

Now his drinking was affecting the business and he knew he had to stop. Good job Chas was reliable and the punters liked her. If he could only make it into the major leagues with the films, he could give all this up and go and live somewhere warm.

His mobile rang. Sweat broke out on his forehead as he watched the phone ringing and vibrating on the desk. He knew there was no way out. Once you were in with these people, you stayed in until they didn't need you anymore. And then, if you had been a loyal servant, they would reward you with more money than you could imagine. If you hadn't... Jed had been very loyal, but he was under no illusion that they would kill him in a second rather than jeopardise their operation.

He spoke to Grigor about the delivery, and then to Irina about the new film. Irina was unimpressed when he told her about the police. There was no way they could change the date or the time, they had actors booked. Didn't Jed realise that they were on deadlines too? She said she would sort something out when they arrived.

By the time the call ended, Jed thought he had convinced them that he didn't have anything to do with Carly's death. But he wouldn't relax until they were gone again with the North Sea between them. There was something so chilling about Irina, like she had a piece missing when they handed out emotions. Abrams had only tried his charm on her once. It was her laugh that had really shrivelled him, that and the stamping on his foot with her boot.

The three Latvians would get off the container ship in the early hours of the following morning and drive the empty van over from Harwich. Jed estimated four or five hours driving time, so they'd be here around nine o'clock in the morning. He swapped the DVDs over and made his way to the bed in the corner. He had to do another few hours at the Studio so he may as well get some sleep while he could.

Chapter 10

Date: Monday 24th April Time: 04:54 Riga, Latvia

Even within the safe harbour of Riga, yellow-frothed waves nipped and harried the sides of the huge vessel. The grey of sea and sky melded on the horizon into a silver line. The ship would sail before daybreak. The 'Kasparov' made the thirty-six hour trip from the Latvian port to Harwich on the east coast of England twice a week, bringing timber and metal to the factories of Britain. Crane drivers, remote in their eyries, shifted containers as a child moves Lego, with slick ease.

There was space aboard the 'Kasparov', occasionally, for fee-paying passengers who wished to avoid any awkwardness that might arise from passing through customs or passport control. The captain had a comfortable arrangement with the Akis family that had already boosted his pension far beyond his needs.

After hiding the black Mercedes van inside an empty container, Grigor Pelakais and Filip Sarkov ushered their employer on board and led her to her usual cabin. She threw her bag on the bed and closed the door in Grigor's face as she squeezed her phone from her jeans pocket. Grigor turned to Filip, his friend and Irina's bodyguard, and raised his eyebrows. Filip shrugged and turned in the narrow space, heading down to the stern. They preferred to berth with the crew.

Later, pausing outside the cracked metal door, Grigor balanced a tray carrying a pot of Earl Grey tea and listened until Irina Akis had finished her call. He didn't know what language she was speaking, but he knew that when she spoke to the person on the other end of the phone she laughed, her voice was warm and she was slow to say goodbye.

Grigor knocked and entered, placing the tray on the bedside table. He looked down at her, waiting to see if she wanted anything else. Eyes cool, expression blank, she thanked him for the tea and dismissed him with a brief nod of the head. To Grigor, she seemed to be able to play two different people as if born to it. One aspect of her was the cool, hard, boss he had to obey in everything she asked or suffer appalling consequences, and the other was the more human personality that she saved for this foreigner on the phone. Grigor nodded back to her and closed the door quietly behind him as he left.

He made his way back to the crew's quarters, where he and Filip would play a few games of cards with the men before attempting to sleep. The sea could be rough this time of year so it was unlikely she would send for him tonight. He expected her to call ahead as soon as they landed to make sure everything was in place for the following day. Superstitious, he touched the wooden rail that ran the length of the corridor. He hummed a children's lullaby to block the distressing images that ambushed his brain every time they made the journey over to England.

Chapter 11

Date: Tuesday 25th April Time: 03:47 The North Sea

The second morning of the crossing from Riga to Harwich was cool and clear. The ship had been weighty enough, the night before, to slice through the waves rather than have to battle over them and they had all managed to sleep for a few hours before they docked. Irina sat on her bed with her feet in Grigor's lap. She loved to have her feet massaged, and Grigor was happy to do it if it delayed her descent into nastiness for the day.

The call to Abrams had upset her earlier. The drunken English fool had got himself involved in the death of a young girl. How stupid was he? They had just spent an hour working out their escape strategy if things turned bad.

To Grigor, she seemed different this trip. It was the same dirty business as usual but he could sense her altered mood, Suppressed excitement was the closest he could get. It worried him a great deal. What had happened to make her so different, and how would it affect himself and Filip?

Grigor ran his thumb down her instep and made tiny circular movements on the pad of flesh under each toe, stroking and kneading until he heard the small sigh of satisfaction and knew that he had done well. She patted his head, like she might a dog, and Grigor slipped a warm sock back over each foot.

In their cabin, Filip waited, packing toiletries into his bag. 'Are you alright?'

'What can I say? She wanted a foot massage. I have no bruises, bite marks or burns. My self-respect, however, is in the gutter.'

Filip smiled, they had had the same conversation many times. Filip was too big and too ugly to interest Irina, and for that Grigor was always grateful.

'She's been talking a lot to someone in a foreign language. I think it might be Swedish. Has she said anything to you about it?'

Filip shook his head. Grigor knew Irina would never engage Filip in conversation, she just gave him orders. Grigor always tried to make Filip feel like he was part of the team, but that was because he loved him. It didn't reflect reality.

Late at night, they both harboured dreams of throwing her overboard, or waiting until they were in England, then killing her and running away. They never did it, and now that they were no longer boys, those dreams seemed childish and impossible.

Filip sighed and took Grigor's hand in his. He repeated the same words one more time, 'We have money saved. We could run away…'

Grigor didn't bother to answer, they both knew that would never be allowed to happen.

Chapter 12

Date: Tuesday 25th April Time: 06:13 Miles Westlake's house

Claire Quick was seething with frustration. She was thirsty, urgently needed a pee and couldn't get the ties off her wrists and ankles. Blood had caked itself around her face and neck and cracked as she moved.

Once she had come round last night, she had done her best to persuade Jamie and Miles to let her go, promising that she wouldn't tell anybody what they had done. Miles was ready to believe her but Jamie showed a level of detachment about her condition that worried her. He had tied her up despite all her reassurances and pleading, and he must have been watching some pretty strange films, as she couldn't get her hands up past her knees without contorting her body into a squat worthy of an escape artist.

Didn't they realise that very soon someone would notice that they were all missing? What was going on in their heads?

Miles had almost convinced her that he hadn't killed Carly, but it was clear that the girl had spent Saturday night and most of Sunday morning at the house with him. It made Claire feel even worse when she admitted to herself what that probably meant. Miles had broken a basic rule of teaching, don't mess with the kids. This was bad enough. It didn't bear thinking about that he may have killed her too.

Jamie, on the other hand, she wasn't sure about at all. His behaviour was so extreme, he had frightened her. And jealousy was a powerful motive for murder.

Would the fear of exposure to the police and the school authorities be enough for them to keep her here against her will? Probably. At least they hadn't killed her…yet. She shuddered. She couldn't see how they were going to be able to let her go now.

Miles had persuaded Jamie to take the gag off if Claire promised not to scream, so she promised. At least she could breathe. And she had slept, folded up on the sofa with her wrists and ankles tied almost together, concussion making it easy for her to lose consciousness for a few hours.

Now, it was dawn on Tuesday morning. Pale light came through the crack in the curtains but there was no noise yet of traffic or people. Claire didn't know whether Jamie had stayed the night or gone home, but she had heard Miles getting into bed above her head during the night. Now was the time to have a proper go at getting away before he woke up.

She could see her bag with car keys and phone on the floor near the fireplace. There was a small multi-purpose knife on her key ring, she just had to get to it. She managed a wry smile, once a Girl Guide… Claire tucked her legs up to the side, and slid off the sofa so that she landed on her knees. The surge of pain from her injured head made her dizzy. She sank down and laid her head on the rug. It took a few minutes for the wave of pain to subside. Claire sniffed back tears that threatened to reduce her to a weeping heap and knelt up again.

She shuffled towards her bag, feeling the blue cord, that she thought could be washing line, biting into her ankles and wrists. Using her teeth, Claire bent over the bag and undid the zip, wincing at each muffled sound. She could see her phone in its little pouch but couldn't think of a way to use it without attracting attention, She'd have to hold it so far away from her mouth that she would need to shout. Better to get the knife.

Her keys were in the bottom of the main compartment. She would have to be careful, as they would rattle when she moved them. With infinite care, she stuck her head into the cavity of the bag and was suddenly overcome with the ridiculousness of what she was doing. She felt like a contestant on 'I'm a Celebrity, Get me Out of Here,' and had to clamp down on the hysteria that was threatening to worm its way out through her clenched teeth.

She located the keys, looped her tongue through the key ring and tried to lift the keys free from the bag. She had had no idea how heavy keys could be. True, she had never tried to lift anything with her tongue before. The giggling was threatening again. On the third attempt, she pulled the bag over and got her teeth onto the key ring. At last.

Once the keys were out and on the floor, Claire picked them up with her bound hands. She had to bend almost double to open the blade and then sat back on her bottom, with her legs crossed in front of her. She was in danger of falling over backwards, so she twisted and wedged her back against the armchair, positioned the tiny blade in her fingers, and got to work. She sawed through the rope a bit at a time, fraying it with the blade rather than cutting it. Her ankles freed, she pushed herself upright by turning onto her knees, leaning on the chair seat to face the door. Almost defeated by the swaying of the room and the pain in her legs, she levered herself upright.

One thing she knew with certainty, she would never sit with her back to a door again.

Now, free her hands, or get out of the house and run? Claire made her way to the door, every sense on high alert. She could hear nothing. She had to have her hands loose, she was too vulnerable without them. She took the minutes necessary to free one hand, unable to concentrate as she strained every sense towards the door. She gasped with pain as the blade nicked the soft, white inside of her left wrist. She had missed the vein, but still it welled and dripped onto the floor. Stifling another overwhelming urge to sink down and sob, she took a huge gulp of air, slit the edge of her white work shirt and cut a strip wide enough to go round her wrist. She looked at the burn marks on her wrists made by the rope. The pain seemed far away at the moment, although the screaming pins and needles in her legs was coming through loud and clear as the blood surged back round the limbs. She held the strip of cloth with her teeth and tied it round her injured wrist, tucking the ends under with her free hand. At least it stopped the bleeding. Sighing, she pushed her hair out of her eyes and grasped the door knob.

It was then that she heard a noise outside the door, a groan or a sigh. Was somebody there? She put her ear close to the door, but there was nothing else to hear. She couldn't wait any longer, even if there was someone out there. The need to get out superseded all other worries. She shouldered her bag, dropping the keys into their compartment and grabbed the poker from beside the fireplace. The sound from outside the room came again.

Claire held her breath and prised the door open a crack. Jamie May was lying across the threshold, covered in a blanket. His arm, which had been resting against the door, fell onto the floor in front of her foot. He was asleep, lost in a mumbling, flailing dream. Reassured, she stepped over him and made for the front door, risking a glance back over her shoulder. The temptation to hit him with the poker was huge. He had hurt her, he had imprisoned her, he may well have killed Carly. Her hand tightened round the blackened metal. She held it out in front of her, like a sword.

She didn't do it. He was just a kid, after all. Someone had to be the adult in all of this madness. He looked so young lying there, asleep.

Leaving the front door ajar, Claire limped as quickly as she could towards the gate and the relative safety of her car parked down the street.

She felt his approach rather than heard it. Half turning, she saw Jamie bearing down on her, his face contorted into a grimace, his teeth chattering, his arms stretching out to grab her like some parody of a zombie in a cheap movie. Claire did the only thing she could think of - she stabbed him as hard as she could in the solar plexus with the iron poker. Jamie stared at her for a second, his eyes wide with shock, then collapsed onto the path, winded. He lay rigid, panic freezing him as he waited for his lungs to recover enough for him to grab a breath.

Claire stared around her wildly, expecting attack on all sides. But the street was still deserted. Birds twittered. A striped cat slunk by, keeping to the protection of the low wall. It was all so normal. She felt the nervous energy which had propelled her out of the house begin to fail, her legs wobbled and a sob began to work its way up her throat.

She fumbled her car keys back out of the bag. She knew it was stupid. She had concussion. But it would be quicker to drive herself to the hospital than wait for a police car to come for her. And she needed to get away now, before Jamie came round.

Chapter 13

Date: Tuesday 25th April Time: 10:00 Royal Devon & Exeter Hospital

Carly Braithwaite lay on the examination table in the Pathology department. Her body was covered by a faded green surgical sheet that emphasized the pallor of her face and neck. Dan nodded at the others; Sally Ellis, Bill Larcombe, Campbell Fox and his three assistants. They were also gowned in green, linked to the dead girl and each other by a shade he guessed none of them would have chosen. The post-mortem room was small, without windows or decoration and lit by a powerful light which bleached all other colour from the watchers. Carly, both eyes closed now, lolling eyeball returned to its rightful socket, looked palely perfect apart from the faint bruising on her face and neck.

In silence, the assistants removed the girl's clothing and passed it to Bill Larcombe, who, with methodical precision, bagged and labelled each item. Dan watched the items go into the bag. There was so little, jeans, tee-shirt, underwear. No coat. Now that was odd. She would have worn a coat, surely, in April? And the scarf they had found at the scene wasn't there with the evidence bags. Not hers then.

Fox spoke first, once he had started the recorder. 'On my preliminary examination of the body yesterday I could find no obvious cause of death. Things are a bit clearer today as the bruising has come out. Can you see the faint marking at one side of her throat, and the finger marks on the right cheek?' He gestured to an assistant who hung back, camera at the ready. 'Take a picture of those, will you?'

The young woman moved in close with her camera, and so did Dan and Sally, but there was little to see with the naked eye. Fox continued his walk around the girl's body, lifting, moving and turning her until he was satisfied that they had recorded all that there was to see.

'External examination shows that she has a tattoo on her left bicep, of a rose and a dagger, but no other distinguishing features.'

His assistant moved the covering over the girl's body as Fox worked, exposing only the part he was examining. Fox glanced over at the police officers.

'You may be thinking that I am preserving the wee girl's modesty, and you would be right.' He took a vaginal swab and handed it to an assistant who took it straight to the lab for analysis.

'She was not a virgin,' he said, 'and she had intercourse very recently, but there are no signs of childbirth or disease.'

He paused the recording and looked round at Dan Hellier, as another assistant took scrapings from under the dead girl's fingernails and went off to process them. Fox removed the onyx and silver ring from Carly's shredded finger and passed it to Bill Larcombe to bag.

'I'm not planning to do a full PM today as it is clear from medical records that she was in good health, unless you have a particular need to see the internal organs?'

Dan gave a quick shake of the head. 'We just need cause and best estimate of time of death please, Doctor. Thanks for sending those samples off to be done straightaway, too.'

Fox nodded. 'I hate to see a young girl at the start of her life lying on a slab in here. I've told my team to prioritise the case.' He resumed the recording. 'She has bruising to the front of her right shin.' He moved up to her arms, gesturing at his assistant to hold a light closer to Carly's right hand. 'She has fragments of glass embedded in her palm and fingers. She was holding something that broke in her hand, or tried to pick up a broken object. Anything found at the scene?'

Dan shook his head. The copse where she had been found was a nightmare to analyse. Too many people had used it and abused it. But as she wasn't killed there, he couldn't add anything useful.

'I'll carry on, then. There are bruises around the biceps above both elbows, indicative of her being held by the arms. A thumb and four fingers clear on each arm.'

Dan interrupted, 'Was she being held from the front or the rear?'

'From the front at this point. A bruise on her shin may be a kick from her assailant.' He turned the body over, exposing a thin back and slim buttocks. 'Interesting. She appears to have two almost circular bruises on either side of her back ribs.' He looked up again, peering over the lenses of rimless glasses. 'What does that suggest, Inspector?'

Sally had seen the signs before. 'She was in a fight. The assailant got her face down and knelt on her back. That's how he managed to strangle her without making so many marks on her neck - she was probably finding it hard to breathe anyway.'

Dan nodded, it seemed plausible. 'So the assailant may have some bruising or scratch marks, too.'

Fox completed his external examination. 'I need to look at her trachea and thyroid area closely, so that is what we shall do now. I'll make the first cut vertically down the centre of her neck.'

Dan swallowed. He was never very good at this sort of thing. He sneaked a quick look at Sally. She looked a bit green too, although it could have been the light reflecting off the gowns. Dr Fox was opening the girl's neck and he watched, fascinated, as he used a scalpel to open the trachea. He swallowed again, and saw Sally concentrate on counting the number of individual bulbs in the arc light above their heads. Only Bill Larcombe seemed unaffected by the scene, as he bagged evidence in the corner.

Fox sliced through the neck cartilage and brought bloodied fingers out from her neck, lifting the trachea and thyroid glands onto a dish. The room was silent then, as Fox examined the trachea. He searched for the small, horseshoe-shaped hyoid bone.

'In an adult this little bone would be broken in most types of strangulation, which makes the diagnosis simple. It's harder to see in a teenager as the bone doesn't fuse across the larynx until adulthood, but you never know, it could help.' His assistant took photographs of the organ, as Fox dissected the individual rings of the trachea.

They waited. Dan could feel a terrible need to run around the room shouting. The quiet, the concentration, the waiting was killing him.

Eventually, Fox spoke again, 'The condition of the trachea and larynx suggests that the victim was asphyxiated from behind. I have found damage to several sections of the thyroid cartilage and the hyoid bone.'

Dan nodded. It was what he expected. He saw Sally nod, too. It confirmed her idea that the girl had been turned over, or that she had been caught trying to run away. There was no doubt now, if anybody had harboured one, that Carly Braithwaite had been murdered.

The doctor continued, 'Her assailant was right-handed. The damage to the thyroid cartilage is worse on the left side of the neck where he or she could exert most pressure. The hand imprint across her mouth was from the left hand. Likely the assailant was wearing something soft on his or her arms which lessened the imprint on the girl's skin but maximised the area of suffocation.'

Dan interrupted, 'Like a hoody or a fleece?'

'That is a possibility. Something that would not leave much of an impression. In order for asphyxiation to occur, the assailant would either have needed to hold on for at least five minutes, which is a long time in a fight for life, or to have struck lucky and stopped blood flow through the carotid artery or the jugular vein at the same time as preventing air getting in through the throat. In those circumstances death can happen in seconds.'

'Could it have been an accident?' asked Sally.

'Aye, that is also possible.' The pathologist scratched his beard. 'But the girl was killed from behind, rather than face to face, which would make it a rather unlikely accident.'

He washed the blood from his gloves in the porcelain sink and leant his bulk against it as he concluded his examination.

'I estimate the time of death as somewhere between four pm and midnight. I'll be able to tell you more when I have been able to study the results. Ye'll have my report and the sample results by the end of the day if we can manage it.'

Dan thanked him. They left the pathologist to complete his work, they had what they needed for now. Bill Larcombe collected his evidence and followed them out of the room.

'Coffee?'

Bill shook his head. 'No thanks, sir, I'll get this lot back and process it. See you later.'

Dan looked at his DS. She was paler than usual. They both needed a few minutes to catch their breath.

'Sally?'

She nodded and they headed for the coffee shop at the entrance. 'At least we only had to see the minor version of a post-mortem,' he said as Sally downed half her coffee in one gulp and came up coughing because it was too hot.

'Yes, not the best part of the job,' she gasped.

'How did the father cope with identifying the body yesterday?'

Sally sighed. 'He was awful. Shouting and angry at everybody. But Foxy calmed him down. I think it's his wonderful Scots accent that does it. He's like a Glaswegian teddy bear.' She laughed and then looked thoughtful. 'It's Jenna I'm worried about. She doesn't really exist for her Dad at the moment. Losing a child is always terrible, but he can't seem to comfort her and she doesn't have anyone else to support her, as far as I can see. I'll try to locate a gran or someone. Might even have a go at contacting the estranged mother, though that could be a waste of time after five years.' She took a more careful sip of coffee. 'How can a mother leave her kids like that? If Paul and I ever split up, I'd take the kids whatever happened. Poor little Jenna. And poor little Carly.'

Dan shook his head in sympathy. Grief took people in different ways, and it was hard to know what to do for the best when there was an awkward character like Alan Braithwaite to deal with, and no mother or close adult to offer support.

'At least we have a cause of death and we should have a closer time of death later this afternoon. So, it seems like the girl was in a fight, but somehow her assailant got behind her to strangle her. We need to check out the suspects for any marks or bruising and find out what she was holding that broke in her hand.'

He thought for a minute, stirring the froth on his drink.

'Will you go and tell the father what the post-mortem has shown so far?' He had a feeling it would come better from Sally rather than him, and a visit was always better than a phone call.

They spent another few minutes in the coffee bar, and Dan realised that this was the first time he had been able to spend a few quiet minutes with calm, competent Sergeant Ellis. It was hard to get a conversation going other than about work, though. He'd had no idea that she had children, nor that she had a husband called Paul. He knew so little about his colleagues, and he had to admit, that was his own fault. He'd been grieving too, in his own way, so he hadn't gone for a drink after work, even when they had asked him. He had asked no personal questions of anyone on the team and answered none. In short, he'd been a twerp. And the fact that he was able to admit this to himself was the best sign yet that he might be getting over his broken heart.

Dan dropped Sally off back at the station to collect her own car and headed for the main office to catch up with Gould and Knowles. He hoped they'd been able to bring Jed Abrams in as requested and had tracked down Jamie May. He squeezed the Audi in next to a patrol car and sent up a prayer that they didn't scratch it as they left.

He allowed himself a little wince at the way last night had played out with Chas Lloyd, and the all-too-familiar flush crept up his neck as he thought about her, and how she had left. He trotted up the stairs, burying the thought to be processed later under "To be dealt with when I stop feeling like a total jerk". He needed to be clear-headed. Jed Abrams was hiding something and he was going to give it up today.

Chapter 14

Date: Tuesday 25th April Time: 12:37 Sally Ellis, the Braithwaite home

Sally rang home as she walked towards her car, wedged into too small a space in the corner of the staff car park. It was her punishment for getting to work late. Her mother answered the phone and told her that the twins were in fine form destroying the Lego castle she had been building with them. Sally laughed, her family were what kept her sane. She was so grateful that she and Paul had finally been able to have kids, and that her mum wanted to help look after them so she could go back to work. She had to remember to tell them that, occasionally.

Scrambling in through the passenger door, Sally swung her legs over the gear stick and bunny-hopped into the driver's seat - not her most dignified entrance. She didn't want to spend too long at the Braithwaites, conscious that Dan was doing a lot of the leg work on his own and, after all, it was a murder inquiry. They needed another body on the ground to do more of the family liaison stuff. She knew she was good at it, but she had taken the sergeant's post with the hope that she could move on to real police work. An extra PC on the team would do, someone looking for the next promotion. She'd have a word with Dan later.

As she cut the engine outside the house, Sally could hear shouting coming from inside. She leapt from the car, skirted the bunches of flowers and messages that had begun to appear at the gate and ran down the path, straight into a black-haired, Gothic looking lad. He pushed her aside and jumped over the hedge, heading for the main road.

Sally yanked herself out of the hedge and shouted for him to stop. Alan Braithwaite came out onto the front step, staring after the boy, giving little away with his eyes but clenching and unclenching his fists.

'Who was that?' she asked, brushing herself down.

Braithwaite looked down at her. 'Jamie bloody May. I'm not having him round here anymore. He's caused enough trouble in this house.' He turned around to walk back inside.

'I need a word, Mr Braithwaite, please,' Sally said and followed him in, eyebrows raised.

In the hallway, she rang through to the station and discovered that Jamie May had been reported missing by his mother at 9.00 p.m. on Monday. An officer had been round to the house and logged it, but not made the connection with the Braithwaite case. Sally tutted. As usual, poor communication was the sword on which they would all fall. She rang Dan's mobile and left a message, then got the call out to beat officers that Jamie was in the area and should be apprehended if possible and brought into the station. She had a bad feeling about that boy. He had looked dreadful.

Alan Braithwaite was standing in the kitchen, staring at an empty box of tea bags. Jenna had only just got out of bed, She was in her pyjamas and a fluffy pink dressing gown standing on the opposite side of the worktop. She looked scared and upset.

'What was all that about, then?' Sally said into the charged silence. Jenna looked to her Dad, but he refused to meet her eye. He opened a cupboard and spoke to it instead of to them as he rooted for tea bags.

'Poking his nose in - asking questions. I reckon he knows more than he's saying, but I'm not having him round here anymore.' He slammed the cupboard door and faced Jenna. 'Now you, go and put some clothes on. You're a disgrace, with your sister lying dead in a morgue and you can't even get your backside off the bed.'

Jenna's eyes, already puffy, flashed with anger, but she held her tongue and pushed past Sally on her way upstairs, tears streaming down her face.

'Mr Braithwaite?' Sally risked touching him on the arm. 'Alan? Just go and sit down in the living room. I'll make us a coffee and bring it through. Go on, it'll be alright.'

He moved then, head down, ashamed of his outburst, and did as she suggested. Sally heard the sound of footsteps above her head. Jenna going into the bathroom.

She took a moment to fill the kettle and put coffee in mugs. She wanted to chase off after Jamie May, but first things first. The fridge was pretty bare and there was little food in the cupboards. If this wasn't a family in dire need of support, she didn't know what was. She could see plastic carrier bags full of empty beer cans in the corner near the bin. Alan's self-medication. She wondered when either of them had last had a decent meal.

Sally rang Victim Support and pushed to get someone over as soon as possible.

Coffee made, she carried the mugs into the living room and sat next to Braithwaite on the sofa. He took the drink in silence and sipped, despite the heat that made her mug too hot to hold.

'We attended the post-mortem on Carly this morning,' she began, keeping her voice low and calm. He gulped in air, like a man drowning.

'Did they cut her open?'

She could hear his anguish and had to fight down her own deep-seated need to make it all better.

'Just one incision on her neck, to see how she died.' She let this hang in the air for a moment. A small step at a time was the best way to do it. 'Do you want to know what we found now, or would you rather wait for another time?'

Braithwaite took another shuddering breath and clutched the coffee mug to his chest, but he nodded for her to continue.

'Carly was asphyxiated, Mr Braithwaite.' His face was bleak, lost.

She rushed ahead, 'But it was probably over very quickly, as whoever did it managed to squeeze her airway and jugular at the same time. No air and no blood to the brain means a mercifully quick death.'

Sally sat then, hand on his arm, and waited. This time he broke, and slid to the floor, heaving out huge sobs and dropping his mug. He clasped his hands round his head, coffee dregs staining the carpet. The only words he could articulate sounded like "Why?" and she wished she had an answer for him. Sally felt her own tears begin to rise, but choked them back. This was his grief, not hers.

She left him where he was and went upstairs to see Jenna. Jenna was washed and dressed in jeans and a tee shirt and sitting on the bed, listening to her dad cry and playing with her phone. She looked up as Sally stood at the door, and slid the phone under the pillow.

'What?' she asked, her tone more belligerent once she was away from her father. 'What did you say to him?'

Sally stood by the door. 'We know how your sister died, Jenna. Do you want me to tell you about it?' Jenna's face pinched closed and Sally could see her jaw tighten where she was clenching her teeth, but she nodded, and let her fair hair fall down around her face. Sally sat next to the girl on the bed. Jenna traced the flowery pattern on the duvet cover with her finger. Sally took her hand.

'Jenna, Carly was asphyxiated. Strangled. Whoever did it managed to block both her airway and the blood supply to her brain and she died in seconds, probably. Once she passed out, she would not have suffered.'

Jenna interrupted in a small, shaking voice, 'You mean she couldn't breathe? Someone was stopping her from breathing?'

'Yes, I suppose I do. It would have been quick.'

The girl crumpled into tears. 'Was it easy to kill her?' she whispered.

'Yes, love, I'm afraid it was,' said Sally, and held the girl's hand tightly as she wept again. This job just gets harder, she thought.

Sally wanted to ask more questions of the girl to establish what had happened on the Sunday. She didn't think any of the team had a clear idea of Carly's comings and goings during that day.

'Jenna, how did Carly get to the studio on Sunday night?'

Jenna sucked in a few deep breaths and let them shakily out.

'She was going to catch the bus with Jamie.'

'What do you mean, was going to? Jenna, did Carly actually go to the studio with Jamie?'

Jenna turned her head away and looked out of the window. Sally could see the hesitation in the hunched line of her thin shoulders.

'Tell me.'

'I don't know,' Jenna admitted, talking to the window. 'I don't know if she got there or not. I wasn't talking to her because she had a real go at me about my friends. She was well out of order. I don't pick on her friends. So I went out for a bit. We had a row.' Her voice was soft, almost a whisper, 'The last time I saw her, we had a row and I didn't even wish her good luck.'

'So, you don't know what time she left or whether she went with Jamie or on her own?' The girl shook her head, eyes on the floor. Sally was sure Jenna knew more than she was saying, she just had to find the right way to get her to talk. Was she protecting Jamie? But if he'd killed Carly, why would he risk coming back here? Or was Jamie trying to protect Jenna from her father? Or even threatening her to keep quiet? Or even, her mind whirled with sudden possibilities, could this girl have killed her sister? Had Jamie gone round there to accuse her? Sally wanted to get a look at Jenna's arms to see if there were any signs of an actual fight rather than just a verbal row.

The doorbell rang. Sally stood, irritated by the interruption, and looked out of the bedroom window. She couldn't believe it. Bloody press. DCS Oliver had begged them to leave the family alone just for a couple of days, and although there were a few hanging about, most had agreed to wait for the press conference and were just using the front of the house for background to their reports. But she could see the zoom lens of a camera pointing up at her through the window of a car parked opposite, and the top of Lisa Middleton's wiry ginger head directly below her.

'I'll go,' she shouted and ran down the stairs, opening the front door just wide enough to see the body in front of it.

'Hello Lisa.'

'Oh, DS Ellis.'

Sally said nothing.

'I didn't think there were any police here,' stuttered the reporter, turning an unflattering shade of pink that clashed with her hair.

'I bet you didn't,' Sally replied. 'Now buzz off. The deal was no press interviews until we have had a couple of days to investigate, and the family have had a little time to come to terms with what has happened. You've already had a detailed statement from Superintendent Oliver. She will keep you informed.' She made a show of looking up and down the street. 'Looks like everybody else was more than happy to agree to it. To show a little compassion, a little human feeling…' She softened her tone, not wanting to alienate the woman. 'Have a bit of a heart, Lisa. You'll get your story when the family are fit to talk to you.'

The reporter turned her back and walked away, but Sally could see she was going to sit in her car with her photographer just up the road until Sally left. She didn't fancy Lisa Middleton's chances with Alan Braithwaite if she tried the doorbell again, though. Maybe she would let her speak to him after all…

Sally rang Victim Support once more. They were sending an experienced advocate and supporter, but she had to travel over from Crediton and would be at least another hour. Sally's phone buzzed, Dan wanted her back at the station. Well, he'd have to wait. She was needed here for the time being.

Chapter 15

Date: Tuesday 25th April Time: 13:09 Jamie May

Jamie checked his phone. He'd got a bit of charge left in it so he texted his mum. He knew she'd be worried, but there was no way he was going to see her. It was better for everyone if he stayed well out of the way. He pulled up his shirt and looked at the bruise spreading across his stomach. It really hurt. He couldn't believe Miss Quick had had the guts to hit him that hard. He'd just collapsed, couldn't breathe at all. Must have passed out for a couple of minutes. She'd gone when he got up.

He was crouched in his own back garden behind the rotting shed where he used to play as a kid, waiting until his mum left for her shift at Sainsbury's. He was planning to sneak in through the downstairs toilet window, grab something to eat, tidy himself up a bit and get out again before anyone noticed.

Jamie was buzzing with adrenaline and lack of sleep and food. His brain couldn't make sense of what had happened in the last twenty-four hours. In fact, in the last thirty-six hours, from the party at Miles's on Saturday night, his life had changed utterly. He'd left his guitar at Miles's house too, and needed go back for it, and that was making him more twitchy.

He hadn't been able to get to see Jenna because of her stupid moron of a father, and he didn't know if he had the guts to try again. The guy had almost smacked him one. If that woman hadn't been coming up the path, he wasn't sure he would still be walking and talking.

Jamie put his head onto his arms and rested them across his bent knees. Carly had been glowing, just beautiful that night at the party. All her dreams were coming true. He'd spent everything he had on a silver and onyx ring and waited until just the right moment at the party to give it to her. He'd taken her outside into the back garden where the music and laughter was like a love song in the background. She had opened the little black velvet box with a funny expression on her face, and asked him if it was a friendship ring.

Jamie's heart was crushed at that very moment. He could still feel it hurting him now, a real pain in his heart. He loved Carly, he wanted her to be his proper girlfriend, not just a 'friend'. But she had laughed at him in disbelief and kissed him on the cheek and said she had never thought of him like that, but that they would always be friends.

And then she had turned around and walked back into the house, and draped herself around the neck of Miles Westlake, who couldn't see him, out there in the night, alone. A teacher. How was that right?

Jamie shook himself like a wet dog getting out of a river. He wanted to howl like a dog too. How had everything gone so wrong? How could he have lost Carly before he had even got her to be his?

He felt his bruised ribs. What would the police do when Miss Quick told them what he had done to her? He may have to go to prison. His heart pounded. His head pounded. He had to think, but the horror was too much for him to bear. He punched himself in the head as hard as he could, wanting to stop the pain, but he couldn't prevent the thoughts from circling round his head like angry biting midges.

The noise of his mum's old Fiesta coughing into life and hiccupping backwards down the drive was his cue to move. He hobbled down the path, wincing as the blood rushed back into his legs and feet, pushed the big wheelie bin under the window and balanced on top of it. He prised open the downstairs toilet window and wriggled, panting and cursing at the pain radiating from below his ribs, through the small gap, down over the toilet and onto the bathroom floor.

Forty minutes later, he had showered, gelled his hair, charged his phone and dressed in his alternative uniform of black tee shirt, black jeans, black biker boots and black hoody emblazoned with a skull and the words “War Death” on the back. He ate four pieces of toast, raided his mum’s gas bill pot and left by the back door, feeling a little better than he had before. He had to get his guitar back, and he hadn’t finished dealing with Westlake’s betrayal yet.

Chapter 16

Date: Tuesday 25th April Time: 13:30 Illusion Studio

The sound of the glass door closing muffled the footsteps of DC Sam Knowles and DCI Ian Gould as they escorted Jed Abrams out of Illusion Studios and off to the station for formal questioning about the death of Carly Braithwaite.

Chas Lloyd stood beside the glass and chrome reception desk, dwarfed by its 1980's opulence. She was scared. Irina Akis rose smoothly from the sofa and took her hand.

'Chas, darling, I would like you to take a long lunch, but the boys and I have work to do and there are no recordings today, are there?'

The girl shook her head.

'Come back at about three o'clock, okay?'

Chas was flustered. Did the fact that Dan had sent other officers to pick up Jed mean that their very brief romance was over? She had been totally pissed off the night before when he'd come over all Jane Austenish and sent her home, virtue intact, but she still kind of liked him.

Why were the police pushing Jed so hard? What did they know? He was such an idiot, but she couldn't see him murdering Carly. She was too old for him, anyway. But they could easily do him for porn stuff if they had a little look around. And what were the Latvians going to do in the studio when she was out?

She didn't dare ask. She got her coat and bag and made her way up the stairs without another word. She knew that Jed made porn films for the Latvians, she'd been in the video room often enough, but she didn't want to know any of the sordid details.

As far as she was concerned, the less she knew the better. She jumped into her Mini and backed out onto Sidwell Street, wondering what to do in her extended lunch hour. Irina waited until the girl had gone and signalled Grigor to remove the CCTV disk. Then she rang Filip to tell him to drive the van into Chas's spot. In less than two hours they had loaded the completed DVDs and removed all of Abram's recording equipment, including forty DVD recorders into the back of their Mercedes van. It paid to be cautious. If the police wanted Abrams for murder, which they might do, they would search the place.

Irina checked the studio over before she replaced the CCTV disk. Tomorrow, she would dispose of the recorders in the North Sea. And in a couple of weeks she would have sold the DVDs and made herself enough money to pay off her father and escape, properly and for the last time, this miserable, disgusting life.

Chapter 17

Date: Tuesday April 25th Time: 13:59 Jed Abrams, Exeter Road Police Station

Dan took the stairs two at a time. He could see Sam Knowles waiting at the top, hopping from side to side like an anxious heron. Dan stopped next to him.

'Got some news, Sam?'

'Sir, we brought Jed Abrams in and he's in Interview Room 1. I collected the security camera DVD from the girl on reception. She's called Chas.' He blushed and Dan felt a bit better about his treatment of the girl the night before. She was more Sam's age, and type, than his. He didn't know what he'd been thinking of.

'Good work, Sam. Where is DCI Gould now?'

'He's stood outside the Interview Room watching Abrams, sir, and having a cup of coffee.'

'Okay, go into the video room and study that DVD for all of Sunday, not just from seven pm. I want to know about anybody who entered or left the building. Got it?'

Sam nodded and disappeared.

Jed felt trapped and not just because he was in an interview room. He'd told the Latvians not to stay in the reception area when the police came, but they had some stupid notion that they would be able to intimidate them somehow by their mere presence. They couldn't understand that the way it worked in their country was a very different beast from the way it worked in the UK. Or, maybe they were sitting there to intimidate him into keeping his mouth shut. As if he needed the reminder.

Abrams realised that the police were on to him, even if they didn't know exactly what they were onto him for. He also knew that if they got into his video room he'd be finished, and in prison very soon afterwards. He couldn't decide whether or not to call in a solicitor. Would it make him look more guilty, or less? They were only questioning him, he reminded himself, he hadn't been arrested. Either way, he was in deep shit. He wiped his face with the hem of his shirt. If he couldn't have a drink, the shakes would start soon.

Why had the stupid girl got herself killed? He was on to such a lucrative contract with the East European markets, and now he could see it all going down the toilet in front of him.

He weighed up his options: talk to the police, probably go to prison for a while, and live the rest of his life on the run from the Latvians. Or keep his mouth shut, close the business in Exeter and move away as fast as he could to start somewhere else. Perhaps Spain. There was no contest.

Gould turned as Dan entered the little corridor that ran alongside the three interview rooms and signalled him to stay quiet. They both looked through the one-way glass at Jed Abrams. He was sweating and using the hem of his shirt to wipe his face, exposing his pale paunch. His eyes were jittery, unable to focus on the statement he was supposed to be preparing for the interview.

'He's a wreck,' said Dan, 'worse than when I saw him yesterday. And why no solicitor? Doesn't he think he needs one? On a murder investigation? That's just weird.'

'That's not all,' replied Gould. 'He stinks of booze, which might explain the jitters, but I think there's something else going on.' He paused to collect his thoughts. 'There were three characters in the studio when we got there this morning. A beaut of a girl, tall with short, spiky blonde hair and cheekbones you could cut yourself on, and two blokes, one with a cauliflower ear and muscles and the other like an extra from a Quentin Tarantino film, all sharp suit and shaved head. I thought they could have been a band, but not when I saw how nervous Abrams was around them. They didn't speak a single word while we were there, and I'll bet my pension they weren't English.

'I think our little friend in there is up to something dodgy, even if he didn't do for the girly.'

Dan bit back the temptation to tell him off about his casual use of language when describing suspects and victims, but he knew Gould came from different times - what was the point? And he had a sneaking suspicion Gould did it on purpose, because he knew it would wind him up.

'So,' he asked instead, 'what do you reckon? Dodgy DVDs? Cheap music rip-offs?'

'What if,' Gould teased the filmy thoughts out of his head, 'what if the girl did go to the studio but Abrams wanted her to do more than just sing? What if he's making porn, and the foreigners are the distribution arm? What if she argued, or said she'd tell her dad, or the police? That would be a reason to keep her quiet, wouldn't it?'

They looked at each other, united for the first time in their shared pursuit of the murderer. Dan nodded, lips pursed as he reached for links, pulling his Mind Map together into a potential answer.

'He could have killed Carly and moved her body in the van without anybody even noticing.' He thought for a moment. 'I didn't see all the rooms in that studio, did you?'

Gould shook his head. 'Sam had a look at the Control room and I went to the toilet, but actually had a nosy round the kitchen and his office.'

'So none of us has been in the Post-Production room, have we? Who knows what we might have found?' Dan angled his head toward the interview room window. 'Let's get in there and see what we can shake from the tree.'

Gould entered the room talking. 'Right, Mr Abrams, let's not mess about. You want to go home and we want to catch a killer, so let's co-operate, shall we?'

He switched on the recorder and the policemen identified themselves and the detainee for the record. Gould sat opposite

Abrams and Hellier sat on his right side, just to disconcert him. The PC who had been watching over Abrams left for a much-needed toilet break with instructions to return with coffee.

'You have already told DI Hellier that Carly Braithwaite did not arrive at the studio last night, but you seem to have no witnesses to that effect. You then told DI Hellier that you went for a drink, but couldn't remember where, until, oh yes, you remembered that you went home, but nobody saw you do that either.' He paused, leaned across the table and glared at Abrams. 'Can you see why my antennae are waving, Mr Abrams? Can you?'

Abrams drew himself up in his chair until he was the same height as the two policemen. He took a breath. He'd worked out exactly what to do.

'Would it be possible for me to go to the toilet, please?' he asked.

Gould shook his head.

'Not just at the moment, sir, as we've only just begun. But, of course you may go to the toilet when we have a comfort break later.'

Dan smiled to see Gould struggling with the proper protocols for looking after a person being interviewed. The Police and Criminal Evidence Act had a lot to answer for.

The door opened and PC Foster came in with a tray of drinks. Dan got him to escort Abrams to the toilet during the disruption. He took a moment in the quiet that followed.

'Ian, don't bully him into talking. He's a wreck as it is, I want anything we get out of him to stand up in court.'

Ian raised an eyebrow. 'Me, bully someone? Never let it be said, Inspector. He just makes my skin crawl. We should be able to break him without resorting to my usual bullying tactics, though.'

He smiled with his teeth to show Dan he hadn't taken offence at being told off by someone twenty years younger and of a lower rank than himself, but the smile didn't quite reach his eyes.

Dan was relieved when Abrams returned. Gould was still touchy, it seemed. The rest of the interview did not go as planned.

Abrams was unwilling to add any further details to those he had already provided about the night of the girl's death. He simply said 'I don't know' to questions he didn't or couldn't answer.

Rolling his eyes, Gould tried another tack. 'Do you do any other kind of productions in your studio Mr Abrams? Films, for example?' He looked hard at Abrams, saw the man's pupils widen. He pressed on, 'Who were those people in the studio this morning? They didn't look like the latest boy band to come out of Exeter. Foreign, weren't they?'

Abrams busied himself putting sugar in his coffee. 'Of course they're a band, that's what I do, record bands.' He stirred clockwise, then anti-clockwise.

Dan felt a small buzz of excitement in the pit of his stomach. Were they getting close? He interrupted, 'It's hard making ends meet these days, isn't it, sir? We all have to look for ways to boost our income, and there's a good market in Europe isn't there? Especially if you can sort out distribution…'

Abrams stopped stirring his coffee and raised teary eyes, 'Ok, I admit I have done a bit of bootlegging of music CDs and DVDs in the past. I know it was stupid but I'm not doing it anymore, honest.' He looked from one police officer to the other. 'Since the kids started downloading music, there's no market anymore, so I don't do it now. I didn't have anything to do with the girl's death, I promise.'

Gould snorted and sat back on his chair, folding his arms over his stomach.

Dan leant forward on the table, twisting round so he could see more of Abrams face. He raised his eyebrows.

'Look,' Abrams tried again, 'I'm an alcoholic. I drink all the time. I passed out on Sunday night, that's why I couldn't remember where I was.'

Gould laughed. 'Didn't take you long to put that together, did it? You won't mind if we have a look in your studio, then will you, sir? We won't be too worried if you have a few fake CDs around the place.'

'I could take you over there now, Mr Abrams,' said Dan, 'get it all over with. Then we won't have to bother you any more, will we?'

Abrams swallowed. 'You'll need a search warrant to look round my premises, Inspector, I believe. I'm not going to let you in just like that to trample all over my stock. I have my rights. I've been as honest with you as I can. Can I go now, please? Or have you got something to charge me with? I've been sat here for almost two hours, and I've got a business to run.'

He signed his statement and looked between the two officers, hands on knees, ready to leave.

Dan looked across at Gould and shrugged. One nil to the suspect. 'Interview terminated at two-twenty pm.' He switched off the recorder and pocketed the cassette tape. Not that it would be much use. He couldn't wait until the new video recorders they'd been promised were fitted, a visual record was far more help. He stuck his head out the door and asked PC Foster to see Abrams out.

The two men sat despondently in the room for a couple of minutes.

'He handled us far better than I thought he would,' admitted Dan. 'He's either very confident or very stupid. He held himself together much better than I thought he could, too. I wonder if he's planning to run?'

Gould looked up from his deep contemplation of the desk and stared at him.

'Who's a clever boy, then? Of course, that's exactly what he'll do. And it will take us at least a day to get a warrant written out and signed off. And that's if we can persuade a magistrate to agree to sign one on mere suspicion of illegal practice.' He drummed his fingers on the desk in a tattoo of frustration. 'I bet the place will be empty by Wednesday.'

Dan nodded. 'If Abrams' visitors are a foreign gang, they are here to collect or deliver something. What? And how does it relate to our murder inquiry?' There was no response. Gould's head was down and Dan could feel the vibrations of furious thought. 'What's going on in that tortured brain of yours, Detective Chief Inspector?'

Gould held his eye. 'What about a little nocturnal visit to check the studio out for ourselves? Tonight? Before he has the chance to empty the place and make a run for it? Not sure how we'd get though that metal door, but the rest looks straightforward enough.'

It was couple of minutes before Dan replied. He knew that if he agreed to such a jaunt, he would be working outside the law he spent his days trying to uphold. He was naturally cautious and knew that Ian was naturally the opposite. Having worked for a time in London, Dan had known officers who cut corners. Sometimes they got away with it, sometimes they didn't. When a bit of rule-waiving got a result, little was said. When it didn't, careers were ruined. But, sometimes you just have to take a risk to get what you want. Like Ian, he just had a feeling that this business with Abrams had to be connected somehow with the death of Carly Braithwaite.

'We may not need to use brute force,' he said at last. 'I might be able to persuade Chas Lloyd to let us in. She must have keys as she gets there first in the mornings. Have to make sure she doesn't talk to Abrams, though.'

Gould gave him an appraising look and Dan had the feeling he had passed a test of some sort.

'Feisty little thing, isn't she, that Chas?' He almost smirked. 'And let's keep this between ourselves, Dan. If we find rip-off music or something worse operating down there, we can pass it on to Vice as a tip off from the general public.'

'Otherwise, we mess it up as evidence, I know.' Dan gave a tentative smile, for the first time feeling a connection with the older man. 'I'll have to see Chas after work. You go home as usual and I'll ring you later when it's arranged. I just hope she says yes.'

Gould smiled back. 'Still life in the old dog, eh?'

It had been a long time since Gould had had the chance to work a murder case. Dan could see he was enjoying himself.

Bill Larcombe waved them down as they entered the office. He was taking notes and balancing the phone under his neck. 'It's the hospital. They admitted a young woman called Claire Quick six hours ago, looks like a car accident. She's the teacher from the school, isn't she?'

Chapter 18

Date: Tuesday 25th April Time:15:15 Exeter Hospital

Bill put the phone down and paraphrased his notes.

'She's just regained consciousness and wants to talk to you urgently. The doc says she's got rope marks on her wrists and ankles, a large contusion on the back of her head, broken ribs and other more minor stuff.'

'What? Which ward is she in?' asked Dan as he grabbed his jacket and headed for the stairs. He was bemused. Rope marks? The English teacher? Gould jogged across to the stairs to catch up with him, earning a weak cheer from the Flowerpot Men. They passed Sally on the stairs, but didn't stop. She would have to wait.

Gould contacted Traffic on the drive to the hospital. Claire Quick had crashed her car just before six am at the traffic lights at the top of Barrack Road. It seemed likely that she was heading for the hospital, but had lost control going round the corner and ended up ploughing into the garden wall of a house on the corner. The car was a write-off.

The police officer at the scene reckoned she was going slowly and had passed out as she reached the corner. She'd only been a couple of hundred yards away from the hospital entrance.

Claire Quick was leaning back against several pillows on the hard hospital bed. In her handbag-sized mirror she could see a neck brace for the whiplash and a bandage on the back of her head, over the swelling caused by the bottle. Both wrists and ankles were bandaged and she had two broken ribs from the accident. Her legs were bruised and cut, but not broken.

When the two policemen entered, a pleasant-looking woman in her fifties stood and introduced herself as Claire's mother. Concern and fear had caused vertical creases between her eyebrows and were tugging down the sides of her mouth. She left with obvious reluctance to get herself some coffee and buy a magazine for her daughter.

Gould seated himself in the only chair, so Dan leant against the wall until Claire invited him to sit on the edge of the bed. He shrugged and sat in the space she made for him by pulling her legs to one side.

'Hi.' Claire looked at Gould, a rueful smile twitching her lips. 'Bet you didn't expect to see me again so soon.'

'Not like this, that's for sure,' replied Gould, and introduced Dan Hellier. 'What happened, Claire? Are you fit enough to tell us?'

She sighed. 'It's completely unreal, and I can't make sense of it, but there are some things you need to know.'

She began with Miles Westlake, the Music teacher, and his affair with Carly and went on to talk about the party on Saturday night.

Dan interrupted, 'So, Carly never went home on Saturday night at all?'

'No, and I don't think Jamie May did either. He must have been horribly jealous of Miles, although I don't think Miles realised how bad he was feeling.' She looked thoughtful. 'This is the end for Miles Westlake, Inspector. He can't get away with behaving like that and just carry on being a teacher. He would realise that I would have to tell the Head about what he got up to with a student.'

'Could Westlake have killed Carly, Claire? Sometime on the Saturday night?' asked Gould, but it was Dan who replied,

'No, I don't think anything could have happened on Saturday night as she was apparently home with her family for some of Sunday… if the family are telling the truth. But Westlake did have a strong motive, didn't he? If Carly threatened to tell anyone about what had happened, he would lose everything.'

Claire nodded, then grimaced with pain. 'No nodding. Nodding is bad. He's already lost his wife, she left him and took their baby six weeks ago. I think that's why he agreed to the party, because she wasn't there, and because he's pathetic.' She clasped both hands across her mouth as a realisation dawned. 'He may have been having an affair with Carly for all of that time. They did enough late nights after school in the Music room.' She looked away and fiddled with the bandage on her left wrist. 'God, what a mess.'

Dan shifted round on the bed to face her. She had the most amazing green eyes. He'd never seen proper green eyes before. She looked a bit like a cat. Some sort of exotic Siamese or something. He realised Gould was waiting for his lead.

'So, how did you get the rope burns?'

Claire flushed pink. 'You're not going to believe this bit,' she said. 'How stupid was I? I went round after school to see how Miles was because he had signed out sick at lunch time and I was worried about him. He wouldn't let me in at first, but when he did it was awful – you should have *seen* the state of the place. It was trashed.' She paused, catching her breath with a wince.

'Those ribs are going to cause you more pain than any of your other injuries,' Dan said with a smile. 'Been there and done that.'

Claire smiled back at him, and shook her head at the ridiculousness of the story she was about to tell. 'I found Jamie May sitting in the living room smoking a joint and drinking a can of lager. Shocked doesn't cover it. I got Miles to explain what had been happening and I started putting two and two together about Carly and Miles, but before I could do anything at all, Jamie came back in to the room and hit me across the head with something hard. I've never been hit that hard in my life. It was such a shock.'

Gould winced. 'He could have killed you if he'd got you on the temple.'

'I know, but he didn't. He's just a kid, Inspector, and I think he was frightened and just did the first thing he could think of to shut me up.'

'Hmm,' murmured Dan. 'He could also be our murderer if he had seen Carly and Miles together and lost his temper.' Not so much of a kid if he can cause that much damage to his teacher, he thought. 'How did he seem to you?'

She hesitated, trying to find the right words. 'Wild, almost out of control. I think he showed how distressed he was when he tied me up and wouldn't let me go. No sane person would think they could get away with that. I think grief has sent him a bit doolally. He's always been a bit wild at school. Well, perhaps more like unpredictable. It's hard to know how he will react to things. In Jamie's case he will always try for the last word or the last laugh. Makes him a pain in the neck to teach.'

'What do you think he was doing at Westlake's house?'

'They were arguing when I arrived, I think, but I couldn't hear properly. Miles tried to pretend Jamie wasn't there but he's no liar - couldn't fool a baby.' She wiped a tear away with the back of her bandaged wrist and smiled down at her wrists. 'Knew these would come in handy for something. Sorry, I'm still a bit weepy. It's all so strange and awful. I know it's a cliché, but things like this don't happen in my world.'

Dan pushed her gently to explain her Houdini-like escape from the house. He was impressed at her contortionist's abilities with the tiny knife blade. She laughed because he did, and Dan was relieved to see her shoulders drop and her face begin to relax.

'Very resourceful,' he said. 'Fancy a job?'

She didn't laugh at that. 'You police may be used to all this physical stuff, but I'm worried. Will I get into trouble for hitting him with the poker? I knocked him flat!'

Dan shook his head, 'You were acting in self-defence, Miss Quick, I don't think you have anything to worry about at all.' He rose from the end of the bed and smiled at her again, just to get one back. She was braver than most people he'd met, and she had a great smile. 'We need to find Westlake and Jamie now, so we'll leave you alone before your mum comes in and tells us off for tiring you out. I'll send an officer over to take a statement from you later. So for now, try to rest a bit, OK?'

She lay back on the bed. 'Yes, I will. I'm really tired, but every time I try to drop off the nurses keep waking me up. I could sleep for England, I can tell you.'

Gould took hold of her hand and squeezed it as they left. 'There's not many people would be defending the person who'd just seriously assaulted them,' he said as they strode down the endless hospital corridor.

But Dan wasn't listening, he was already on the phone.

Chapter 19

Date: Tuesday 25th April Time: 14:35 PC Lizzie Singh

Lizzie Singh turned up the radio attached to her black bulletproof vest, as high as the volume would go. She whispered into it, resisting the temptation to throw it at the wall when the desk sergeant stage-whispered, 'Receiving,' back to her.

'For goodness' sake, Sarge, be serious. I'm following a Jamie May; white male, sixteen years old, black hair, brown eyes, 5'8", wearing black everything. Wanted in connection with the murder of Carly Braithwaite and he's been missing for two days. So, stop mucking about and get me a bit of back up.' She gave her location and general direction of travel and then turned the radio down.

Jamie was walking fast along Pinhoe Road, hood up and head down. Lizzie had only noticed him because of his unmistakeable 'War Death' hoody, otherwise he was wearing the perfect disguise in a city with 20,000 students. She didn't want to get too close, and had had to abandon her patrol car in a small cul-de-sac to follow him on foot. Sergeant White had promised her an area car with a couple officers. But, until they arrived, she was on her own.

She watched Jamie cross the road under the Polsloe Bridge and head down Hamlin Lane. Lizzie hesitated. It was a winding road with several straight sections where she would have nowhere to hide if he turned round. The last thing she wanted was to frighten him into running. Should she wait on the corner and flag down the area car? She had no idea when they would arrive, and he could disappear in that time. She couldn't work out where he was heading, either, which didn't help.

When Jamie moved out of her line of sight, she made her mind up, she would have to bring him in herself. Jamie knew her and would probably be calmer with her than with two burly uniformed coppers, anyway. She jogged to catch up with him.

Jamie saw PC Singh pass him in her funny little police car on Pinhoe Road. He tried not to panic, but she had slowed down, so it was clear she had an idea it was him. He tried to walk fast but not run, to keep his head down and look purposeful.

So far, he had not seen or heard the police car so he thought he was safe. He hadn't dared look back, but as he rounded the first bend on Hamlin Road, he risked a glimpse over his shoulder. She was there! Standing pressed up against the hedge at the end of a side road. She was on foot, not in the car. Jamie's heart fluttered. He couldn't get taken by the police, not now. He ran.

The sudden turn of speed caught Lizzie by surprise. She switched her radio back up, shouted her location then shot across the road, following Jamie up and over the crumbling stone wall into the cemetery.

Sergeant White had clearly decided that discretion was no longer an issue. Lizzie heard the comforting wail of a siren heading towards her as she stopped in the middle of the main road into the cemetery. She made a complete circle, using her ears as well as her eyes, straining to detect movement. Had he run straight through, or was he hiding? Great place to hide. Still she didn't move. She called in and asked for the other officers to go to the far entrance and move back towards her. She was going to try to flush him out. Bit like hunting rabbits with her granddad when she was a girl.

She crept towards the older section of the cemetery, to the part where the Victorians had made an exhibition of death with massive ornate stone memorials and crypts. She jumped onto a raised, flat, weathered gravestone and shouted into the quietness, 'Jamie, we need to talk to you. I know you're frightened, but you have no need to be. Come out now, please. I need to let your mum know you're safe. You're not in any trouble. I just want to talk to you.'

She hoisted herself up onto the roof of the nearest crypt and waited for a sign of movement. There was a tentative rustling beneath her feet. She held her breath.

The space into which Jamie had jammed himself was tight and oppressive. He was down inside the crypt, squashed between two stone coffins with statues of dead people lying on the top of them. He heard the sirens and pushed even deeper into the tiny space, hands over his ears.

When he heard the police officer shout, he almost laughed. What did she mean, he wasn't in trouble? Then he understood. The teacher hadn't told on him. Well, she hadn't told yet, he corrected himself. The temptation to give himself up was huge. He couldn't cope with what was happening to him.

Into the silence came a shuffling sound above his head. Had she found him? His instinct, as in all cornered animals, was to run.

He levered himself out of the space and peered through the metal grille of the door. Nothing. As quietly as he could, he edged towards the crumbling stone steps and poked his head over the top step. Nothing. He crept up the steps and paused for a moment at the entrance to work out which way would get him closer to Westlake's house. Then he set off at full speed to cut across the cemetery.

Lizzie launched herself off the crypt roof and took him down in a flying rugby tackle. Jamie crashed onto his face with a thump of exploding air. Lizzie sat astride his back, kneeling on each arm in turn as she yanked one wrist into a handcuff, then the other. She was surprised to find that she was snarling. Jamie gasped for breath, his face pushed into the gravel. He bucked backwards to throw the officer off him, rolling onto his side and scrabbling to get purchase on the stone chippings. Four black-booted feet appeared in his line of sight, and Jamie May found himself hoisted six inches off the ground by two large, uniformed police officers.

'Okay, lad, calm down,' said the older of the two, PC Peter Salter. 'We just want to talk to you down at the station, no need to cause all this fuss.' He sighed at the stream of abuse and shook his head sadly in the direction of Lizzie Singh. 'Swearing with all the monotony of teenagers whose vocabulary stretches no further than from C to F. I do apologise for the whippersnapper, PC Singh.'

The officers lowered the boy back to the ground and held him steady. PC Adam Foster nudged Lizzie. 'You may well get a commendation, Lizzie. And a place on the Exeter Chiefs' next line up. Very impressive bit of arresting, that.'

'Do you mean you just stood there watching and let me jump him without helping me?' Lizzie spluttered, outraged.

'Didn't look much like you needed help,' laughed Foster, 'and no need for all of us to get our uniforms dirty. Way to go, Lizzie!' He patted her on the back.

She stared at them. Sometimes equality wasn't all it was cracked up to be. Finally, she laughed too, to stop her bottom lip trembling, as she felt the adrenaline wash out of her body in waves. She brushed dust off her trousers and patted her vest to make sure she had everything.

'Can I have a lift back to my car? And promise not to tell Whitey that I just abandoned it?'

The call from the Major Crime Unit came in as they drove out of the cemetery. Jamie May was wanted for kidnapping and assault on the teacher, Claire Quick. Apprehend on sight.

Lizzie twisted in her seat and stared wide-eyed at the boy sitting behind her in the car. 'What on earth have you been up to, Jamie?'

Pete Salter stopped the car, and PC Singh arrested and cautioned him.

Chapter 20

Date: Tuesday 25th April Time: 17:02 Exeter Road Police Station

Sergeant White passed the news on as Dan walked in through the station door. Jamie May had been apprehended by PC Singh just before the notice for his arrest had gone out. White had arranged for the boy's mother to be brought to the station and the duty solicitor had been contacted.

Dan nodded, pleased that they at least had one suspect in custody. He wanted to be off again to catch up with Miles Westlake, but they all needed a re-cap, especially in the light of Claire Quick's statement.

Having gleaned the story of the arrest of Jamie May from the two beat officers, Gould stopped Dan in the main corridor. 'D'you know, Daniel, my boy,' he said, 'that girl Singh is an asset to this force. Why don't we steal her for a couple of days? She knows the kids and the area and she's not scared of getting stuck in and doing what needs to be done.'

Dan agreed. They could do with a little local knowledge, and PC Singh seemed willing and keen. He rang Colin White and gave him the bad news, he would be one uniform down for the rest of the week.

'Do all these gung-ho women make you feel a bit inadequate, Ian?' Dan asked, as they headed for the incident room.

'You have no idea,' Gould replied, raising his eyes towards Julie Oliver in her top floor office.

Sally Ellis and Bill Larcombe were busy with the Mind Map on the wall. Bill had spent all morning re-doing it. The picture of Carly was at the centre. He had used colours to represent the different people involved with her. Sally was writing up the main headings from the Braithwaite meetings. Dan passed on the Abrams interview tape to Ben Bennett who didn't take long to transcribe it.

Dan stood and stared at the wall, wolfing a tuna sandwich and slurping from a mug of surprisingly good coffee. He raised the mug in a salute to Sally who had thrown out the old stuff and started again from scratch. He stepped forward and added the information he had gained from Claire Quick to the board, then stood back.

He was looking for a pattern that just wasn't there.

Maybe Jamie May was the killer. Perhaps Claire Quick was right about jealousy being the motive. But surely he would have killed Miles Westlake, not Carly? Or maybe that was why he was at the teacher's house yesterday? Finishing the job. Was Alan Braithwaite just a grieving father, or did his argument with Jamie May earlier that day mean something?

And how did Jed Abrams fit in? Or was he just a distraction? Should he pass their suspicions about Abrams straight onto Vice and let them deal with it?

He found himself chewing at the fingernails on his right hand, a habit he thought he'd conquered when he was a child. He kept the nails long on his right hand and clipped on the other for playing the guitar. If he carried on, he'd have none left on either hand. He could feel anxiety spreading across his chest, a fluttery sensation. He and Ian should not be going to the studio without a warrant. The murderer was still out there. He should tell Oliver what he was up to and have the decision taken away from him. He took a long, slow breath.

He understood something in a brief flash of clarity. The truth about leadership was that sometimes you had to manage the decisions and their consequences, all by yourself. And he'd made a decision that he was going to have to see it through, whether he had second thoughts or not. He couldn't back down in front of Ian Gould, not if he wanted to hold his head up in front of the older, more experienced officers he was supposed to be leading.

The buzz of his phone interrupted his thoughts. Message from his mum. Had he found out anything about Alison? He didn't want to tell her. He really didn't want them rushing off to prison to see her, getting themselves all wound up again, giving her all their savings, letting her steal from them and treat them like dirt, all over again. This way, they had over a year of peace and quiet before she would be paroled. Maybe the prison would get her on one of their programmes and get her addiction under control. Maybe. His finger hovered over the tiny keyboard as he prepared the lie, '*No news yet, be in touch soon as I know something. D xx*'.

He wondered what it would be like to be an only child, and whether it was worse to know that your sister was dead, like poor little Jenna Braithwaite, or to wish that she was, like poor little Dan Hellier. He stared guiltily at the now empty bin next to his desk, paper evidence destroyed. 'A few days won't make any difference, I'll tell them at weekend,' he said to the bin.

The subdued bustle of people going about their jobs, discussing the latest information, enjoying the Lizzie Singh story and typing up notes, ballooned up behind him. He took a moment to appreciate that he hadn't had to do anything to make this bunch work as a team, except to be part of the team himself. He hoped that the compromises needed to be a leader were ones that he could make. He banged his empty mug on the table.

'Right, everyone, gather round.'

Sam Knowles loped in from the video room. 'Sir, I've scoured this disc from early on Sunday morning to midnight on Sunday night. Carly Braithwaite didn't go into the studio. Abrams at came in at twelve-oh-six pm. A couple of lads with guitars arrived at about one forty pm and left at five forty-three pm. Abrams left a bit later than he originally said he did, at nine thirteen pm.'

'So, no sign of Carly Braithwaite or Jamie May?' Sam shook his head. Ian Gould looked disappointed. It would have made life a whole lot easier if they had had a genuine need to search the premises as part of a murder enquiry.

'How much more stuff is on there?' asked Sally.

'I got there to collect the disc at about five thirty pm yesterday, so I suppose it's got all Monday's visitors on it, as well as the previous couple of weeks.' He stopped as they looked at him in disbelief. 'It's a sort of stop-motion camera. Only records when there's movement at the door, then switches itself off. Quite sophisticated kit, I'd say.'

'Thanks, Sam, and I hate to do this to you, but could you go back a bit further and see who visited earlier in the week?' asked Dan.

Gould asked for any footage of the foreigners arriving on Monday or Tuesday, and any signs of anything being moved out of the studio.

Sam shrugged, not looking excited by the prospect of more hours in front of a computer screen. His face brightened, 'I could go over to the Studio and get some more discs, sir, if you want me to?'

Dan smiled but shook his head. He understood why that would be a journey Sam would like to make, but he would have to do his chatting up of Chas Lloyd on his own time. 'I think there's more than enough on the disc you've got, Sam.

'Well, ladies and gentlemen, it seems we have to take Jed Abrams off our list of murder suspects for the moment, as we don't have enough on him to charge him with. If the girl didn't get as far as the studio, then we have no reason to suspect him.' He flashed a look at Gould. 'But we keep him on the board, because all my little grey cells tell me that he is up to no good in that studio, and so he remains a person of interest.'

'It's young Jamie looking favourite, though, isn't it?' asked Sally. 'He was with the girl at Westlake's on Saturday night, and presumably he was there Sunday morning. Maybe he found out that Carly was having an affair with her teacher and flipped. Both Claire Quick and Jenna Braithwaite said he was keen on her.'

'But why kill Carly, and not the teacher?' asked Gould.

'Did Alan Braithwaite say that Carly had stayed out all night?' asked Dan.

'No, he didn't and neither did Jenna. Maybe she sneaked in early in the morning? If the empties I saw in the bin were anything to go by, I doubt Alan Braithwaite hears a great deal in the early morning.'

'And why,' added Gould, 'would Jamie feel the need to assault and tie up the English teacher? It was the Music teacher having the affair with Carly. What was he so frightened of that he had to resort to violence towards a teacher?'

Silence greeted him. None of it made sense.

'Was Jamie at the teacher's house because he intended to hurt him? Jamie must have known that Claire Quick would tell the police he'd been there,' put in Sally.

Dan nodded at her. 'That's where I'm heading too. Westlake may still be our man. It makes sense if he told Jamie what he had done, or if Jamie witnessed the murder and was there to extract revenge. But we still need to search Jamie's room while we've got him here in the station, in case we find anything, so let's do that first. Sally, see if his mother will co-operate, will you?

'Also, what did the Braithwaites say about Sunday?'

'Not a lot,' replied Sally, consulting her notes. 'Dad said she was excited and took ages to get ready. He went to the pub in the afternoon to watch the footy, admits he didn't get back until late. Jenna went out because she and Carly had had a row over friends, so she didn't see her sister leave. Neither of them could be clear about timings for the day.'

The door opened to admit Lizzie Singh, and, much to her embarrassment, she received a round of applause, and a wolf whistle from Gould. She stood in the doorway, having changed into her own clothes, brown eyes huge, looking a bit lost.

Dan stepped forward. 'PC Singh, great to see you. Good job out there. I've spoken to Sergeant White and he's happy for you to be seconded onto the team for the rest of the week at least. Take a seat over near Sergeant Ellis and she'll brief you. We think your local knowledge of the area and the young people in it will be invaluable to the investigation.'

Lizzie did as she was told, pulling up a chair next to Sally and keeping her head down until the heat faded from her face. She took out her notebook from her handbag and fumbled around her breast pocket for her pen, then remembered she was in civvies and poked about to get it out of her bag.

Dan pulled their attention back to the wall behind him. 'It's still early days, only two days since the murder. I know we have lost one potential suspect, but we have one in custody and soon we'll have another one, Mr Miles Westlake. We're just not quite there.' He sighed.

'The problem is that we still have no real motive for this murder except the jealousy angle. It doesn't seem right that young Jamie May would kill the girl he professed to love. More likely that he would kill the teacher.' Several nods and grunts confirmed his speculation. 'Which leaves us with Miles Westlake, if we can work out how he did it. And, more importantly, when he did it.' There was no reply this time - they all had the same information.

Dan searched their faces and risked another speculation, 'I think we have all the players on the pitch already, ladies and gentlemen. This was no random killing. So, we'll stop the house to house and school enquiries and focus on the three in the frame.' He crossed to the board and circled their names. Westlake, May and Braithwaite.

'Yes, I know what you're going to say,' he said when Sally raised a hand, 'but we don't write off the father yet. He's volatile at the moment obviously, but we don't have a clear understanding of his movements on the Sunday, and his violent outbursts may be hiding guilt as much as grief.' He frowned, consulting his mental list and chewing his bottom lip.

'Right. Sally, take Lizzie with you this evening and pick up Miles Westlake, bring him in under arrest for a formal. We have him for possible kidnap and assault, too. We'll keep him in overnight.'

Sally nodded and smiled at the young officer next to her.

Dan continued, 'Bill, the Post-mortem report is on my desk but I haven't got a minute. Go through it with Ben and dig out the relevant details for the wall before you go home tonight, please. Can you see if the forensic team got any decent tyre or footprints from the scene? I'd still like to know what vehicle transported her.' And, where it is now, he thought. 'We'll push back the formal interviews as far as we can tomorrow, to give us time to do a bit more sleuthing.' He gave the team time for a snigger. 'What? Don't we sleuth anymore? I bet DCI Gould sleuths, don't you?'

'Certainly do. The old ways are the best, as I keep telling you whippersnappers. If it was good enough for Sherlock, it's good enough for me.' He patted his stomach and smiled round the room, enjoying the brief release of tension.

'Jamie May is definitely going down for kidnap and assault unless Claire Quick withdraws her statement, so we can keep him here for twenty four hours anyway. Then we'll see if we need to extend or release him on bail once we have Miles Westlake's statement.

'Ian, you speak to the boy's mother and I'll just pop into the interview room to see if I can get anything out of him before the solicitor arrives.' He paused and consulted his notepad, all jobs allocated.

'Right, that'll do. There's overtime in this - so don't skimp on anything. I want thorough work and no mistakes. Let's do an eight o'clock briefing tomorrow morning.' He slid off the desk and made his way back to the dishwasher with his mug, signalling the end of the meeting.

As they all got to work, Dan felt in better control. At least there were no snide looks or remarks for him to pretend to ignore, and they did have a couple of suspects to interrogate.

His anxiety about the evening ahead retreated to a small nagging voice.

Chapter 21

Date: Tuesday 25th April Time: 17:18 Jamie May, Exeter Road Police Station

The air conditioner sucked old air from the windowless room and replaced it with older, recycled air. Even though no smoking had been allowed in the interview rooms for years, the stink of tobacco was ground into the brown streaks on the ceiling and the crumbling round burn marks in the linoleum floor.

Jamie May sat, head bowed, tracing the grooves etched into the formica table with his thumb nail. Sandra May stood outside in the corridor looking at her son through the window. A thin woman with dyed red hair and deep wrinkles, she looked like someone who had given her life to looking after her son and not spent any time or money on herself. She looked up as Dan and Ian approached, wiping her nose with a tissue.

'He won't see me,' she said. 'What's he done? Why won't he talk to me?' She looked up at the men, tears pricking at the corners of her eyes, appealing for answers they couldn't give.

Dan watched Gould take Mrs May aside. The poor woman was going to be in a real state when she found out precisely what her only son had done.

He entered the interview room without notes or files. This was not a formal interview. He just wanted to make contact with the boy, but didn't intend to frighten him.

Jamie looked up through his black fringe, took in the slim, dark-haired man and looked back down at the table.

'Jamie, I'm Detective Inspector Hellier. I'm in charge of the investigation into Carly Braithwaite's death.'

Dan studied the side of the boy's face. Jamie stiffened when he heard Carly's name, but there was no other reaction. Dan picked up a chair, took it round the table and sat next to the boy, so he could at least see part of Jamie's face.

'How close were you to Carly, Jamie? Did you know her well?' The boy did not look up. 'I think you can help us to work out who may have killed her, Jamie. We know how she was killed and we have a good idea of when it happened. Can you tell me what you know about it? About what happened on Sunday?'

There was still no response. Dan's instinct was to press on. 'If you tell me the truth now, I can help you with the other charges. You know, for assaulting your teacher and keeping her against her will. They are serious charges.' He waited for another minute. 'Don't you want me to help you with them?' He was becoming angry at the lack of response, even though he could see the boy twisting one leg round the other in a mammoth effort at self-control. Dan pushed a little harder.

'Jamie, did you actually like Carly? It's just that it seems to me that if you were a real friend, you would want to help us to catch her killer. Carly would want you to help us, I think. We are on the same side, you know.' He bent his head round into Jamie's sight line and softened his expression. 'Help me out here.' Still nothing.

'When did you last see Carly, Jamie? Were you with her on Sunday afternoon?'

Jamie shuffled on his chair to face away from the detective, hunching into his hoody.

Frustrated, Dan slapped the table top and raised his voice. 'Okay, if you don't want to talk about Carly, tell me about Miss Quick, your teacher. You must really hate her to have tied her up like that. I bet she's a really nasty piece of work, eh? Was she going to tell us about what you had done, Jamie? Did you need to shut her up?'

The boy exploded out of his chair, knocking it backwards and stumbling over it towards the door. Dan leapt backwards from his own chair and threw himself in front of the door to stop the boy leaving. He was pleased to have caused some reaction, but he just might have pushed the boy too far for a first meeting. So much for not frightening him.

'Sit down, Jamie,' he said, 'you're not going anywhere, sunshine.'

Jamie glared at the man in front of him. He swivelled around, took two steps to the one-way window and banged his head and fists on it, kicking the wall with his booted foot and yelling an incoherent stream of abuse to anyone who might be listening outside. Dan heard footsteps in the corridor and stepped away from the door. He had to admit it was a pretty impressive way to bring an interview to a close.

Gould burst in, followed by Jamie's mother. She ran across to the boy and swept him into her arms. This time there was no resistance. Jamie let his mother hold him, and tell him how worried she had been about him, and how it would be alright now.

Gould raised his eyebrows at Dan but he just shrugged. He hadn't found anything out and it was unlikely to be alright for Jamie May ever again. Gould ushered them both back to the table and proffered tissues.

The duty solicitor arrived in a flurry of paper work and Calvin Klein's Obsession. As she read the charge sheet, she kept glancing up at Jamie May as though finding it difficult to equate it with the boy sobbing in his mother's arms. She introduced herself to the Mays and to Dan, and nodded towards Gould, whom she called by his first name.

Before she got a sentence out regarding the charge, Dan jumped in. 'We're keeping him in, at least overnight. We haven't charged him yet, but you can see the charges for yourself, and they are serious. The plan is to interview and charge him formally tomorrow afternoon when we have had time to verify the charges and collect witness statements.'

Vanessa Redmond bristled, and re-arranged the tortoiseshell glasses on her nose. 'My client is barely sixteen. It is wrong to lock juveniles up and this one doesn't look like he's a danger to anybody at the moment. You should let him go, to be returned here tomorrow on his mother's recognizance. He looks like he needs a good night's sleep.'

'And,' Dan continued as though she had not spoken, 'we have a badly injured witness in hospital who can tell you that he is certainly not the sweet, innocent boy you might wish him to be, so he will be staying here tonight. I'll think about letting him go home tomorrow or Thursday, if you want to start bail proceedings after the formal interview tomorrow.'

Jamie followed the exchange, hope fading to despair on his face when he realised that he would have to spend at least one night in a cell. His mother uttered a quiet, 'Oh, Jamie,' and held onto his hand.

Vanessa Redmond held Dan's eye for a moment, then gave a reluctant nod, and sniffed her displeasure. 'I suppose that will have to do. Can you leave me alone now with my client and his mother, please?'

Both men rose and left the room. Dan posted a PC outside.

Gould glanced across at Dan as they headed back towards the main office.

'You handled her well. She's like a Rottweiler normally.'

'Yeah, I spent a lot of time dealing with solicitors as a sergeant. You have to get in first. I don't like locking kids up either, but I'm not sure Miles Westlake will be safe if Jamie's out and about. Plus a night in the cells might encourage him to talk to us. He's still our number one suspect. I have to give the kid credit - he held out well against me in there.'

Gould gave a short laugh. 'What were you saying about me not bullying witnesses?'

Much to his embarrassment, Dan felt heat around his collar rise up into his face. 'Just shaking the tree. He knows what happened, I can feel it.' He paused at the door to the incident room. 'Why don't you go home now, Ian? Have a couple of hours break, get something to eat. I have a few things to sort out here, then I have to get Chas to agree to help us. It may take all my powers of persuasion. I'm a bit worried that I may have to arrest her to get her to co-operate.'

He smiled to show that he was joking, but he wasn't entirely sure she wouldn't smack him on the nose.

'I thought she was a real little cracker, myself. Is she going to be so difficult? Would you prefer me to go and see her and use all my charm?' Gould grinned, licking his lips and rubbing his belly.

'Err… tempting offer, but no thanks all the same. I need to do this myself.' He felt another warm flush creeping up his neck and turned to enter the office so Gould wouldn't see. He didn't want to admit to him what had happened the night before with Chas. He'd just laugh at the opportunity wasted and at the thought of the DI being a wimp and having 'finer feelings'. Questions about his masculinity, never mind his ability, would be round the station before he could blink.

Gould sauntered over to his desk and Dan stood in front of the whiteboard again with a felt-tipped pen. He drew a red triangle to connect Carly, Miles Westlake and Jamie May, and wrote 'love' along the line from Carly to Miles, and 'jealousy' along the line from Jamie to Miles. He wrote the same words on a similar line connecting Carly with her sister and father. Then he thought about how to connect Jed Abrams to the main characters, but however hard he tried, he couldn't. Abrams was a wild goose chase. Interesting in his own right, but not connected to this case. He would be happy to pass it over to Vice in the morning.

It was six thirty. The office was quietening down. Bill and Ben had added the results of the post-mortem to the wall before going home. Carly had definitely had sex on the Saturday night. Sally had scrawled across it – 'with Miles Westlake' and had drawn a line to connect up the information. Had Jamie caught them at it? He wrote the question on the wall. Jamie was struggling emotionally. He wrote that up, too. Would he even be coherent in a formal interview? They had to find a way to get him to open up and trust them. He wrote 'Trust?' on the board. In his heart, Dan didn't think Jamie had killed Carly, but he thought Jamie knew who had. He sat at his desk, took out his notepad and doodled while he thought some more.

He was hesitant to bring in the father for a formal interview so soon after the death. He wouldn't be reliable, he was too angry and emotional. Sometimes that could hide guilt. Sometimes it was genuine. He was relying on Sally to get the family's trust and persuade them to open up to her over the next few days. Jenna would probably crack first. Poor kid needed a mother figure, especially now, and might shed light on the relationship between her sister and father. In the meantime Braithwaite was below Westlake and May on the list. He looked down at the pad. He'd doodled the name 'Abrams' and circled it many times with swirling patterns of leaves and thorns. Nice design, he thought, but what did it signify?

Dan checked his phone but there were no missed calls or messages from Sally, so he assumed she was on her way to Westlake's house. Nothing back from his mum. She'd be disappointed in him. He brought up Chas's number, suffered another tremor of embarrassment as he touched the screen and wondered how best to play it.

Chapter 22

Date: Tuesday 25th April Time: 19:10 Miles Westlake home

The battered Fiat Panda that Sally Ellis called her own was not the best vehicle for picking up a suspect in, having just two doors and a pair of child car seats in the back. So she had signed out a new Ford Focus from the pool. It was smooth, spacious and comfortable. There was no need to force the gearstick into third, there was good visibility, the brakes worked. Sally felt she had died and gone to car heaven. And it was only a Ford for goodness' sake. She was very tempted to go to the police station at Heavitree Road via Taunton, just for the ride.

'The boss said the English teacher was pretty badly hurt,' said Lizzie Singh, shifting about in her seat. Sally smirked at her attempts to work out where to put the kit that was usually attached to her uniform.

'Yes,' nodded Sally, 'but it seems that Jamie did the hitting and the tying up, not Westlake, and we've got him in custody, thanks to you.'

Lizzie grimaced. 'I'm hoping that my one act of madness in arresting Jamie May hasn't given you all the idea that I'm some sort of superhero. I'm still feeling a bit wobbly round the knees, to be honest.'

Sally laughed, 'Don't knock it, kid. Better that the blokes think you're handy - might stop them getting ideas...'

Lizzie put the handcuffs into her handbag with her radio.

They drew up outside the house. Westlake's car was still in the driveway. The front room curtains were partly drawn but there was no other sign of life.

'Lizzie, go round to the back door and wait for me to call you. Stop him if he makes a run for it.' Lizzie straightened her coat, threw her bag over her shoulder and stepped past two overflowing bin bags on her way to the back of the house. Sally rang the doorbell.

Several minutes later, having rung the bell, banged on the door and shouted through the letterbox, she realised they were not going to get a response. She worked her way round to the back garden to find Lizzie chatting to the next-door neighbour over the fence. The neighbour was certain that Westlake had not left the house as she had been waiting to have a word with him about the noise from the party on the previous Saturday night. The woman was enjoying a chance to complain about her neighbour, so Sally took a step backwards and allowed Lizzie to take down the complaint.

Sally took a moment to think. Westlake could be hurt inside the house and unable to cry for help. He could even be dead. If Jamie May was the killer, he could have killed Miles Westlake after Claire Quick had escaped early that morning. Her head snapped up. She cut straight across the woman's complaints.

'Lizzie, we have to get into the house, now. Find a brick or something to break the window.' Lizzie, caught on the hop, looked about her, picked up an ornamental stone squirrel from the rockery and hurled it at the glass kitchen door as hard as she could.

'No good,' said Sally, 'toughened glass. Go for the window.' This time the glass cracked.

Using her coat to protect her hand, Lizzie pushed the shards of glass into the kitchen sink, balanced one foot on a protruding brick to give her a lift up, and clambered over the sill and onto the work surface, scattering dirty plates and cans onto the floor. She found the back door key still in the lock and let Sally inside.

'Good work, Spiderwoman,' said Sally as she entered.

'It's no good, I am marked forever,' Lizzie sighed as they stared at the mess around them. 'The next thing I know I'll be transferred to the SAS. And look at the mess - I've probably destroyed evidence all over the place.'

'I wouldn't worry about it, Lizzie - if this guy had a party, there'll be fingerprints and other DNA evidence all over the other rooms, too.'

Sally led the way to the sitting room. The place stank like a brewery. What the hell had been going on? It was no wonder the neighbour had complained. They stopped at the door and peered in. The room was empty but she guessed the guitar in the case might be Jamie May's. There were CDs all over the floor and more discarded mess from the party. She spotted blood on the floor near their feet - evidence from Claire Quick's injury, no doubt. An empty vodka bottle lay on the carpet.

'Wonder if that's what May used to hit the teacher over the head?' asked Lizzie.

Sally nodded, 'Could be. He hasn't tried to clear up at all, then. That'll make it easier for forensics.' There was nothing else to see on the ground floor, so they made their way up the stairs.

The front bedroom was also empty but the bed had been slept in. Looked like it hadn't been changed for weeks. The second bedroom was a nursery for Westlake's baby daughter, Emily. The cot had been filled with empty beer cans and there were stubbed out roll-ups on the pink carpet. Sally felt angry that someone could treat a baby's room like that, could show so little respect.

'Bloody disgusting,' she whispered, rolling her eyes at Lizzie and shaking her head as they backed out of the little room.

They found Westlake in the bathroom, slumped on the floor with his back against the bath and his legs splayed out in front of him. An empty bottle of vodka lay by his side. Ripped packets of aspirin, paracetamol, cough medicine, and old unfinished prescription medicines were scattered across the floor.

'Dear God, Lizzie, he's taken every bloody thing in the cupboard,' breathed Sally. She dropped to her knees next to Westlake and listened, her ear close to his mouth. There was a faint rattle of breath in his chest, and a weak pulse in his neck.

'Ambulance! He's alive. Call it in, fast.'

Sally dragged Westlake out of the bathroom and onto the landing, where she put him into the recovery position and waited for the ambulance. Lizzie held his head, in case he wanted to be sick, but he seemed to be too far gone to act on simple reflex. Sally willed him not to die.

The wail of the ambulance broke the silence. There didn't seem to be much to say when they arrived. Lizzie went in the ambulance, leaving Sally to lock up and leave the house safe. He hadn't died yet, but who knew how much of him would be left after they had tried to save his life? There was no way to know whether he had taken a lot of pills, or was just sleeping off a bottle of vodka.

She took the number of Westlake's wife from his phone and rang her. Sophie Westlake seemed like a nice woman, but she hadn't known what to say, and Sally had the feeling that she would rather not have known. If Miles had been Sally's husband, she would have wanted to know, even if she had left him.

Then she rang Dan's phone, but had to leave a message. She checked her watch, gone seven. Fair enough, she thought, he's gone home and I'm going home. Report will do in the morning and Lizzie wanted the overtime so she could look after Westlake at the hospital tonight. She rang the duty sergeant and arranged for someone to relieve Lizzie later.

'I just hope the dirty, cowardly bastard doesn't die on us,' she said to the cracked picture of a baby hanging off the wall.

She stepped outside the door to a gaggle of neighbours. Whole families were out on the pavements, gossiping, chatting, and enjoying the spectacle of the ambulance on their quiet street. She resisted the urge to berate them and pushed past to the borrowed car, keeping her head down and avoiding eye contact, answering no questions – stuff community policing, she thought.

Sally had a sudden, urgent need to see her daughters, to hold them, to play a game, to give them their baths, to eat with her family, to be normal for just a few hours and to restore a bit of innocent joy to her world.

She knew she would never really want to do anything else, but sometimes her job was a dirty business.

Chapter 23

Date: Tuesday 25th April Time: 19:26 Chas Lloyd

Dan stood in the doorway under a cracked oak lintel. He had to admit that even after three years at university in Exeter, he had never been in this pub. The walls and ceiling were covered in beer mats that appeared to have been signed by famous people. He amended that on a closer inspection to people who had played for the local football team and a couple of now dead minor celebrities. There were several small rooms and a brass-covered semi-circular bar around which they radiated. He walked through the main lounge area and spotted Chas sitting alone in a back room with a beer. He made a "want another one?" gesture and bought two beers to take through with him.

Dan reassured himself that spurning an attractive young woman's advances did not make him a bad person, although possibly it made him a stupid one. He slid onto the bench next to her and decided to disarm her by going straight for the apology. 'I am so sorry about last night, Chas. I wasn't thinking straight.'

'Looked like pretty straight thinking to me. You practically threw me out.'

Truth was, she had terrified him the night before. They had enjoyed pasta, wine and more beers, giggles and stories about music and past histories, and then gone up to his flat. Big mistake.

It had been alright at first. She had teased him about the 'new minimalism' of only possessing one armchair. She had had a go on his guitar and got him to sing her a couple of songs. He had been flattered, and a bit drunk. But when she had climbed up him like a monkey up a tree, looping her legs around his waist and clamping her hands on either side of his head, he had panicked. She was nineteen years old, a possible witness, if not an actual suspect in an active case, and he was about to take her to bed. It was self-preservation as much as concern for the girl that had broken through the haze of alcohol.

Within five minutes she had been dumped back on the floor, and Dan was calling a taxi.

He took a swig from the bottle and tried again, a telltale slow flush creeping up his neck. 'We were both a bit drunk, and I do find you very attractive.'

Chas sniffed, breaking into his prepared monologue, 'So what was all the "I just can't do this," nonsense?'

'Look.' He decided he had to be at least partially honest, but he couldn't look at her, focussing instead on the brass rim that bound the table edge. 'I've just come out of a relationship that I thought was going to last forever. The kind where you have two kids and a dog and a house in the country. I just hadn't realised that it was a total fantasy not shared by the other party in the relationship. She doesn't want kids ever, she wants Manolo Blatniks or whatever they're called, a flat in Hampstead and a job that pays a hundred and twenty grand a year.'

He stopped and twisted round on the leather bench to face her. 'I'm still hurting, Chas, and I don't want to get hurt again.' He hadn't quite intended to say the last bit, but he could see from her face that his confession had touched her.

Chas reached across and took his hand. 'Okay. Well, I'm sorry too. I can be a bit much for people to take. I tend to see what I want and go for it. Shall we have another go at being friends first?' She smiled to see the relief on his face.

'Yeah, I would like us to be friends,' he said, smiling across at her. 'That would be great. Give me time to get my mojo back, or something.'

It was more than he deserved. His behaviour had been crass and juvenile. But it was the fact that Chas forgave him so easily that made him feel queasy again. She was so young and so easy to manipulate. She really did need someone more her own age and experience, not a fast-becoming cynic like him.

She laughed at last, a little sound that encouraged him to press on.

'The thing is, Chas, I need a favour.'

'Favour? What kind of favour?'

'I need to have a look round the studio without Jed being there.' He raised both hands to quieten any response, 'just to eliminate him from our enquiries, nothing else. I don't think he had anything to do with Carly's death but he won't let us in to look round without a warrant, and we wouldn't be able to get one until Thursday, I wouldn't think. I don't want to wait that long. I've got a murderer to catch.'

Chas's eyes widened. 'I can't. Jed would sack me. And I need that job.'

Her eyes radiating alarm, she backed away from him. She looked ready to run. Dan reached for her hand.

'He would never need to know,' he said, soothing her by stroking her fingers with his thumb, like you might a frightened animal. 'Just give me the keys and tell me the alarm codes. I won't leave any prints or take anything with me. I just need to know if Carly Braithwaite was in the studio on Sunday night. I can get the keys back to you later tonight. You will be genuinely helping me, Chas.'

'What if he's working late?'

'Ring him and see. Does he have anyone booked in for tonight?'

'No, but you never know.' She swirled her beer in its bottle. 'I don't want to do this, Dan.' She looked at him properly for the first time that evening, shaking her head with each word to emphasise her worry. 'I'm scared of what might happen.'

Dan tried for a smile. He was quite worried about what might happen, too. 'Please? Give Jed a ring now and we can see if it's possible. Perhaps you could suggest meeting up for a drink? That way, I'll know you're both out of the way. If he's working late, I promise I'll wait until I get the warrant and then you won't need to do anything. We can just go back to getting to know each other. Okay?'

He knew he was pushing her hard. He also knew that he had no intention of ever seeing her again. He was surprised at how easy it was to lie to her.

He watched as the girl weighed up the pros and cons of betraying her boss to her new boyfriend. She was struggling with it. He drank his beer and gave her time, holding lightly onto her hand.

'Okay, I'll do it,' she said eventually, having reached some sort of conclusion in her head. 'I'm going to the Ladies, then I'll ring Jed. If the studio's going to be empty, I'll give you the keys, but I want them back before midnight, so I've got them before I go to bed. And you promise me, he will never know I let you in?'

Dan promised. Another lie. How easily they came. She gave him her address.

'You must promise me you won't tell Jed,' he said. 'We probably aren't going to find anything anyway, so no point in annoying him.'

She smiled at him, and nodded, 'Got it.'

He watched her head off to the toilet and rang Ian. They arranged to meet at the entrance to the alley at nine o'clock assuming Chas gave them the all clear. Dan needed time to get home, change out of his suit and into something more appropriate for breaking and entering. He wasn't entirely sure he liked this new person he was turning into.

Chas made her call when she returned. Jed told her he was going out to see a band later that evening and was at home, now. Did Chas want to go with him? Dan nodded at her - she couldn't be implicated in the B and E if she was in a club with the owner of the studio.

Chas said she would head over to his place and ended the call. She passed over the keys, and wrote the alarm code on his hand. She kissed him on the cheek and rose to leave.

'Don't forget to give me back the keys.' She winked at him. 'I could always pop over for them later, save you coming over to me,' was her parting shot.

Chapter 24

Date: Tuesday 25th April Time: 20:54 DI Hellier and DCI Gould

Marilyn Gould looked across the top of her knitting at her husband. She couldn't figure out what was going on. He was sitting at the dining table dressed entirely in black, like the Milk Tray man, but with a paunch and a bald patch. On the table were a big Maglite torch that had been police issue years ago, his phone, a pair of latex gloves, and what looked suspiciously like a balaclava. He was trying to squash all of it into the pockets of his fishing jacket.

'Are you going to tell me what you're up to, Ian?' she asked, inwardly cursing as she realised she'd dropped a stitch and now had to undo the whole row.

'Up to, my love?'

'With the James Bond routine. Have you got a beautiful blonde and a fancy car outside?'

Gould laughed. 'I wish. No, I'm just going out with Dan Hellier the new DI, for a drink. Thought it was about time I introduced him to the delights of Exeter's nightlife.'

She regarded him sceptically. He used to be much slicker at lying. But things had been so much better between them over the last few years, and if he wanted to go out on a little adventure without telling her what he was up to, she wasn't going to stop him. If it was police business, he wouldn't tell her anyway.

Marilyn focussed on her knitting again. It was a complicated cable pattern but it would look fantastic as a baby blanket for Laura's first one. It could go with the bonnet and socks she'd already got in the drawer. She could hardly wait to be a grandma.

She was going to be looking after the baby three days a week so Laura could go back to work. That would get her out of the house for a bit while Ian found his retirement feet, so to speak. She found her mind wandering back to how Ian was going to occupy himself when he retired. He liked fishing, so that would get him out of the house. Maybe they could travel, go to New Zealand to see her sister or India or somewhere?

Gould's phone rang. He stood up, listened, said a few words back, kissed his wife and headed out the door.

'Don't wait up,' he called as he pulled the door behind him.

Gould couldn't help whistling the theme tune from the James Bond movies as he waited in the music shop doorway for Dan to arrive. The night was cool and wet, puddles reflecting the streetlights on the main street, but inky in the blackness of the alleyway. He also couldn't help leaping out at Dan from the shadows and making him jump.

'Ian, you nearly gave me a heart attack. You're not five,' muttered Dan, waiting for his heart to subside.

Gould snorted a quiet laugh. 'D'you know, I genuinely didn't understand that being Chief Inspector would mean that I would spend far more of my time behind a desk supervising investigations than carrying them out. Perhaps that's why I've been so unhappy in the job recently. Planning and writing reports just doesn't interest me.'

He dragged the balaclava out of one pocket and placed it on his head, just above his ears. Dan didn't respond to the chatter, which he put down to nervousness, although it could have been excitement, but Gould didn't seem to notice how quiet he was.

'I feel positively frisky,' he continued. 'Marilyn had better not be asleep when I get home.' He glanced at Dan. 'Have you brought gloves?' Dan showed his gloved hands. Gould had brought some, of course, and pulled them on with relish.

'Ok, boy wonder, lead on,' he said, and they slipped into the gloom of the alleyway, pulling hoods over their heads.

Dan had a feeling that it would be pretty easy to identify the bulk and gait of his partner on CCTV even without facial recognition, but it was the best they could do at short notice. He kept his head down and clung to the darkest wall as they groped their way to the entrance. Gould held his torch over the lock of the heavy, scarred outer door. Dan fumbled with the key and grimaced at the muffled tut from behind him.

'It won't go in,' he said, 'I…' It wouldn't go in because the lock was already undone. Dan backed away from the doorway as if he'd been burnt. 'It's open,' he whispered, 'let's get out of here.'

Gould was not so easily put off. He checked the inner door and it was firmly locked. 'I reckon Abrams forgot to lock the outside door, the rest is locked up fine.' He squinted through the glass door. 'I can see a faint red glow down there, probably a security light. There aren't any other lights on and it's as quiet as the grave. Come on.' He gestured impatiently at Dan to give him the keys.

Swallowing his reluctance, Dan passed them over and crept in behind the older man. The alarm began to beep a warning signal. He was reassured that the building was locked after all. Breathing more steadily, he fed in the code and waited for the beeping to stop. Gould unlocked the glass door and wedged it open a fraction with the doormat.

'Always keep your exit free, basic training manual, page one.'

'Basic breaking and entering manual, page one, too,' muttered Dan behind him. He followed Gould down the carpeted stairs. Neither man wanted to put the lights on until they were inside the studio, so they traced pictures on the wall with the wavering beams of their torches as they descended. Gould unlocked the final glass door at the bottom of the stairs and handed the keys back to Dan.

'For your girlfriend,' he whispered, and chuckled as he stepped round the corner into the spacious reception area, torch held out in front of him.

The room was lit only by the interrogative glow of a red light on the alarm box high in the corner of the ceiling. Gould located the main lights and padded across the room to the bank of switches on the control room wall.

Dan took more care as he peered around the doorway, staring into the red space, his uneasiness magnified by the dream-like light. And saw what he most dreaded. A blackness, shadow within shadow, figure from a child's nightmare, rose up from the floor behind the desk.

'Ian! Get down!' he screamed, but could only watch as in a horrible slow motion the creature raised its arm and he saw the unmistakeable outline of a gun against the crimson flicker on the wall.

Gould was slow, far too slow. But he dropped obediently to his knees, and felt the bullet as a point of heat where it entered his chest, and as a seeping cold as he tumbled to meet the floor.

A scream came from inside the control room, an incoherent yell of anger. Chas Lloyd came hurtling round the corner and leapt onto the back of the shooter, scratching at his head. She clamped her teeth onto the huge gunman's ear and attempted to pull the arm holding the gun back over his head. The man growled in pain and used his free arm to grab the back of the girl's coat and throw her over his head like a child's toy. She smacked into the metal corner of the reception desk and fell quiet.

Dan reacted on an instinct fleeter than thought. He yanked his baton from his pocket, whipped it open, ran up and over the leather sofa and smashed it down on the gunman's forearm. The big man dropped the gun, screaming in pain and shock. Throwing himself to the floor, Dan used the stick across the back of the gunman's knees, bringing him down too. The man scrabbled crab-like for his gun, howling as he tried to wriggle across the floor on deadened legs.

Dan rolled and twisted himself up onto his hands and knees next to the gunman. He straddled him, pinning the gunman's good arm under his knee, and rammed the baton as hard as he could into the man's temple. He watched the man's eyes roll up into his head. He screamed into the man's slack face, 'I hope I've killed you. I hope I've killed you, murdering bastard.'

He fell away panting, dropped the baton, and half-crawling, half-creeping scrambled over to the dark lump that was his colleague. Gould was still breathing, but it was ragged, stilted breathing. The bullet seemed to have pierced a lung.

'Can't breathe…' he gasped, struggling to sit up.

'Stay quiet, mate,' Dan said, scrubbing tears from his face. 'We'll get you to hospital. It'll be alright.'

Gould's eyelids fluttered and he sank into unconsciousness.

Dan looked up as he heard a noise from the kitchen and leaned back ready to grab the gun. Jed Abrams came out, quivering and shaking with his hands in the air.

'I never meant...' he began, and then stopped as he saw the limp body of Chas Lloyd by the desk. Whimpering, he crossed the room and knelt beside her, trying to straighten out her twisted limbs.

'I'm sorry, I'm so sorry,' he repeated.

Dan turned his phone on. There were so many messages wanting his attention. He rang for an ambulance. 'Officer down,' would bring them quickly. No need for an armed response unit. Too late now. He shrugged off his jacket and bundled it up under Gould's head. On the floor next to the desk, Abrams had gathered the broken body of Chas Lloyd close to him. Dan couldn't tell if she was alive or not, but he couldn't spare the emotion to check.

He knew he had to make sure there was no one else there. Shock was protecting him now, but it would wear off. He placed Gould's head back onto the rolled up jacket, and wiped a small trickle of blood and fluid from his chin. Rising to a crouch, he checked the other smaller rooms and found they were empty.

Lastly, he went to the post-production video room and was not surprised to find that it was also completely empty. No DVDs, no CDs, no recording machines, nothing but empty shelves, a table and a chair. Abrams had emptied it already, or there had never been anything there in the first place.

Dan sank back down next to Gould and held his hand while they waited. He could hear the rasp of his breath and the rattle of fluid in his lungs as he struggled for air.

It slowly seeped through his dulled senses. Chas had set them up. He had been a total, gullible idiot. She had probably rung Abrams when she went to the Ladies. Why had he not seen that coming? Had he been that easy to deceive?

But then, in the middle of the shooting, she had tried to save his life, and had quite possibly given her own whilst she did it. Hard to make any sense of that. She must have thought the shooter had shot him rather than Ian. He stared around him at the bodies on the floor. The big guy fit Gould's description of one of the foreigners he'd seen earlier in the day. Where were the others, though? Was this a warning from them to keep out of their business? Had the gunman thought that Ian was armed? His torch could have looked like a gun, he supposed. So many questions banged against his brain. He couldn't begin to process them.

But the truth was inescapable: there was nothing here that could help them with their investigation. It had been a total red herring.

From his position in the entrance of Blockbusters, across the road from the studio, Grigor Pelakais watched, rigid with shock, as police cars and ambulances arrived. What had gone wrong? It should have been a simple warning to the police to keep out of their business. They were behaving illegally by breaking in. Abrams just had to pretend he was working late, and then make an official complaint when he found the officers on his premises. It should have been simple.

He felt impotent as he watched his friend being carried into an ambulance. There seemed to be a drip being supported by a medic next to Filip's arm, so maybe he wasn't dead. And by the size of the body on the second stretcher, the little girl Chas, had also been hurt. Jed Abrams had been shoved into a police car and driven off.

He should have gone in with Filip, no matter what Irina had said. And now… What if Filip died? How could he carry on living without him? It would suit Irina if he died. She would have Grigor to herself. Filip would be too frightened to tell the police anything even if he lived. As usual, she would be safe from the chaos she caused.

Grigor turned his head away as the police car reversed onto the main road, and then he ran for the van. He didn't know which of the policemen was on the last stretcher to come out of the studio but he didn't want to hang around to find out about him. He had to follow the ambulance with Filip in it to find out where they would take him.

Chapter 25

Date: Tuesday 25th April Time: 23:35 Royal Devon & Exeter Hospital

Marilyn Gould sat on a hard plastic chair at the other end of the corridor from Dan. She stared at the linoleum floors, polished to an unnatural shine and winced at the slap of rubber clogs and the squeak of rubber wheels. She wrinkled her nose at the attempt to disguise death with a flowery curtain and a can of air freshener.

Dan kept trying to catch her eye, but she avoided his gaze. He thought she was wondering why her husband had been shot and not him. And now Superintendent Oliver was in with Ian and wouldn't let Marilyn in to see her husband. He checked his watch, it was gone half-eleven. Marilyn had been in bed when he rang. He gave her no details, just told her that there had been an accident and that someone would pick her up in an area car and take her to the hospital. The one question she had asked him was how someone gets shot taking the new DI out for a drink in Exeter. And that question he could not answer. So she blanked him.

The door to the side room opened and Julie Oliver came out. Dan watched her go up to Marilyn Gould, sit next to her and take her hand. They talked for a few moments until Marilyn stood up and went in to see her husband.

Oliver turned and looked at Dan. He couldn't make out the expression on her face. She walked back towards him, and seemed to be struggling with what she was going to say. Her voice, when it came, was a flat monotone. 'Ian has given me a statement. He insisted that I took it down there and then.' She waved a piece of spiral notebook paper at him, the torn edges fluttering. 'He claims full responsibility for the little prank you pulled this evening. He says it was all his idea, that he had to force you to go along with it and that you only agreed because he would have gone to the studio on his own anyway.'

She finally looked down at him. Dan started to speak but she cut him off. 'Don't even try. I know this whole mess wasn't just Ian's idea. I'm not stupid, but he has saved you from instant dismissal. There will, however, be serious consequences for your actions, Detective Inspector. I'm going now. Be in my office at nine tomorrow.'

Oliver turned, body erect, head held high, and strode away. Watching her back as she walked, he saw her shoulders slump as she passed through the swing doors.

Dan leant forward in the plastic chair and rested his elbows on his knees. He scrubbed his face with his hands. He should go but he didn't really have anywhere to go. He had been in to see Chas Lloyd, who was alive but had fractured her back when she had landed on the corner of the reception desk. It was too soon to tell if she would walk again. She would be operated on in the early hours of the morning. He had held her hand until the doctor told him to go away and let her rest.

He'd been in to see Claire Quick. She was sleeping peacefully, lying on her back. They were going to let her out in the morning. The first bit of good news he'd had all day.

Abrams was in custody. If Chas had told him about the proposed nocturnal visit as soon as she left Dan in the pub, he'd had two hours to shift any stuff before they got to the studio. Thinking about it logically, Dan knew there had to be more to find and that they had been on the right track, otherwise why would one of the foreign gang have been there waiting for them? And why would he have been armed? What were the other two up to and where were they? Why had Chas betrayed him, and then tried to save him? Where was the van that Abrams had used to move the stuff? It had been outside the studio yesterday.

He shook his head and rested his burning eyes in the heels of his hands, pressing his eyeballs until streaks of blue and orange light lit the darkness.

The injured foreign gang member was also in the intensive care unit. The blow to his temple had caused bones to crack and a small piece was embedded in his brain, causing a bleed. Part of Dan still wished he had killed him. On the other hand, it would be cathartic to see him punished for shooting Ian Gould. And it would be far better for Dan if he didn't have an unlawful killing charge to face. He hadn't bothered going to see the foreigner, who was under guard anyway.

He switched his phone back on and scrolled through the messages, trying to determine their importance by who had sent them. He sat back in his chair as he stared at Sally's message from seven o'clock. He couldn't believe it. Another one in hospital. Shaking his head, he slowly walked the short distance to the other end of the intensive care unit. Concerned about him, the nurse at the desk called out the young PC who had been set to guard Miles Westlake until he came round, or died. It was Lizzie Singh.

'You alright, sir?' she asked. 'Only you're not looking too good.'

'No Lizzie, not alright at all. How is Westlake?'

'Pretty good. He's breathing on his own so he'll live, but he swallowed all sorts of stuff, so they don't know about organ damage. I think we got to him quickly, though, sir. And he's young and fit.'

'I'm sure you did everything you could. When are you being relieved?'

'In about ten minutes. I'm pooped, I can tell you.'

'You should go home and get some sleep then. I'll see you in the morning. Briefing at eight am.' He turned to go.

'Sir, who's in the bed down the corridor? There's a guard on him, too. Is he something to do with our case?' She looked up at Dan. She trusted him. Trusted that his decisions were wise ones, expected him to act as the leader of their team, to protect them and support and guide them. What a joke.

'Yes, Lizzie, he's got something to do with our case, but I'll tell you all about it in the morning. Here's your relief, off you go.' He nodded at the newly arrived officer and set off back towards Ian's room.

The sound of a quiet but insistent bell and urgent, whispered voices brought him round the corner at a run. The crash unit was in the side room. Marilyn Gould stood outside, the back of her fist in her mouth to stop herself from screaming. She glared at Dan with such venom he took a wide arc around her.

He got to the door just as the crash team disengaged the paddles from Ian's ruined chest. One of them gave the time of death as four minutes past twelve, on Wednesday the 26th April.

Dan walked home. He didn't know what else to do. He took off his shoes, lay face down on the bed and let exhaustion drag him into oblivion.

The slow creep of dawn in the intensive care unit disturbed the sleeping sick, setting up a chain reaction of groans, coughs, murmurs, sighs and turnings over. The staff nurse on duty rose from her chair, padded round the table and looked out along the corridor. A tired constable smiled up at her from the chair outside the door. She looked in at Mr Westlake and saw that he was awake. It was never easy to predict whether they would survive the night, and even harder to predict how they would cope with still being alive if they came round. Thanks to the police, the team had dealt with him promptly, a couple of hours or so after he'd taken the stuff, and he was young and fit. Suppressing a sigh, she opened the door.

Miles could only move his eyes at first. He felt like he was under water, with a great weight on his limbs. The slow rise to consciousness had been the hardest part. Most of him was fighting to crawl back down again. Because he couldn't, really couldn't, think about what he had done to his wife, to his daughter, and to Carly. Beautiful, talented Carly.

He also couldn't work out how he had ended up in hospital. Somebody must have got into the house, yet he was sure he'd locked all the doors. He'd obviously made a mistake somewhere in his planning, but nothing would come clear.

They would take him to prison as soon as he was well enough. It would be in all the papers. He could see how it would pan out. His name on the news, his reputation ruined. Sophie's reputation ruined. No, he couldn't cope with that. He couldn't cope with that at all. He tried to move his arms and felt them fight against him.

A nurse entered the room smiling at him.

'Glad to see you're awake, Mr Westlake,' she said. He couldn't answer. His voice was still refusing to respond and his range of movement was minimal. 'Just take it easy, you'll get a bit more feeling back over the next few hours. Then the doctor will be in to see you. You're a very lucky man.' She lifted him up onto the pillows and gave him water, which he kept down. She adjusted the speed of the drip to help rehydrate him more quickly.

He could see another shape behind her in the background, standing near the door. As the nurse moved to write on his chart, he saw it was a policeman. He was being watched, but they hadn't handcuffed him or anything. The policeman left with the nurse and he saw him sit down outside the room. If he was to get out of here, and he was determined to get away one way or another, Miles was going to have to be a lot cleverer than the police. With gentle persistence, he began to flex his fingers and toes.

Two floors down, Chas Lloyd was also awake, having swum up through layers of nightmare to face the dawn. She would swear that she could feel the waves of morphine entering through the drip and strapping her as effectively to the bed as any material restraint. She knew that was a bad thing. You would only give someone morphine if they were seriously hurt. It was weird then, that she was seriously hurt but couldn't feel anything at all. She flexed one hand and then the other. So, she had some movement in the top half at least.

With an effort, she remembered everything from the night in the studio up to the point where that Latvian monster had shot the policeman that she had thought was Dan. After that it was emptiness.

Chas knew that Dan had been to see her in the night, and held her hand and stayed with her. She felt tears prickle and leak from her closed eyes when she thought about how she had betrayed him. Betrayed him for so little. A few pathetic thousand quid towards her course at college. How cheaply that Latvian bitch had bought her.

Her mother had always said Chas would come to nothing, and this time she'd be right. She knew full well what the Latvians were like, and how scared of them Jed was. None of it was worth the taking of a life. None of it was worth betraying Dan for. In the deepest, darkest part of her, she had to admit she had done it for revenge, to ease her anger at the way he had responded to her the night before. And look how it had turned out. What kind of woman was she, that she could want revenge on a man who had simply treated her with respect?

Chas looked towards the doorway. She could see a doctor in scrubs talking to someone. Her mother and father had arrived. That meant they would be operating on her soon. She felt the tears begin again.

Chapter 26

Date: Wednesday 26th April Time: 07:03 DI Dan Hellier

Dan woke up. A great lurching, falling thump into the day. Seagulls were strutting on the roof, calling out threats and bragging to other birds across the water. He rolled over to sit upright on the bed and rubbed his face with his hands. Just for a second, he forgot about what had happened the night before and looked down in confusion at the rumpled clothes he still wore. Just for a second. Then the gunshot and the blood and Ian shuddering for each breath on the floor flew back in through the little gap he had left open and pinned him back down onto the bed, under the duvet, shaking and shivering with the shock of it all. It took all his effort and all his will to force himself up from that place of safety into the shower.

The face in the mirror gave so little away. If you ignored the black rings under his eyes, he still looked fit and healthy and ready to face the day. His own thriving, alive image made him feel sick as he ran the razor over his chin.

After he had dressed, he ate cereal and toast and drank tea on the balcony, feeling strangely and unreasonably disloyal to Ian for taking time to eat when there was work to be done. But, he was starving, and self-preservation had set in. He might well end the day suspended and under investigation for gross misconduct or, worse, incompetence. He knew that he had to be calm and rational when he arrived at the station. He wanted to break the news about Ian to the team himself and he needed to have a plan of action ready for the team to get cracking on, even if he wasn't going to be leading them. With Carly's murderer still not charged and a violent gang running free, there would be no point in them sitting round feeling miserable.

The morning sun caught the edge of the tiny metal table as Dan planned how to tell his team that he had been responsible for the death of their friend and colleague.

Lizzie Singh arrived first. She threw her bag in the corner and got started on a fresh pot of coffee. She gave the brown-ringed, stained mugs a scrub and dug a packet of Hob Nobs out of her bag. She didn't need to be told that "last in" made the drinks.

Dan arrived to find her standing at the wall, tracing possible connections with her finger. It almost hurt to see her so keen to be part of his team. He guessed he was not more than ten years older than her but it could have been fifty the way he was feeling at the moment. He slipped past into his own office and waited there until they were all assembled before going out.

As usual, Sally was last to arrive, rushing to drop her bag and smiling her thanks at Lizzie as she placed a steaming mug in front of her. Sally liked to take the twins to nursery when she could, but it meant she was always cutting it fine. She opened her notebook and looked around . 'Where's Ian?' she asked of no one in particular. 'You can never get the bugger to do overtime but he's usually in early.'

At just after eight o'clock, Dan appeared from his office and began the briefing. He motioned to Lizzie to sit down when she attempted to pour him coffee. He stood at the head of the table and spoke: 'Last night, Detective Chief Inspector Ian Gould was shot and killed in the line of duty. He died bravely…' He didn't get any further for the gasps and denials around the table. Bill Larcombe, who had been one of Ian's closest friends, laughed in disbelief.

'Shut up, all of you,' shouted Sally, and into the abrupt silence she asked the most important question, 'How?'

The thing that had become most clear in his quiet hour of thinking that morning was that he had to tell the team the absolute truth. They had to know now, before the press and the station gossip got hold of it and twisted everything. They also needed to know what they had to do next. The bit he couldn't do was to reassure them that he would still be leading them in an hour's time.

'Ian and I were pursuing a hunch about Jed Abrams. So we went to the studio last night to have a look round to see if there was anything dirty there. We thought porn, or maybe rip-off music. Ian also had a thought that Jed Abrams might have killed Carly and used his van to transport her body.'

'So it was a legitimate part of our investigation then?' asked Sally.

'Yes, it was. But... we didn't want to wait until we had a warrant. No magistrate would have granted one simply on a 'suspicion' of illegal activity, and we knew that Abrams would empty the place if we left it any longer. The plan was to pass it straight on to Vice if we found anything. It should have been a quick in and out.' He flushed as he heard the crack in his voice. 'I got the key from Chas Lloyd, the girl who works there. But, she evidently tipped off Abrams and the gang of foreigners who Ian and Sam saw at the Studio earlier in the day.'

Dan looked over at Sam Knowles, who had turned white. The young officer nodded, 'I reckon they were Russian or something.'

'Well, one of them was waiting for us. When Ian went over to switch the lights on, the guy shot him in the chest, through the lung. He died of a heart attack later in hospital.'

Lizzie Singh stared at him, her mouth open. The others looked anywhere else. He rushed to finish before he chickened out. 'Chas Lloyd and Jed Abrams were hiding in the kitchen. Chas came charging out and tried to stop the gunman. He threw her over his head like a... like a string puppet, and she broke her back on the metal desk. She's in hospital.'

'But alive?' asked Sally.

'Alive, but facing a major operation this morning. She may never walk again.'

'What about the gunman, boss? Did he get away?' asked Sam.

'No, I hit him pretty hard across the temple with my baton. It's a bit touch and go whether *he* lives or dies. They're operating on him this morning, too.'

'I wish you'd killed him.' Sam's unsteady voice was echoed by others.

'Sam, so do I. But I'm in enough trouble already. I need him to live. We've got Abrams in custody, too.'

He stopped then, and gave the team a few minutes to absorb the information. Sally comforted Bill Larcombe, who looked devastated. The pair of them wiped away tears. Lizzie leant back in her chair to talk to Sam, who was clenching his fists in his efforts not to cry.

It was Ben Bennett, the quiet one of the team, who put two and two together. 'Boss, as there's been an officer killed, will you be suspended?'

Dan looked at the clock. 'I'm seeing DCS Oliver in half an hour, when she will make the initial decision. There will certainly be an investigation and a post-mortem for Ian before his wife can bury him.' He took a breath and let it go. 'I shall, of course take full responsibility for what happened. It was my bad call to go ahead with it when I found the outer metal door at the studio was unlocked. They couldn't have locked that as it's padlocked from the outside. Should have followed my intuition and got us out of there.' He stared at the table top. 'But I didn't … And I am so, so sorry.'

He took another deep breath. 'So, let's get you sorted out before I get my marching orders. We still have a murderer to catch, and we have to avenge the death of our colleague, if you'll pardon the old-fashioned use of the verb. I'm still in charge of this case at the moment, and I'm now convinced that Jed Abrams has something to do with Carly's death.'

He let the lie slip out, and hated himself for his weakness. Hated himself for needing to validate his terrible decision to go along with Ian's mad suggestion. How desperate had he been to earn the respect of his senior colleague? His brain had been stuck in a reel all morning: it wasn't a red herring. It can't have been a red herring. We were right to look. It was the right thing to do. But his heart didn't believe it.

He asked Sally to update them on the arrest of Miles Westlake.

'With the evidence from the post-mortem, it's clear that Westlake probably had sex with Carly on the Saturday night. Although, we can't rule out Jamie May on that count. Westlake is still a murder suspect, though, especially since he tried suicide.' She paused. 'Is Alan Braithwaite still in the picture, boss?'

'Well, you spent a day with the family, what do you think?'

'I don't think he did it. He seems too genuinely upset to be faking it. I'd hate to be the one that did kill her, though, if Braithwaite catches up with him first. I think he was just over-protective of Carly and aggression is his first mode of attack.'

Dan nodded. 'I think we have the killer either in custody or in the hospital. We just need someone to tell us which of our likely suspects is the guilty party, or get one of them to cough. Okay, let's get to work. I have to see DCS Oliver in twenty minutes.'

Dan set Bill Larcombe to organising Forensics to search Abram's studio and then to go to the Westlake house.

'Sam, you have to continue looking through the studio security CDs. We have to know for sure if Carly went to the studio, or we're stuffed. Well, I'll be stuffed. Could Abrams have sneaked out earlier in the day?

'While you're out, have a chat with the music shop staff, see if they have noticed anything odd happening. First though, you and Lizzie get over to Jamie May's house and give it a good looking over. We should have done that yesterday, but God knows how we'd have fitted it in. Anyway, get it done today.

'And someone find me Jed Abrams' van – it needs a thorough going over.'

Ben Bennett nodded, that was his area.

'If I'm still your DI in an hour, Sally and I will interview Miles Westlake if we're allowed, and speak to Jed Abrams about the foreigners. We should also go and see how Chas Lloyd is, and pop in on Claire Quick.'

He scanned his notebook. 'We have to either formally charge Jamie May or let him go by four thirty this afternoon. And I'm not letting him go unless he tells us something, so I have asked for a twenty-four hour extension. Let's meet back here at about five.'

Dan looked up at the clock. Time to face the music. He didn't see the sympathy on the faces of his team as he walked out of the room.

Julie Oliver tapped her pen against her teeth and contemplated her office door. What a mess. She couldn't take Hellier off the case without bringing in a DI from elsewhere. Her other Major Incident team was up to their necks in a people trafficking case, and without Ian, she didn't have anyone else at the appropriate rank to lead a case. The advert was already out for a replacement for Ian, but they weren't even planning to interview for another two weeks. She didn't want to bring in a DI from a totally different area at this crucial stage in the case, and, if she was being honest, she didn't want to admit that she'd made a mistake in assigning the case to a rookie Inspector in the first place. How else did you learn the job?

She'd endured the call to Marilyn Gould as best she could. The brief affair with Ian had been over ten years before, but she had still had a soft spot for him. Marilyn was hurting, and wanted a public humiliation of Hellier. Well, that wasn't going to happen.

As Chief Superintendent, she was Dan Hellier's line manager, and it was initially up to her to investigate the misdemeanour and decide on its severity. It was pretty clear-cut though, that suspension was the next step.

Oliver looked down at the statement signed by Ian just before he died. Technically, it let Hellier off the hook as Ian took all the blame for the visit to the studio. But Hellier was a senior detective. He should have refused to do something so stupid and come straight to her. She would have rushed through a warrant application, if they'd had real cause. She sighed. It was so typical of Ian to do something stupid. It was why she'd taken him off active duty in the first place. She did believe they were onto something major, though. Why else would there have been a guy waiting for them with a gun? Why would someone have emptied the video production room? How did the two pieces of this jigsaw come together?

She sighed again and, shaking her head, pulled across Hellier's personal file. It read well at first. He had had commendations for bravery whilst doing a stint in the Drug Squad and he was well thought of in the Met. He'd done a stint in Vice. Apart from one time when he went a bit overboard arresting a drunk, he'd never stepped out of line until he beat seven bells out of some bloke who was chatting up his girlfriend. The file detailed the inquiry. He had been lucky to be offered a transfer. The psychologist had said the attack was out of character and had been a stress reaction to a particularly harrowing case he'd been on at the time, so they had shunted him out of London. I hope I've not lost Ian and replaced him with another maverick, she thought.

A light knock interrupted her thoughts. It was two minutes to the hour and the slim outline of Dan Hellier wavered through the rippled glass of her door. He entered and hovered near the doorway. He was finding it hard to look her in the eyes. Had it only been two days ago that he had promised not to let her down?

'Sit down, Detective Inspector Hellier,' she said, indicating a simple straight-backed wooden chair facing her desk. She called in her secretary to note the meeting.

Dan sat, took a deep breath and let it out slowly.

'Ma'am, I…'

'No, Inspector, that's not how it works. You sit and listen, and then I'll give you the chance to put forward your version when I have finished.'

She signalled Stella to begin writing.

'This is the first meeting of the investigation into the death of Detective Chief Inspector Ian Gould and the serious injury of

Chastity Lloyd and an unknown assailant. You have the right to be accompanied by a federation representative or a supportive friend if you wish.' She glanced up at him but Dan shook his head. 'Very well, noted. It is my understanding that you wilfully flouted the Police Code of Conduct to enter the premises of Jed Abrams without waiting for a search warrant, because you believe there is a link between the death of Carly Braithwaite and potential illegalities at the studio. You took this action because you believe there is something going on as we speak, and that there was no time to wait for the appropriately signed warrant because the suspect would have emptied the studio of evidence.' She looked at Dan.

He nodded. 'Yes, Ma'am.'

'Once you were inside the building, Ian Gould was shot once in the chest and Chastity Lloyd was thrown against a metal table, breaking her back. You incapacitated the gunman with a blow to the temple, which could yet prove to be fatal.'

Dan nodded once again, his face bleak.

'When the building was searched, you found nothing of any use to us in the investigation. Is that correct?'

He barely moved his head in acknowledgement.

'The breaking and entering part of this fiasco is worthy of a charge of gross misconduct on its own. Because of your poor decision, we have lost a serving senior police officer and two members of the public have been severely hurt. I can accept that you disabled the gunman appropriately as you were unarmed apart from your baton. I just hope, for your sake, he doesn't die.

'I note, for the record, that the totally empty video room does suggest that the suspect had prior knowledge of your arrival and removed items before you entered the premises, which does provide some validation for your hypothesis.'

She looked up from her notes and surveyed him over the rim of her glasses. 'PACE makes it very simple, Inspector Hellier, you should be suspended whilst an investigation is carried out.' Dan raised his head and tried to meet her eyes.

She stared back at him. Then she turned to her secretary. 'Off you go, Stella, type that up for me. I'll make my own notes for the last part of the meeting and get them to you in an hour or so.' The secretary left. She sat back in her chair.

'Right, I am now flying by the seat of my pants, as they say. I will have to take you off the case as far as the ACC is concerned, there is no way to avoid it.' She watched his face fall into resignation and his shoulders slump. 'However, as we are so short-staffed at DI level, there is nothing to stop me stepping in and taking over, at least on paper. You can 'advise' me as you have all the knowledge, and I can then keep you on active duty in this 'advisory' capacity. I'm going to have to be very creative in the reports I send in.'

Dan interrupted, 'Ma'am, don't put your own future on the line for me. You shouldn't cover for me. I broke the law and an officer died, I know the rules.'

She allowed a smile to lift the corners of her mouth. 'I want to catch these bastards, Dan, and I want to catch the murderer of Carly Braithwaite. Ian explained why you ended up breaking into the studio and I will give his note as evidence in your hearing. He took all responsibility. Just makes you look naïve and inexperienced, rather than incompetent. He was the senior officer, after all, and should have known better.

'The way I see it, you are my best chance to solve this case. So, if I have to fudge the truth a little to achieve those aims, then it's my decision.'

'But, how?'

'No going anywhere on your own, or interviewing anyone on your own. Someone with at least the rank of Detective Sergeant to accompany you, and no writing up of your own reports, I'll do those. Oh, and keep your mouth shut.'

Oliver cocked her head to one side, assessing the man in front of her.

'You now have one hour to explain to me exactly what has been going on, and give me a detailed breakdown of your reasoning, the intel you have so far, and what your gut is telling you. I need to believe that you have the ability, in fact the capability, to solve this case. If you do a good job in persuading me you are competent, then that will go in your favour as well. Then you can help me draft yet another statement for the press, which I'll deliver later this morning.'

Dan took out his notebook and flicked briefly through the pages, but she noticed he didn't refer to it again. She was pleased to note that he had all the salient facts in his head. She was simply going to help him get them into order.

Forty minutes later Julie Oliver sat back in her chair. 'Ok, I think I get it. We are looking at either two separate cases, or there may be a link between Carly and Abrams that we haven't yet found. So the nocturnal visit was a genuine part of your investigation.'

Dan agreed. 'I can't give you a solid reason why just yet, but it just feels right. There is a link. Abrams removed stuff from that room, and it is important to the case. I bloody well hope I am right, after what happened.'

'And we need to find out about this foreign crew and what they are doing in Exeter. We need to eliminate or charge Carly's father, Jamie May or Westlake. Currently, murder seems a bit strong for a girl who was having an affair with her teacher. After all, if we believe the Daily Mail, this sort of thing happens all the time, right? So we need motive and opportunity.'

Dan nodded again. 'The motive could be jealousy, as we originally thought, or it could be something totally different, related to some dirty little dealings going on at the studio.'

Oliver sniffed and sat in silence for a moment, assimilating the information. 'Okay, Dan, I'll let you carry on, as long as you stick to my rules. The younger members of your team don't need to know about our arrangement, just tell Sally. I know this has been a disaster so far, but I also know you're onto something.

'You promised me on Monday that you would do everything you could to catch Carly's murderer, didn't you?'

He nodded.

'Right, then, you'd better get on with it, and lord help us if this all goes tits up. I'll second another person onto your team to help out, and I will act as SIO instead of Ian, bless him. Then you can get back out there and catch me a killer.' She paused and checked her notes. 'I think that covers it. So, anything else you want to say?'

'Thank you,' said Dan. 'I want to say thank you for letting me have this chance and for not throwing me out, even though we both know I deserve it. I want to say I'll do better and I will find out what's going on. Thank you, Ma'am.'

'Ok, enough mushy stuff.' Oliver pursed her lips and sighed. 'What on earth can I say to the press that will show them we are on top and in charge, and know exactly what we are doing?

The Incident room was a hive of pretend activity. Dan entered the room and found the whole team still there, shuffling paper, writing up notes and pretending to talk to people on the phone. So busy were they at the tasks he had appointed them an hour before, they pretended not to notice his arrival, too. Sally 'suddenly' noticed his return.

'Oh, Boss, there you are. Everything alright?'

All sham activity ceased and they looked up at him, their faces leaking their emotions. Dan was surprised and touched that they had waited for him. He was even more surprised when he smiled and they let out a cheer.

'So it was alright, then?' Sally said, 'you're not suspended or anything?'

He shook his head.

'Right,' she grinned, 'Sam, get that coffee pot on. Lizzie, open the biccies. Let's have a mini-celebration.'

Dan was itching to get on. He wasn't entirely happy that they had all disobeyed his orders and were sitting on their backsides, but he understood why. Even a rubbish DI was better than breaking in a new one halfway through a case, and they did need to know what the Superintendent had decided. The fact that Oliver thought he was still in charge meant that they could trust him, and they would work better with that knowledge.

He perched one buttock on the edge of the table as they gathered round, holding out stained and drained mugs for a refill, relief clear on their faces. He didn't think he would be able to shake the darkness from the eyes of Bill and Ben, though. They had been Gould's men, had worked with him for years. And they were right in their unspoken accusations. It was his fault that Ian had died. In his head, he marked up the list of people damaged or killed because of his bad judgement, Ian and Chas, and because of his anger, the gunman. He knew those worries would come back into his dreams and haunt him, but that was a worry he would have to bury for another day.

Dan dunked his biscuit and threw the whole thing into his mouth before it dropped into the hot drink, earning applause from Sam Knowles.

'So, you all on strike, or what?' He spoke with a mouthful of soggy biscuit. The door opened and a sheepish Adam Foster entered followed by Julie Oliver. The younger officers shot to their feet and Adam took a bow, blushing when he realised they had stood for Oliver, not him.

Oliver drew up a recently vacated chair to the table and smiled. 'Just carry on,' she said, 'I'm giving you young Adam for a week or so to help out and I'm here to take DCI Gould's place as SIO. I know it's been a long time since I did any actual detecting, but I used to be quite good at it.' She looked over at the flowerpot men and gave them a sad smile. 'I just wish it was under different circumstances. We will all miss Ian, but none of us more than the flowerpot men, or me. He was my first sergeant when I was a rookie WPC.' She stopped for a moment and wiped a tear away with her finger. 'How on earth we got away with some of the stunts we pulled in those days, I'll never know. He seemed to have no sense of fear or self-preservation.'

'Well, definitely no sense,' observed Ben Bennett in his dry rumble, a wry shake of his head the only emotion he would allow to surface.

Bill Larcombe managed a small smile in return.

'He was a fool sometimes, and I don't think he ever read the rulebook, never mind stuck by it. But I'll miss him. By God, I will.'

Dan kept his head down. He could hear the snuffles and the blowing of noses in the room, but felt he could play little part in their shared grief. He'd hardly known the guy, and for the three weeks they had shared an office, Ian had barely spoken to him other than to wind him up. But he could not escape the feeling that he was responsible for the total cock-up the night before. He should never have agreed to such a stupid stunt. Stunt was indeed the right word for it. And the worst thing was that he had stood in this very office and had known that it was a mistake. And he had ignored his intuition. Well, he wouldn't do that again. He would find a way to atone for this pointless death.

He drank his coffee to the dregs and looked up to find Julie Oliver staring at him.

She smiled an encouraging smile. 'Before you all go off,' she said, 'I wanted to say that despite what the tabloids would have us believe, it is not common for an officer to die in the line of work. Inspector Hellier has assured me that this late-night visit to the Illusion Recording Studio was essential to the Carly Braithwaite investigation, and judging by the reception they got, he is absolutely right that there is something going on. Linking that slime-ball Abrams to the murder of Carly Braithwaite is as important a priority as nailing her murderer, and will be the best tribute you can pay to your colleague and friend.

'So, I am your SIO. Send back everything as you get it. I'll make sure I'm up-to-date with everything we've got so far.' She stood and walked across to the whiteboard. 'What have we missed?' she asked, but she was talking to herself. The office had emptied behind her as soon as she'd left the table.

Chapter 27

Date: Wednesday 26th April Time: 09:48 Jamie May's house

It was quiet in the car. Sam Knowles felt he could hardly start a conversation with Lizzie about the weather, but he thought he'd have a go. 'It's going to be a nice summer if it stays like this.'

Lizzie ignored him.

'Are you going anywhere on holiday in the summer?' Still nothing. He turned pink. She was torturing him. It was bad enough that he fancied her, but if she didn't even admit to his existence, then what chance had he got?

She negotiated the roundabout and signalled left, stopping at the pedestrian crossing. 'What?' She saw his discomfort. 'Sorry, Sam, I was miles away. I just can't get my head around Jamie May being involved in Carly's murder. How much would I love to be able to find something out? You know, to really help with the investigation.' She paused. 'What were you saying?'

'No, nothing. Just making conversation.'

'Right.'

They drove another mile in silence until Lizzie relented. 'So, have you searched a house before?'

Sam smiled in relief, a reprieve. 'Yep, on several occasions, actually.'

'Good. Tell me what to do, 'cos this is my first.'

They took a moment to walk the street before coming back to the battered front door. The May household was a terrace in the middle of a typical long row of houses in Heavitree, one of the older parts of town. It had a small patch of grass at the front, and a long back garden leading out to an alleyway that met up with a road at one end and the cemetery at the other.

'I wonder if Jamie was trying to get home when I intercepted him at the cemetery yesterday? It's just down the road.'

'It's likely. He must have been devastated.'

Sam eyed the front garden, turned into a muddy drive for the aged maroon Fiesta parked at an angle in front of the door. He rang the doorbell.

'I still feel a little strange being out of uniform,' Lizzie laughed, finding a place for the car keys in her bag. 'I don't expect people to take any notice of me now I'm in plain clothes.'

Sam smiled. 'Oh, I don't think you're going to have any problem at all, Wonderwoman.' He slipped neatly to the left to avoid her elbow.

'Oh,' Sandra May said as she opened the door. 'I thought it would be the older policeman I met yesterday.'

Sam replied, 'No, just us underlings, Mrs May, to do the house visits. Hope that's alright?'

He didn't wait for an answer as they followed her into the living room. Sam was surprised at how empty it was. There were no pictures on the walls, no ornaments, no soft cushions, nothing that would turn this room into a home.

'What a lovely tidy room,' said Sam, deciding that in this case, banality was exactly what was required.

'I don't like stuff everywhere.' She looked at the floor when she spoke to them. 'It's hard enough having to work forty hours a week and bring up a boy on my own without having to spend all my free time cleaning and polishing. It's got what we need.

'So what do you want to see? I need to get back to the police station for Jamie.'

'We would like to see his room please, Mrs May, and anywhere else he's likely to leave his stuff.'

She sniffed. 'Right, you'd better come upstairs. But we weren't expecting visitors, so you'll have to take us as we are.' She led them up a narrow staircase, the wall burnished to a dull yellow sheen from the brushing past of countless hands. 'I know it needs decorating, but everything costs money, doesn't it?'

She stood back in the cramped space at the top of the stairs and let them go through into Jamie's room.

'Thanks, Mrs May,' said Sam, 'we can manage from here.' She sniffed again and made her way downstairs.

To Sam, the contrast between Jamie's room and the rest of the house was more marked than it would have been in a typical home. Jamie had been through the upstairs of the house in a hurry, there were clothes on the floor, open jars of hair gel and canisters of deodorant and aftershave on top of the chest of drawers. The walls were covered in posters for heavy metal and death metal bands, and there were CDs and even vinyl records on every surface. 'This is more like it,' he muttered to Lizzie as they stood inside the door.

'Shouldn't take too long,' he added. 'It's not a big room. You start on the left and I'll start on his laptop, so we won't get in each other's way.'

'Sam, what are we looking for?'

'I don't know, but we will when we find it. Put everything back where you get it from.' She put her tongue out at him.

The search was as methodical and thorough as they could make it without taking everything out of the room. Once Sam found Jamie's laptop, it took him three minutes to work out that Jamie's password was 'Napalm Death'. After several further fruitless minutes searching folders and browsing history, Sam shook his head, 'Nothing. You'd think there'd be something here that would help us.'

'I know we're missing something,' Lizzie said. She gingerly checked the boy's underwear drawer, the place where most teenagers would store personal stuff. She found tobacco, bits of cardboard he used for filters for his roll-ups, and an unopened packet of condoms. 'We asked Sandra May not to touch anything. So, what is it we're not seeing?'

There were hand-written song lyrics, and a demo CD, and at one point Sam played a couple of Jamie's songs off his computer, which weren't bad. It was a poignant moment to hear the strong voice of Carly Braithwaite belting out vocals as if she was just in the next room.

'She could really sing, couldn't she?' said Sam, pausing in his perusal of the CD rack.

Lizzie slapped his arm and let out a little squeal.

'Got it! There's no guitar in the house, is there? I wonder if the guitar I saw at Westlake's house was Jamie's? I wonder if that's where he was heading when I arrested him yesterday? I thought he was coming home, but Westlake only lives a mile or so away. I knew we'd missed something.'

'What does it mean, though?' asked Sam.

'Don't be a numpty. If the guitar was in the house, then Jamie had to have been there with it, at the party. It's corroborating evidence, isn't it?'

Sam nodded at her. He didn't want to destroy her excitement too early on, but Jamie had already admitted to being at the party. Still, she was making deductions, and that was good.

The sound of the music brought Mrs May unexpectedly up from the kitchen with tea and biscuits, which they drank and ate standing in the small room. Sam could see that Sandra May wasn't a cold woman, just one who had been worn down, and who was worried sick about her son.

'Mrs May, where are the clothes Jamie was wearing on Saturday night?' Lizzie asked, eyes bright. Sam stared at her. What was she getting at?

The woman looked confused. 'He was wearing black jeans, like he always does, a white tee shirt and his grey hoodie.' She thought for a moment. 'I think he must have come home when I was at work yesterday and got changed, though, because he was wearing his hoodie again when I saw him last night at the police station.'

'So what does he usually do with his dirty clothes? I can't see any here in his room, which is weird if my brothers' habits are anything to go by.'

Mrs May led them out to the small bathroom across the landing. There, on the top of a laundry basket under a stripy towel was a grey hoodie, some dirty jeans, a white tee shirt, socks and underwear.

'Was this what he wore to go to the party on Saturday night?'

Sandra May nodded, 'I think so. Course he came back late on Sunday night, and never came back on Monday night at all. That's when I reported him missing, so that's probably what he was wearing all weekend.'

Lizzie lifted the trousers off the pile and tried the pockets, then she tried the deeper pockets of the hoodie. There, squashed deep down in the right hand pocket, was a black ballet pump.

Chapter 28

Date: Wednesday 26th April Time: 10:44 Royal Devon & Exeter Hospital

Sally slid into the Audi next to Dan. She'd felt an inexplicable anger at her old Panda ever since she had borrowed the new Ford from the Pool the day before, and it had felt good to leave it behind in the car park. She'd have to speak to Paul when she got home about trading it in.

Dan didn't start the engine straightaway. He half-turned in his seat and looked at her. 'Sally, I just wanted to say how sorry I am that I didn't tell you about what Ian and I were up to. I didn't want to compromise you. I know you worked for Ian and for my predecessor for a long time. I suppose I want you to know that I'm not some sort of reckless idiot who goes off the rails all the time.'

She gave him a level stare. 'First, you need to know that I had little time for Ian Gould. He pestered me when I was a young copper and ignored me when I got promotion. He was slack about paperwork, and if you really want to know about crazy recklessness, read his file. DCS Oliver got him off active duty and into the station as soon as she took over. He would have loved going out with you on a daring nocturnal mission, and he died the way he would have wanted. What on earth would he have done when he retired?' She paused and shrugged. 'There. Does that make you feel a bit better? Because we all need you to be at the top of your game at the moment, not feeling so guilty you can't think straight. He was a grown man. He'd have gone and broken in that night anyway, whether you were there or not.'

'OK, 'nuff said. Thanks, Sal.' Dan cracked a rueful smile. 'There's just one more thing that I need you to know about, but I'd prefer it if you didn't tell the others.' Sally's eyes widened. 'The boss hasn't just let me off. Ian wrote her a note before he died and took all the blame for the incident. But I still messed up, and I will have to face a disciplinary committee when this is over. Officially, I'm off the case and just assisting her. It means I need you or one of the other sergeants with me on interviews, visits etc. Okay?'

She nodded, subdued. 'Right, let's get over to the hospital and see who we can talk to.'

Claire Quick sat, fully dressed, on the side of the bed, her feet dangling a couple of inches above the polished linoleum. She'd had a shower and removed her head bandage. Her hair fell in a shiny drift tucked behind one ear, and her wrists were freshly wrapped. She was talking into her phone, so they waited. She seemed to be setting work for her classes.

Sally tucked her own untidy curls behind her ear and cast a glance at Dan. He seemed to be staring. He sat himself next to Claire on the bed, waving Sally into the single chair. Claire finished her call.

'You look much better today,' he said.

Sally noticed that Claire's eyes were the most remarkable shade of green, like cats' eyes. She really was rather attractive.

'Feeling better, too. I'm being let out today.' They smiled at each other.

Nothing like being a gooseberry, thought Sally. She introduced herself and took out her notebook ready to take down the teacher's statement.

Dan stopped her. 'I've had a better idea. Claire, why don't you come back to the station with us and do it there? Then I can make sure you get home safely.'

Claire laughed. 'Well, I gather there isn't much left of my car. I was going to ask mum to collect me in her lunch break, but that would be fine if you can spare the time.'

'I think we can spare the time, Sergeant, don't you?'

'Yes, sir, if you say so.' Sally smiled. She had been watching the couple's body language. Lots of eye contact. She smirked into her notebook, and drew a heart with an arrow through it.

'I'm a little concerned about what might happen when I get back. Is Jamie still out and about?' Claire tried to hide her worry under a smile, but Sally saw the tension in her shoulders and heard the wobble in her voice. 'I'm no hero, Inspector. I'm terrified he'll come after me once he knows I'm out of hospital.'

'No,' Dan replied, 'please don't worry. He was arrested and charged with assault and suspected kidnap yesterday. He is being detained for the meantime.' He hesitated for a moment. 'Claire, you need to know that he's our main suspect for Carly's murder, too.'

Her face lost its colour. 'My God, I don't understand what's happening. Why would he kill Carly? I thought he loved Carly. Was he jealous of Miles?' She flicked her eyes between the two officers and said, 'That's it, isn't it? He found out about Miles and Carly and killed her.' Her eyes filled with tears. 'What will happen to him now?'

Dan glanced across at Sally. 'He may not be the murderer at all,' he said. 'The evidence is looking bad for him, but it is all circumstantial. If he would talk to me, we could try to get to the truth. I do think he knows what went on, and he's either shielding the murderer or is frightened that he is in danger, too. Unfortunately, if I have to charge him without his telling us anything about what happened, I don't get another chance to speak to him before the trial.' He shook his head. 'It's so frustrating. I really need him to open up and need him to do it today.'

Claire nodded. 'I understand, but Jamie won't respond to shouting or being told what to do. He'll talk, I'm sure, but you have to give him space to say it in his own way. He must be in a terrible state, poor lad.'

Sally snorted. 'Poor lad? That 'poor lad' assaulted you and kept you prisoner. Don't feel too sorry for him.'

'I know. I just feel this has all got out of hand. I can't believe he killed Carly, even if he was jealous,' She shook her head. 'But what do I know? When I got up on Monday morning, I never thought I'd be sawing my way through ropes and crashing my car into a wall.'

Dan, reached out to touch her hand. 'You've been incredibly brave, and we'll do everything we can to get to the truth, Claire, I promise you that.'

She stared into his eyes and seemed to find the reassurance she was looking for.

'I haven't been discharged yet. Got to wait until the consultant comes around and signs me off. Hoping I can go back to work in a couple of days. I hate having time off.' She winced and yelped as she turned to grab her handbag.

'Ribs sore?'

'You could say that.'

'Why don't you just wait here? Sally and I have a couple of other people to see and we'll call back for you later.'

'Who?' She was curious. 'Who else is here? People to do with Carly?'

To Sally's amazement, Dan took hold of Claire's hand and told her about the suicide attempt. She was astonished not just because the DI was such a fast worker in the romantic stakes, but because he was discussing a major suspect with a major witness in the middle of a major case. She relaxed when it became clear that Westlake was a close friend of Claire's, not just a colleague. It would be better for her to hear about Westlake from the Inspector now, than to watch it on the news later. So much for not breaking protocol. She would have to reassess her initial impressions of her new boss when she had a moment.

They left Claire Quick with tears in her eyes, trying to contact Westlake's estranged wife, Sophie.

Their attempts to see the foreign gunman were thwarted by a terrifying sister in the intensive care unit, who would tell them nothing more than that an operation had been carried out that morning. She did go so far as to tell them that the patient was stable and had regained consciousness. That fragments of bone had been removed from his brain and the bleeding had stopped. That there was no way of knowing how serious his injuries were until he was much better. That he would not be feeling much better at any point today.

Dan gave up arguing, got on the phone and arranged for someone to come and photograph and fingerprint the suspect. He could at least distribute the details to Interpol and see if he was known in Europe. They stared through the glass window at the still figure, attached by a manacle to the metal railings of the bed. Shaven head, cauliflower ear. Muscular, not fat.

'D'you know what I think, sir?'

'What? And just call me Dan. I don't mind Boss, when we're with the team, but I hate sir. Except from junior staff, of course.' He put on a posh accent. 'One has certain standards to maintain.'

'Sure thing, sir.' She glanced across at him, winking. 'I reckon he's a boxer. Maybe we could find out more by looking on the boxing websites, especially the international ones.'

'You're a genius, Sally. There may just be something in that.'

She felt herself blush. First bit of praise felt good.

The officer on guard duty stood as they left the ward. Dan stopped for a word. 'The guy's out cold, so I'm not worried about him escaping, but you need to keep an eye out for anyone visiting this end of the corridor. And I mean anyone. Don't say anything to them, just get onto hospital security straight away and apprehend them. Understood?' The young officer stood to attention as they left.

They clattered up another two flights of stairs and along another interminable corridor to the side ward where they found Chas Lloyd attempting to drink from a cup through a straw. She seemed delighted to see Dan and reached out a hand towards him. He took her hand, sat on the bed and gave her a peck on the cheek.

Blimey, thought Sally, he's got another one.

This time, Dan introduced her and took a moment to explain to Sally what had happened the night before, and how she had tried to save his life. He left out the part where Chas had sold him out to Jed Abrams, but she didn't. Although weak from anaesthetic, Chas was clear-headed.

'I wasn't brave, Sergeant. I told Jed about Dan going to the studio. I feel so bad about it. When I realised that stupid Latvian had a gun, I just went mad. I thought he'd shot Dan.' She hung on to his hand, fighting back tears. 'Jed and I just thought he was going to frighten you off, to get you away from the studio, not shoot you. Did…did the other policeman die?'

'Of a heart attack, late last night. The bullet went through his lung. We got the shooter.'

He gave her a moment to absorb the news.

'So, they're a Latvian gang?'

She looked up at him. 'I'm so sorry, Dan. They gave me two grand for grassing you up.' She broke off and tears filled her eyes again, spilling over her cheeks. Sally passed her tissues pulled from her bag. 'Not much use to me, now, is it?'

'Was the operation a success this morning?' said Sally.

Chas blinked back tears and whispered, 'They don't know yet. I can't feel anything below my waist but the doctor says it can take weeks or even months for the nerve endings to knit back together. They seem happy with the result. I, well, I just don't know.' She broke down again. Sally handed over more tissues.

'Sorry. I'm so sorry. I feel like a right idiot.' She blew her nose and sniffed. 'I'm going home to Cardiff in a week or so. They have a great rehab centre in the hospital apparently.' She wiped her eyes. 'So I guess I won't be seeing much of you, then.' She peered up at Dan, hope and need writ loud on her puffy, tear-streaked face.

'I'll pop in and see you again before you go. Sergeant Ellis will take your statement now, if you are up to it. We know Abrams was up to no good, so it will be better for you if you tell us everything you know about his dealings with the Latvians. Alright?'

Sally watched Chas gulp down the last of her drink and observed her internal struggle as she panicked over what to say. It would be interesting to see if she finally told the truth about Jed Abrams. She was sure Chas was more scared of the Latvians than she was of Dan, Abrams, too. She had a feeling they would have to wait until they got her into court to get the truth out of her.

As Sally prepared to take the girl's statement, Dan stood.

'I need to pay my respects to Ian,' he said. 'Sally, I'll see you back at Claire's ward in half an hour.' He let go of Chas's hand and went out of the room.

In the corridor, Dan felt like a total jerk. He'd intended to walk away anyway, but to leave her helpless like this, felt cruel, even if she had put his life in danger and caused the death of his colleague. But sometimes you have to hold the line.

He rang the station and told them the foreigners were Latvians, of all people. Bill would try to find him an interpreter, and get started on the boxing angle. There was yet another message from his mum. He had to tell her where his sister was at some point, but not now. He put the phone back in his pocket, and tried to ignore the itch of guilt.

What kind of a man am I, he asked himself as he strode along to the mortuary, that I prefer to seek out the company of a dead man rather than deal with my emotions regarding the living?

Chapter 29

Date: Wednesday 26th April Time: 11:27 Irina Akis

Irina Akis finished her cigarette and ground it under the toe of her knee-length black leather boot. She had positioned herself outside Blockbusters' Video and Game store and was watching the alleyway leading to the studio door through the reflection in the window. She adjusted her focus and noticed that her hair, usually dead straight and almost white, was curling and going frizzy in the drizzle that had begun to fall. Adjusting her focus again, she noticed that the two youths serving in the shop were beckoning to her and grinning. She gave them the finger and stalked away.

The police had been in the studio for hours. The British police weren't armed, were they? So how had Filip lost his gun? He was as strong as a moose. And Filip wasn't answering his phone either, so she had to assume it had been taken away.

She made her way up the High Street and found Grigor waiting in Nando's. He'd ordered her a coffee. She took a seat opposite him. 'The investigation team is packing up, but they will have taken everything they could find, so I don't see the point of trying to get in to look around.'

Grigor checked if anyone was within listening distance.

'Don't be paranoid, nobody is listening, idiot.'

'I am worrying that if Filip is in prison, he will talk to the police and leave us to take the rap.'

Irina laughed again, a light, tinkling sound, ' "Take the rap!" You're beginning to speak like an American movie star. This is England, not LA.'

She shrugged her leather-clad shoulders. 'Anyway, we will not worry too much. Filip will be able to hold out against the English police without too much trouble. We just need tonight, then we are finished. I shall meet the actors later and prepare them at the house. You will be doing the filming instead of Jed. You do know how to do that, don't you, darling?'

Grigor nodded. He was temporarily unable to speak as Irina had pushed the pointed tip of her boot up under the table and was pressing it hard against his testicles.

'We should aim to be on the boat for the sailing early tomorrow morning. The finished DVDs are in the van already so we will just upload the master copy for tonight's film from the laptop, then drop that machine and all the others into the North Sea - untraceable.' She frowned, a little crease appearing between her fine eyebrows. 'We will have to arrange for a different method of production when we get home. Abrams is no longer of use to us now that he is known to the police. It is such a shame. This business arrangement has been very lucrative for us.'

Grigor shifted to his left, wriggling away from her grip. 'Won't the police be round to search Jed's house? They have him in custody. He will talk. It's too dangerous to continue.'

Irina fixed the shards of blue ice that passed for eyes onto Grigor's handsome face. 'For you, it is too dangerous not to continue. Jed will not talk. He is more frightened of me than any English "bobby". She shook her head and smoothed down the damp frizz. 'No, we will continue. Jed will give the address of his city centre flat, not the address of his parents' house, to the police. He is not completely stupid. Why should they even know about it? We use the house. They are away. It's easy. Stop worrying. I do the worrying, darling.'

'What about Filip?' he persisted.

Again the laugh. 'He has always been just the muscle, Grigor, you know that. If he survives whatever injury he has sustained, he has enough sense not to talk to the police. He may have to spend some time in prison, but an English prison is like a holiday camp, no? If he does well, we will reward him. If not, we will take his family, one at a time. We all know the rules when we join the team.'

She wandered outside to smoke a cigarette and answer her phone, leaving Grigor to stir the froth on his cappuccino and ponder, yet again, what gods he had angered.

Grigor often wondered who the 'we' in the team were. He had only known Irina and her father. He had grown up with Filip in a village outside Saldus in the country south west of Riga. There was no work on the family farm so they had both headed for the bright lights of the city. Within days they had lost their money at cards, been assaulted, propositioned and robbed. Only a residual spark of pride had prevented them from crawling home.

Being found by Irina had felt like winning the lottery. She had said she was twenty-five, also from the country, and that she was looking for two honest young men to protect her in the big, frightening city. They could not resist the slim blonde with the longest legs they had ever seen, even if they tried.

So, she dressed them, fed them, trained them at the best gyms, boxing clubs and firing ranges. They never questioned where she got her money. Filip, always a large, strong boy, found his vocation in boxing and became quite well known on the circuit. Grigor was better with guns.

Then, after a year or so, she took them into her 'family' and their lives had been a living nightmare ever since. They had met Pavels Akis, her father, just once. Grigor could not forget the fear that had been instilled about what would happen to his family, one by one, if he betrayed Irina. There were even pictures of his mother and his sister in a file with his name on it. There was no going back, that was abundantly clear.

Irina was one of the most damaged people Grigor and Filip knew. She claimed to belong to this wealthy old Latvian family, but they had seen no sign of aristocracy or gentility in the four years they had worked for her. Pavels Akis ran the port of Riga and took a cut from every ship that landed there. He had Irina in a grip just as tight as the one in which she held Grigor and Filip.

Also, Grigor had come to realise, there was no way that Irina was twenty-nine. When he looked closely, he could see the flat features of Botox and the too-white teeth of the cosmetic dentist. He thought she must be in her late thirties at the least. She had snared them as easily as any spider might snare an unsuspecting fly.

He stared at her now, back through the window of the café. She was waving her arms about and shouting between puffs on her cigarette. She liked to hurt people, and he did not like to be hurt.

Her exploitation of the burgeoning market in child pornography, something that made Grigor sick to even think about, had made her a fortune and destroyed dozens of young lives. She liked to direct the films herself. Filip was convinced her father had probably abused her as a child. But, it didn't matter why she did it. They were both as lost as she was now, too far into the filth to escape. They could never be clean again.

The move to production in England had come at exactly the right time, as the local police had begun to notice the rise in kiddie porn available in Riga.

Jed Abrams had been in the city, promoting a band. The meeting between him and Irina at a nightclub in the centre of Riga, gave her all the contacts she needed to set up in Exeter, and clean up her business at home. From her offices at the docks, she shipped her films all over Europe under the cover of being a courier for a Swedish film company. She had made a fortune over the Internet.

Irina came back inside and sat down, looking at him from under her eyelashes. She had drunk her cappuccino and crunched the little biscuit, and was scooping out the froth with her finger.

'What are you thinking about? Are you worried about Filip?'

When Grigor nodded, she laughed again. 'It is about time you two were separated for a while. Anyway, I have news for you. This will be my last trip. I am leaving the family business. It has been agreed that you will take over my role in the film production and liaise directly with my father. He is sorting out the details ready for when we return.'

She smiled again … a different smile. A smile that said she had somehow persuaded Pavels Akis to let her go.

For Grigor, it was the first moment in his life that he considered suicide.

Chapter 30

Date: Wednesday 26th April Time:12:30 Royal Devon & Exeter Hospital

Miles Westlake endured the nods, tuts and warnings of the consultant. He made the appropriate noises to the psychologist, reassuring her that the suicide attempt was a terrible mistake, an impulsive response to a dreadful situation. As feeling returned to his body, he was allowed out of bed. He took his medication and ate a little breakfast. Odd that he could feel no pain, although he knew his organs must be damaged.

He was allowed to visit his small bathroom, as long as he pulled the drip along with him on a trolley. The consultant said that he had sustained some permanent damage to his liver and kidneys, and that he may need a transplant in the future. He also said that a fast recovery was a sure sign of someone who had a strong desire to live. Miles really had a strong desire to die, and possibly to kill. But to do either, he had to get out of the hospital.

He noted the change of guard as the young police officer was replaced by an older man with greying hair and the beginnings of a paunch. He knew the police would be in to interview him at some point during the day, and that he would go to prison as soon as he was signed out of hospital. His clothes, minus his belt and shoelaces, hung in the alcove. He had to be ready for any opportunity.

As soon as the orderly had removed his lunch tray, Miles staggered out of bed and headed for the bathroom making as much noise as he could. The head of the policeman guarding him appeared in the window, was happy with what he saw and disappeared again. Miles heard the orderly giving the guard a cup of tea. He disconnected himself from the drip and, crouching, passed by the door again to grab his clothes from the hooks. He dressed in the bathroom and put his hospital issue gown on over his jeans and shirt, hiding his trainers under the bed.

Then he got back into bed to wait for fate to intervene, as he knew it would. He had to finish a task, and he knew that was why he had been allowed to live for just a little longer. Then, he would be allowed to be with Carly.

Grigor Pelakais sat in the black Mercedes van with the blacked-out windows in the car park opposite the main entrance to the Royal Devon and Exeter Hospital. Dozens of people had arrived and left in the half hour he had been sitting there.

Grigor had good English, it had been taught as the second language in his school, and he did most of the talking on their journeys to and from the country. But he didn't know whether he could bluff his way into and out of a hospital. He shrugged. If his plan worked, he just had to get in. Even if it was dangerous, he had to know if Filip was dead or alive, so it was worth the risk of being caught. Filip had never been very good at schoolwork, and Grigor doubted that he could remember enough English to speak to the doctors. Or the police. He needed Grigor.

What had Filip been thinking, shooting a police officer? Shooting anyone? Grigor handled the guns, not Filip. Had Irina given Filip a gun? Had she told him to shoot the policemen? He wouldn't have put it past her to want Filip to be captured. She was jealous of their friendship. And it could explain why she was so relaxed about what had happened.

He looked at his watch, twelve thirty pm. He'd left Irina at the house, getting the rooms ready for the filming. He'd got the rest of the afternoon to himself before she wondered where he was. Grigor glanced down at the seat beside him. He had found the Army and Navy Stores easily and soon realised that they were pretty much the same all over Europe. The lab coat had cost him ten pounds, the soft clogs another fifteen, and the sheaf of notes and diagrams had been printed from a medical website. If he'd walked in there in his Gucci shoes and Armani suit, he would have stood out like a black bear in a petting zoo. He changed in the van. As he turned to lock the door, he picked up the last part of his disguise - the lanyard and name tag, slung it round his neck and headed for the main entrance.

Grigor didn't pause in the atrium and did not approach the information desk. Instead, he walked straight through, down past the shops and cafeteria until he came to a junction. There he pretended to look at his notes while he scanned the massive wall for signs for something he might recognise.

PC Will Rowntree was helping his colleague, PC Andy Waters, to complete the Daily Mirror crossword. They were at either end of the intensive care unit, guarding the two prisoners. Waters thought his guy would survive. He was getting out of bed and going to the toilet on his own, but Rowntree wasn't so sure about his guy, the big foreigner. He hadn't moved much, although the nurse said he had regained consciousness a few minutes ago. He must be a tough bugger, thought Will. Rumour had it that their new DI, Dan Hellier had battered him with his baton and crushed his skull when he saw that the guy had shot Ian Gould. Nice one, thought Will. He wondered if they taught you to do that in the Met.

His attention was pulled back into the corridor as he noticed that Andy had stopped whistling under his breath as he wrestled with the clues. He was looking left, past Will's chair. Will followed his gaze to see a tall doctor standing at the end of the corridor, carrying a sheaf of papers. He wasn't one of the team that had come round earlier in the day. The man moved towards Will slowly, reading from one of the papers in his hand. He stopped in front of the constable.

'I have to examine the patient. I am a specialist in brain injury. I come from Ukraine.' Will squinted at his name tag, it was different from the usual hospital tags. He stood up, glancing towards Andy for support.

'I'm sorry, sir,' he said, 'nobody can enter the room unless I have their name on my list. And I cannot see yours here.' He glanced down at the sheet, never seeing the blow that sent him falling down to a mute slump on the floor. Andy Waters leapt to his feet and banged the emergency button to alert the security team. Without pausing, he ran down the corridor and leapt in front of the door to the prisoner's room.

'Get out of the way,' said Grigor. 'I do not want to hurt you, but I have to see that my friend is Okay. Understand?' Waters heard the sound of running feet, and the low insistent siren calling for support. He just had to hold out for a few seconds.

'Sorry, mate,' he said. 'You can't see him, he's under arrest, and so are you.' Waters moved to flip out his handcuffs but, as he would recount later, the speed of the guy was incredible. He chopped Waters across the side of his neck, to briefly cut off his oxygen, then held onto him as he slid down the wall.

Grigor opened the door, entered and wedged a chair under the handle to hold it shut. Filip was awake and looking at him, though only his eyes seemed to be able to move.

'You came,' Filip croaked.

'I had to see that you were alive,' said Grigor, 'but I have just a few moments before they come.' He held Filip's hand and kissed him on the forehead. He could not stop the treacherous tears from rolling down his face. 'You must live, Filip. I cannot go on without you.'

Filip lifted a hand to touch the bandage that covered his head. 'My head hurts.'

'Why did you shoot the policeman, Filip? What were you thinking?'

'I thought he had a gun. I thought the girl had betrayed us and that they were armed. Irina gave me the gun, in case anything went wrong.'

Grigor wiped his tears away. 'What a mess our lives are.'

'Run, now, or they will catch you, too.'

'But that is what I want. Then we can be together. Better prison in England than any more time spent doing this terrible work.' He held Filip's hand tighter. 'She's leaving, Filip. Somehow, Irina is able to escape. I am supposed to take over the business. I cannot do it. I will not do it.'

'Our families?' Filip's face contorted as he tried not to cry.

Grigor shrugged. 'I don't know what will happen. Let us see what the British will offer in exchange for our co-operation. Perhaps they will offer them protection, too.'

They had a few more minutes together before the security team broke down the door and arrested an unresisting Grigor.

Nobody noticed the tall, skinny man with the mane of red-gold curls slipping along the corridor, unlaced trainers slapping against the linoleum.

Chapter 31

Date: Wednesday 26th April Time: 12:16 Exeter Police Station

Dan raced up the stairs to the incident room, leaving Sally to escort the injured Claire Quick at a more sedate pace to an interview room. Julie Oliver was waiting in the room with Lizzie, Bill and Sam as Dan burst through the door.

'Show me,' he barked as he crossed the floor. Lizzie held up the black shoe, now encased in a clear evidence bag. He stopped and breathed for a second. A breakthrough? Dared he even think it? 'Where was it?'

'In Jamie's hoodie pocket. The one he was wearing on Saturday and Sunday.'

'Well done, Lizzie, great work.'

'Sam was there as well.' Lizzie added generously.

Dan took the evidence bag and waved it at Oliver. 'Ma'am, do you think we have enough to charge Jamie May with murder?'

She looked at him. 'Whoa, there, cowboy. We might be able to charge him with being an accessory, because this shoe puts him with Carly at the right time and the right place, but we still don't know where Carly was killed or how she was transported to the woods at the school, or, indeed, why she was killed.' She rubbed her forehead. 'And, we've got serious suspicions about Jed Abrams....' She bit her lip. 'No, I just don't think it would stick.

'Somehow, we have to find a way to get the lad to talk to us before we charge him, because it'll be hard to change it once we've done the formal, and we can't question him again then until the trial. We've got the poor kid on enough as it is to send him away for years.' She paused for a second. 'Sixteen years old, and a life ruined. It doesn't seem right, somehow.

'Oh, yes. Alan Braithwaite's car has come up clean, just got the results through now, so he's in the clear. Forensics are in the Carly's bedroom now. Jed Abrams' van will be in a car park somewhere in Exeter, or still back at his flat as no one's had a moment to look for it yet. But I'll bet you a tenner it will tell us a pile of secrets.'

'Maybe Jamie can drive,' put in Sam. 'Maybe he took his mum's car and moved Carly's body himself after killing her.'

Dan acknowledged the input with a purse of his lips. 'Or maybe we need to be looking more seriously at Miles Westlake as the murder suspect, or at least finger him for providing the means of transportation.' He paced the patch of threadbare carpet between table and wall and thought aloud. 'It could have been a shared job between May and Westlake - that would put a huge strain on both of them. And it might explain why May was round at Westlake's on the day they kidnapped Claire Quick.' He gave a little shake of the head. However much progress they felt they were making, they were no closer to a confession. 'Where's young Adam?'

'Right behind you, sir.' Foster pushed his way through the door carrying printouts from Interpol and pinned them to the whiteboard.

'Right, leave that. I've got one forensics technician over at the hospital taking prints from the Latvian guy. Take a car, go and get him and take him to the Westlake house. Go over Westlake's car with a fine tooth-comb. If you find any traces of the girl's presence in the car, Bill will arrange for it to be brought in for further examination. Scoot!'

Foster scooted.

Dan turned back to Oliver. 'We've brought Claire Quick in to give her statement. She's with Sally in interview room 3 at the moment. She's unconvinced about Jamie, and knows him better than we do.'

Oliver looked sceptical. 'I'm becoming more and more convinced, myself. Whatever happens, we need to persuade him to give up what he knows. I'm prepared to keep him in for another twenty four hours based on the statement from the teacher and the ballet pump before we charge him, but it would be better not to have to.' She turned to Bill Larcombe. 'Is the solicitor here?'

'Yes, Ma'am, she's been here for half an hour and we've just let his mum in, too. So you can go in any time. I'm not having any luck with Latvian speakers, by the way. Currently, I've got a Lithuanian speaking Russian specialist from the University who reckons the guy might speak some Russian, but that's it.'

Dan sighed. It frustrated him to know that something was going on with Jed Abrams and his visitors, and that he wasn't able to grasp it. But he had to concentrate on one thing at a time. He rose, picked up the evidence bag containing Carly's shoe, and followed the Superintendent and Sergeant towards the Interview rooms.

Sandra May and Vanessa Redmond, the solicitor, were standing in the corner of the room in conversation when the officers entered. Jamie was slumped as far down as he could get on a plastic chair and had his eyes closed, blocking out his mother and everyone else in the room.

Dan brought in two more chairs from the corridor and they sat around the scratched and furrowed wooden table. He started the tape, placed the bag on the table and waited in silence until Jamie opened his eyes. As the group identified themselves for the record, Dan kept a close eye on Jamie's face. The boy stared at the evidence bag, trying to identify the contents. There was no recognition on his face, just curiosity. He was so distracted that he said his name without needing to be prompted by the solicitor.

Vanessa Redmond took out a sleek fountain pen and prepared to make notes on a pale yellow legal pad. Dan watched her eyeing the contents of the evidence bag. He knew that she knew she'd be passing this case onto a barrister in a very short period of time.

Dan started. 'Jamie, can I ask you again to remind us what you were doing on the evening of Sunday the twenty-third of April?' Jamie looked at him, but didn't speak. 'Because, as you can see, we have found Carly's missing shoe.'

He studied the boy's face. Jamie looked down at the floor as he thought about the shoe, but then he shook his head.

'And we found it in your hoodie pocket. The hoodie you changed out of when you went home yesterday afternoon. The hoodie you were wearing on Sunday when you saw Carly.'

Jamie looked from Hellier to the solicitor. 'But? What? I dunno… I dunno where it came from. I didn't know she hadn't got her shoe on. I didn't know.'

Sandra May wept once more. 'Jamie,' she pleaded, 'please talk to them. Explain how the shoe ended up in your pocket. Please, love, please. They think you killed her. Tell them that you didn't kill Carly.' She reached across the table and grasped his hand, but Jamie shook her off, clasping both hands together between his knees and shaking his head. A moan like a low keening escaped from his lips.

'It would be in your own interests if you could explain how this shoe came to be in your pocket, Jamie,' said Dan. 'Otherwise we can only think that you were involved in Carly's death. Just tell us what you know. When did you last see Carly? Did you argue? Did you fight about something? Was the whole thing an accident, Jamie? Did Carly die by mistake? Tell us if it was a terrible mistake, we'll help you.'

Vanessa Redmond was becoming jumpy. 'Inspector, please could you ask one question at a time and stop harassing my client? Give him time to answer.' She put her hand on Jamie's arm and though they all saw him flinch, he let it stay.

A small step forward, thought Dan, he's accepted that he needs help.

'Jamie,' Redmond said, trying to catch his eye, 'you do not have to answer any questions, but if you can help the police to find out who did kill your friend, then you should do so. Your mum and I, we believe that you didn't kill Carly.'

Gathering himself with a breath snorted through his nose, Jamie shouted, 'I didn't kill her. I loved her, why would I hurt her? I don't know how her shoe ended up in my pocket. I stayed at Westlake's house on Saturday night, and Monday night. I didn't see Carly after Sunday morning.'

He looked at the floor, and then towards his mother for support. 'It's true, mum, I didn't kill her, I swear. I swear on Gran's grave.' He made eye contact then, scanning the table for a friendly face. 'Someone must have put the shoe in my pocket, to frame me for the murder.' His voice rose again and he slammed his hands flat onto the table top, 'It wasn't me. I didn't do it!' The yell sank away into silence. Jamie slumped back into his chair, swearing under his breath, and shoved his hands into his pockets. 'No point saying anything. No one believes me anyway. Just makes it worse,' he muttered, and clamped his eyes shut again.

'But you do know who did it, don't you, Jamie?' Dan said, but the boy had closed down.

Superintendent Oliver stopped the recording at that point and motioned to Dan to follow her from the room.

'He's lying,' she said, keeping her voice low. 'It's not looking good for him.'

'Yeah, true, but Carly could have lost that shoe at any point during the Sunday and he could have picked it up. Maybe he helped Westlake to move her and picked it up then? Or maybe Westlake helped May to move the body after he had killed Carly?' He shook his head and banged his fist on the wall. 'I don't think we can charge him for the murder, Ma'am, even though I really want to. You were right. All our evidence is circumstantial. We still have so many questions.' He banged the fist again, taking comfort from the pain in his hand. 'Christ, this is frustrating. We've got to get him to talk to us.'

He'd been sure they'd nailed him when he saw the shoe. 'Jamie said that he didn't see Carly again after Sunday morning, and neither Jenna nor her father admits they saw him at the house. So where was he? At Westlake's? Or are we being lied to? By all of them?'

'All of that's possible,' agreed Oliver. 'Maybe Jamie didn't kill Carly, but he doesn't want to tell us about Westlake. He could have helped move her body, though, couldn't he? It would be a kid thing to do, to think of hiding her at his school, where he felt he knew the territory.'

She bit the skin round the thumb nail on her right hand. 'We just don't have enough evidence to charge either the boy or the man with the murder without a confession.'

She turned to face the wall and mimed hitting her head against a peeling poster which warned them about the dangers of contaminating evidence. 'You'd better get back in there. Keep at it. I can't hold him forever.'

Chapter 32

Date: Wednesday 26th April Time: 12:54 Irina Akis

The room looked just right. In one corner she had set up a small table for refreshments and a pile of cushions for the children to sit on. In the other corner was Abrams' king size waterbed, covered with a red silk sheet and black lace cushions. The daylight was obscured by heavy curtains, so that the room was lit by lamps. It looked seductive and sensual. She was pleased with the effect. It was much better using Abrams' parents' house than the studio, even if it was a way out of the city. She left the door to the en-suite bathroom ajar so that a little more light fell into the room, and opened the old casement window, leaning out to breathe in the soft afternoon air. Spring was here already.

Irina had been determined that her films would be of a better quality than the rubbish usually available, a standard that had repaid her efforts handsomely over the past four years. A standard that would, at last, allow her to get away from her father. He had held her body and soul for thirty-six years, had taken her mother, her brother and would take her child if he could find him. But now, she could pay back all that she owed him and walk away. She would join her son in Sweden and they would have a different, cleaner life.

Irina had shrugged off any guilt about her methods for paying off her debt years ago. No one had cared what her father had done to her when she was a small child. No one had stopped him parading her and finally selling her to his friends. There was no loving mother to spirit her away like she had spirited her own boy out of the country. So why should she care about squalid children in a foreign country? They were well paid. She checked her reflection in the mirror and removed a tiny piece of fluff from her black top.

Turning away, Irina parted the curtains and looked out onto the drive again. She had a nagging feeling that Grigor had not gone shopping at all, but had tried to find Filip in the hospital. Her heart thumped as she considered that he might try to rescue Filip and return him to the house. They could have the whole of the British police force after them if he did something stupid. She should never have taken on two such close friends to assist her. She knew better than anyone that the ties that bind you to the past are the strongest. Until you break them, that is.

Irina pulled out her phone and tried to call him, but the phone went straight to voicemail.

'Answer the phone, Grigor,' she shouted. 'Don't you ignore me. Answer the fucking phone!' Enraged, she threw the phone onto the bed. Nobody ignored her and walked away. She picked up a china figurine from the window ledge and hurled it to the floor. It bounced on the thick carpet. She screamed at the ornament for not breaking. Screamed at Grigor for caring more about Filip than he did about her. Screamed at her sick bastard of a father. Screamed at her mother for dying instead of saving her. Screamed for herself until the clamour faded to a hoarse whisper and she could lie on the bed, spent and whimpering. She slept for an hour.

Calm after her outburst, Irina rinsed her face and re-applied her make-up in the bathroom, helping herself to Abrams' mother's creams. She smoked a joint in the over-stuffed living room. It was all going to be fine. The last job. The last trip. It would be fine.

Grigor would return. He would be too frightened of the consequences to run away. She was not going to take Filip back with them whatever happened. He had to stay and pay the price for being caught, the fool.

Irina checked her watch. Three hours until they would start filming. She had drinks, drugs, and snacks to prepare. She wanted the new ones quiet and compliant.

Chapter 33

Date: Wednesday 26th April Time: 13:09 Exeter Police Station

Grigor Pelakais found himself bundled into a police van, driven at speed to a police station, charged with assault on two police officers and locked into a cell before he was able to explain to anybody that he spoke English and that he needed to speak to the officer in charge about what had happened the night before in the studio. Once he had been allowed to speak, the duty sergeant asked no further questions. He got straight onto Detective Chief Superintendent Oliver and called her downstairs as soon as he could.

Julie Oliver took Sally Ellis into the cell with her to talk to the Latvian. She was experiencing a slight sense of panic that everything seemed to be happening at once. It looked likely that Jamie May might start to talk, and now she might get a real clue as to the identity of the murderer of Ian Gould. It was odd that the guy had practically asked to be arrested, but stranger things had happened.

She had scanned the reports from Interpol. Nothing concrete. The woman appeared to be an Irina Akis. She was known to them and wanted in connection with prostitution, but all had been quiet for several years and she was not a top priority. The one in hospital had been a well-known boxer on the European circuit, Filip Sarkov. Whatever this gang was up to, it was either happening within the confines of their little Baltic country, or they were very clever indeed to have escaped detection. Oliver tended towards the latter interpretation.

As she entered the cell, Oliver thought Grigor Pelakais was the walking cliché for "tall, dark and handsome". He had removed the fake doctor's coat he'd been wearing and was sitting in a silk shirt, expensive looking trousers and rubber clogs. She introduced herself and Sally, and they stood near the door. Two officers stood just outside.

'I believe you wish to speak to me about the murder of Detective Chief Inspector Gould, Mr Pelakais?'

Grigor was at a loss. He didn't know how to address this woman, and he needed her to listen to him urgently. He rose, intending to show respect for her seniority. The officers responded with frightening speed. One shoved Pelakais back onto the concrete bed base and towered above him, baton raised. Both women were simultaneously yanked out of the cell and placed behind the other officer.

'Please,' Grigor said, hands up in the universal sign of submission, 'I will not hurt you. I want to help. I have information to give if you will help me and my friend, Filip Sarkov.'

Oliver hated it when her officers over-reacted, but she guessed that they were all a bit jumpy at the moment. She rolled her eyes at Sally and resisted muttering "boys" as she entered the room for the second time.

'Just take your time, Mr Pelakais, and stay seated. What do you want to say?'

Grigor spilled the whole story, from his lowly beginnings in rural Latvia to the sordid mess that was now his life, and the 'warning' that had gone so badly wrong the previous night.

Sally interrupted. 'So, if we help Filip Sarkov in his trial for murder, you will tell us what Irina Akis is doing here in Exeter?'

'Yes, and I wish to claim asylum for myself and my friend.'

'We'll see about that later,' muttered Oliver. 'For now, tell me what you are doing here in Exeter.'

Grigor thought hard. It was important to give the correct information and to make them see how important it was that they should listen to him. 'We are making pornographic films for sale in Europe.'

Oliver glanced at Sally, a question wrinkling the skin between her eyebrows. Why come all the way to Exeter to make a porn movie?

'I thought they were made in Eastern Europe and exported to England,' said Sally, 'not the other way round.'

'These are special movies. They are made with children. Sometimes little children. Sometimes the children do not live.' He felt tears come to his eyes and focussed his gaze on the concrete floor. Perhaps it was now time for him to grieve for the lives he had helped to ruin. 'Irina, she cannot do this in Latvia anymore. She met Jed Abrams and they agreed to make the movies together. Filip and I, we are the muscles. We handle distribution and any problems. Abrams finds the children.'

'How many?' asked Oliver. 'How many times have you been here? How many films have you made?'

'We come every three months, for three years. Twelve films. Today will be the thirteenth.'

Oliver took a step forward. 'What do you mean, today?'

'We are filming this evening.' His eyes skittered between the two women. 'If you guarantee us safety and a fair trial, I will tell you where it is happening.'

Oliver turned to the officer standing outside the door. 'Get this man a drink and some food, and tell the desk sergeant to organise a solicitor for him.' She turned back to face the prisoner. 'I will call a meeting of the detectives involved in the case.' She paused and glared at him. 'You had better not lie to me, Mr Pelakais.'

'No madam, I will not. My life and the life of my family and friend depend on it.'

Oliver found Dan with his nose pressed against the glass of the interview room, trying to lip-read what was happening inside.

'Jamie said he would talk to his mother and Sergeant Larcombe if I wasn't there,' he said. 'I didn't like leaving them but it seems calm enough, and he is talking to the solicitor and his mother, although you could stuff a mattress with the number of tissues they've got through in the last half hour.' He noticed the expression on Oliver's face and stopped talking. 'What?'

'We've got Grigor Pelakais, the other male Latvian in custody. They're involved in child porn with Abrams. That's why they're here, and it's going down tonight. He'll help us in exchange for a fair deal for him and the one you almost did for, who's called Filip Sarkov. Put Sally in the Jamie May interview and get to my office in fifteen minutes. I've got an idea.' With that, she turned and was gone.

Dan allowed himself a moment of panic. It was all happening very fast. He looked back in through the window. Jamie was listening and nodding. He was talking, too. It was the breakthrough they wanted. He wanted to get back inside and make the little git tell him what he knew. On the other hand, he needed to solve the murder of his colleague. He had known all along there was something bad about Jed Abrams, and it was no surprise that it was child pornography. He'd like to know where the contents of that production room had disappeared to.

Sally was in the main office, taking a call from the front desk. 'Boss, we've just been informed that Miles Westlake has escaped from hospital. In all the fuss over Grigor Pelakais, they didn't notice he'd gone until the nurse went in to check on his drip.' She listened again. 'He could have been gone up to an hour.' She put the phone down, 'Do I put out a shout for him?'

Dan stared at her. Could this case get any worse? 'Just what we bloody need. He'll probably go home. People generally do. Adam Foster and the forensic guy are there at the moment going over his car, aren't they?' Sally nodded. 'Get in touch and ask them to keep an eye out, and bring him in if they see him. And put out a general shout to detain and bring him in. If he's fit enough to leave the hospital, he's fit enough to come here and be charged.'

'I'm more worried about him trying another suicide attempt before we get a chance to interrogate him,' Sally said.

'Well, I can't worry about him at the moment. Get in to the Jamie May interview and see how things are going. DCS Oliver wants me in a meeting in a few minutes. I think we may be going after Jed Abrams and the Latvian gang.'

Sally raised her eyebrows. 'Action? Count me in, boss.'

'Thrill-seeker. How's Abrams been this morning?'

'Complaining about everything. He's just asked for a solicitor. Must have dawned on him that this might be serious. Bennett's with him now, listening to the complaints. We've got him until midnight tonight before we need to charge him, so I suggest we leave him to stew for a while and let his brief take the complaints.'

'Fine. Try to find out what Jamie's hiding, Sally. He finally seems to be talking, now that I'm not in the room. And interrupt my meeting if you have any news.' He turned away then swung back. 'Can you make sure Claire Quick gets home safely, too? I'll be in Oliver's office. Good luck.' He smiled at her before striding towards the door.

He felt a flutter of excitement in his gut as he headed up the stairs to the top floor. They were getting somewhere, even if it did feel out of control.

A perk of Julie Oliver's senior position was that she had room in her office for a conference table with ten seats. As the meeting began at two thirty, eight of them were occupied.

Present in the room were DCI Tom Garrett and DS Duncan Lake, members of the Special Operations Armed Response team, DS Alison Yelland and DC Geoff Short from the Child Protection team, DS Carl Manley from Vice, DI Dan Hellier and Oliver's secretary, Stella.

Under guard, Grigor Pelakais sat on a chair outside the office in handcuffs, outwardly calm and composed, but inwardly panicking. He had no idea what was happening, but he could see that the people going into the room were not ordinary English bobbies. They were going take notice of what he said, and for that, he was grateful, and hopeful.

In the office, they all stood as John Pallister, Assistant Chief Constable in charge of Operational Resources entered the room and took a seat. If there had been any doubt in Dan's mind about the level of the meeting to which he had been called, he felt no doubt now. The big guns were out.

Oliver summarised the conversation she'd had with Pelakais earlier in the afternoon. Dan found himself subject to close questioning about the events of the night before and Ian's death. ACC Pallister's jowly glare pierced Dan. He could see that the Chief was angry for the loss of his officer, but mostly, he suspected, for the expense he was about to agree to if they went ahead with Oliver's plan.

Grigor was called in to say what he knew. The films were made in the recording studio, but because of the police interest, Irina had made him agree to do this one at Jed Abrams' parents' home on Church Hill, near Poltimore, on the outskirts of the city. The 'actors' would arrive early evening, and it would be over in time to get the children home before parents asked questions.

Dan interrupted, 'From my records, it appears that Abrams has a flat in the city. Would his parents agree to letting their house be used like this?'

Pelakais raised his eyes to look at Dan. 'The parents are away on holiday. They know nothing.'

The sergeant from the Child Protection team, Annie Yelland, asked if the children knew what they were going to do when they got there. Grigor could feel the tears welling up again. He looked at the floor when he answered, 'Not at first. Irina gives them Ecstasy and alcohol and sweets, sometimes heroin, so they relax. Just tiny amounts at first, she is very skilled.

'Some of the older ones help to find the younger ones. They want the money, the attention from the pretty lady. She makes them feel special. That what they are doing is right. And, of course, she gets me to take pictures of their families, as she has of mine. If they tell, she says she will kill their mother, or their father. It is simple. They come back again until they are too old and not needed anymore. By then they are ruined.'

Grigor paused as he heard clothes rustling and felt the atmosphere in the room change. 'By the time the filming starts, they are unable to put up a fight.' He looked up and stared at Oliver.

'It is very bad. I have been very bad to do this. It must be stopped. She must be stopped. Please.'

'That's what we're here for, mate,' put in the Vice Officer, Carl Manley, 'and you are going to be stopped. Permanently, if I have anything to do with it.'

Julie Oliver intervened. 'Yes, thank you, DS Manley. Mr Pelakais is co-operating fully, so there's no need to threaten him. This is not a Vice case. You're here out of courtesy.' The officer held his tongue, but the atmosphere in the room changed as she stared him out until he dropped his eyes.

The Child Protection officer asked Pelakais another question, 'What about the adults in the films? Do you take those parts yourselves?'

Grigor looked shocked. 'No, I could never…' he controlled himself. 'No, they are friends of Abrams. They pay lots of money to Irina, and Abrams gets his share. They will arrive later, around seven pm, when the children are ready...'

There was a hot, sick silence in the room. Dan wondered if the others felt like he did, that a swift left hook to the Latvian's face when he was led from the room and seated back out in the corridor would make him feel a whole lot better.

'You do realise that if they've made twelve films, there are potentially dozens of abused children in the local area? Children who desperately need help, but are too frightened, or too messed up, to tell anyone.' Oliver put her hands over her eyes.

'Abrams uses his singing competitions as a front for grooming, doesn't he?' asked Dan. 'All those youngsters keen to do anything he wants them to.'

Pelakais nodded.

Oliver's mouth dropped. 'The scale of this operation is shocking. But what's more shocking is that we knew nothing about it. Nothing at all. How can that be?'

'It's a secretive world, ma'am. Very few people manage to penetrate it, and with the rise in on-line porn, it's even harder to track them down,' said DS Yelland.

'Right. Dear God, I despair of humanity sometimes. Well, we know the time and place. Now we need to plan. Please escort Mr Pelakais outside, PC Short, and then come back in. We may need him later.'

The Assistant Chief Constable spoke before the door had even closed on Pelakais. 'Superintendent, I shall expect your written strategy on my desk in an hour, before you do anything at all. Understand?'

'Yes, sir.'

'You can have all the resources you need, but after last night's fiasco, if we're going to catch these swines at it, it must be done by the book.' He stood and moved towards the door, his eyes issuing a warning to Dan that his role would be "Advisory capacity only."

'Thank you,' he said to the room, 'don't get up,' and he was gone.

Oliver suppressed a sigh of relief. 'Right, ladies and gentlemen, as I said, we know where, and we know when. Let's see if we can work out how to catch them. We have,' she checked her watch, 'two and three-quarter hours to get into position, so don't promise me what we can't have, give me what you've got.

'Dan, get your team organised. I want uniforms and cars ready in one hour. Get Bill Larcombe onto it. Also, we need good quality maps of the house and surrounding area and traffic need to arrange to block the road on my command. Straight back to me.'

Dan strode from the room, heart hammering.

'DCI Garrett, we need an Armed Response Vehicle and at least two long-distance rifle operatives.' Garrett nodded once and took out his mobile phone as he and his sergeant, Duncan Lake, moved to the rear of the room. Special ops teams were always ready to be called for terrorist threats or major incidents such as this one. He spoke quietly into the phone.

'DS Yelland, I need a couple of people who can come with us tonight. We may have several traumatised children.'

'That will be me and DC Short, ma'am,' replied Annie Yelland, indicating her companion, a broad, sandy-haired officer with a genial, open face. 'We're on duty. Just tell us where you want us.'

'Okay.' Oliver let out a long breath, aware that the decisions she made now were crucial. But that's what they paid her for. She looked around the table and felt confident. It was a good team. 'Let's decide exactly how we're going to do this.' She turned to her secretary, who so far had stayed quietly in the corner.

'Stella, we'll need coffee and sandwiches, up here and in the incident room, as soon as is humanly possible, please. Then I need you to write down everything I say during this planning session and use your magic to transcribe it into proper sentences for our Lord and Master up at the big house.'

Stella smiled her assent, scuttled from the room and met a pink, puffing Bill Larcombe on the stairs, carrying an arm full of maps and print-outs.

'All go round here, isn't it?' she said, and twinkled a smile at him as he gasped for breath on the landing.

'I think I'm a bit past rushing about, Stella, to be honest, but I want the gang who did this, so I'll do whatever it takes, even if I have to shoot the buggers myself.'

'Oh, I don't think it'll come to that, Bill, love. Madam's got everyone running around and jumping when she squeaks in there.' She cast a backward glance at the door. 'Best get going, or I'll be in trouble, too,' she said and skipped down the stairs like a woman half her age.

Chapter 34

Date: Wednesday 26th April Time: 15:42 Miles Westlake

The journey from the hospital felt much further than the couple of miles it actually was. Miles felt weak and strangely light, like he had left most of his real body behind in the bed and had been left with the little bit of skin, flesh and bone he needed to complete his task before he could let it all go, forever. He struggled to focus, to bring himself back to the mundane task of placing one foot in front of the other.

A group of children from the local primary school charged past him on their way home, laughing and giggling, and he had to lean against a wall until they had gone. They shouted at him, 'Alright, mate? Had one too many, eh?' and laughed in his face. Their noise was too much for him to bear. Pedestrians flashed him curious looks as they rushed past. His senses on fire, his skin hot to the touch, his eyes burning, Miles watched them go until there was some quiet once more.

Clutching walls and hedges for support and ignoring the stares and comments, Miles Westlake stumbled onwards.

PC Adam Foster was on the phone to DI Hellier. Westlake's car was providing a wealth of evidence that Carly had been in it.

'Sir, the forensic guy has found long, dark hairs which might be Carly's, and a whole pile of prints which are less helpful. Westlake's wife has arrived but she's blonde and so is the baby. I found her in the kitchen washing up. Forensics haven't even started on the other rooms for evidence in the Claire Quick case, so I've banned her and told her to go back to her mum's for the time being, once she's finished washing up. Can't seem to shift her away from that. She's in shock, sir.'

'Okay, Adam, get her out of there as soon as you can. We'll bring the car in for forensics to have a go over later. Any sign of Westlake himself?'

'No, sir. He'd be a bit mad to show up here though, we have quite an audience in the street and there's a fair bit of chat about what the local kids think happened. I reckon they're getting pretty close, too. The kids knew he was having an affair with Carly, even if his wife didn't.'

'But they didn't think to tell anyone?'

'Well, you don't do that if you're a kid, do you, sir? They all idolised Carly by the sounds of it. Thought she would end up on the telly. No way they'd tell an adult and risk getting her into trouble. Until now, of course.'

'Of course. Now that it's all over the news. Right, Adam. Stay there until the forensic guy gets going on the main rooms and I'll see you back here by five pm. We'll need you and your oppo, Pete Salter for tonight, we've got a job on.'

From the corner of the road, Miles Westlake could see the activity around his house. A man in a blue plastic suit was doing something to his car, and there was a cop talking to his horrible neighbour and a pile of nosy kids. Looking for evidence of Carly, thought Miles. Well, let them look.

He turned and entered the garden of the neighbouring old people's flats keeping close to the wall. All the back gardens on the row were connected with old privet hedges and he thought he would be able to push through them and get to his own back door unseen. Taking care to make no noise, he pulled the old shrubs apart and slipped through into the next-door garden, glad that she was out bending the ear of the policeman at the front of the house. He pushed through her hedge into his own garden, scratching his arms and face on a bramble and coming to a stop in the farthest corner behind the shed. A workman in overalls was whistling through his teeth as he finished puttying the kitchen window in place.

It wasn't the workman who caused him to catch his breath, however. There behind the new window, was Sophie, washing dishes. He knew that meant she would have Emily with her. Probably Emily would be in the baby car seat on the table behind where Sophie stood, laughing at something the workman said. Miles felt the ground lurch under him. She had come back. After all he had done, she had come back. He took a step forward. He wanted desperately to see his daughter one more time.

He froze and thought again. The thoughts were so slow to come. Maybe she had come back because she thought he was going to die and she wanted the house back. That was a more likely reason. They'd parted on very bad terms. She'd accused him outright of sleeping with Carly and he'd admitted it. It would have been impossible to deny since she had caught him in bed with Carly. She'd moved out that day back to her mum's, and he'd only seen Emily twice since then.

He was going to leave her anyway. He'd been waiting for Carly to leave school, so they could be together. Properly together. He felt a deep howl growing at the back of his throat, but held onto it. Only a little more time, and they would be together.

He turned away from his house, his wife, his child, his life, and weaved back the way he had come. He would have to finish his task in whatever way he could. There was nothing left for him here.

Chapter 35

Date: Wednesday 25th April Time: 16:18 Exeter Road Police Station

It was unlikely that the Incident room had ever contained so many people. Dan had rounded up three patrol cars with two officers for each one plus members of his team to be shared between them. They would be strike teams One, Two and Three. There were two Armed Response vehicles and two vans ready for arrests. Child Protection had their own vehicle. All relevant officers were in attendance, except for Sally Ellis, who was still in the interview room with Jamie May.

DCS Julie Oliver stood at the front of the room flanked by Dan Hellier and DCI Tom Garrett from Armed Response. The enlarged map of Jed Abram's family property had been tacked to the wall behind her. 'As you can see, the Abrams family lives in an old farmhouse on a quiet lane, about a mile from the main Cullompton road. Their neighbours to the right are the Farmers- they really are farmers called Farmer - and they have kindly agreed to allow us to set up a base in their farmhouse and park our vehicles in their yard.

'There is no access or egress from the rear of the Abrams' house. The drive goes up the right side of the house into a yard at the rear and to get out you have to go back the same way. There are fields behind and to the left.'

She indicated the areas that would need cover. 'When we get there, you are to take up position as quietly as possible and await instructions. There will be armed officers at each location. Pelakais will drive back as if nothing has happened, in the black Mercedes van. He will leave the van at the rear of the house with the keys in for us. If we are to make the conviction of Jed Abrams stick, it's very important that we retrieve everything in the van, and one of you will have that as their priority.'

'The attack plan is for team One to go through the back door, which Pelakais will leave open, and go straight for the main bedroom where we can take them unawares.'

She numbered the named teams and showed them their positions. 'Team Two will go in through the front door and stop anybody leaving that way. Team Three will take up position at the rear of the property and prevent any suspects leaving through the fields.

'Our sharpshooters,' she nodded at two young, serious-faced officers leaning against the rear wall, 'will be ready to cover any other eventualities. One of you will be on the roof of the barn.' She pointed to a rectangular building which butted up against the hedge directly overlooking the front drive to the farmhouse, 'if it holds your weight.' She raised her eyebrows at the snigger. 'The second officer will be positioned on top of the milking parlour here at the farm to cover the rear of the property.'

'Sergeant Lake will lead Team One. DI Hellier, I want you in that team. No shooting until you have the order either from myself or DCI Garrett. Please follow protocol. No heroics. Allow armed officers to lead when you enter the property, and do not go further until they have cleared the way.'

She eyed her team. 'I don't want to lose anybody. Got it?' They nodded.

Dan, from his position at the front of the room, saw feet tapping and heard throats clearing. He felt his own adrenaline rush as a wobbling of the knees and a swift fluidity in his gut.

'DCI Garrett will take over running the operation as soon as I say go. Is that clear?'

There were murmurs of assent round the room. Dan had heard that Garrett was the best they had. He'd make sure they were okay.

'DCI Garrett and I will remain in the farmhouse and direct ops from there. The Child Protection team and two patrol cars will be positioned near the gate to the farm, so they can go in to get the children out as quickly as possible.

'I have released Grigor Pelakais to return to the house.' She got ready to glare at any who might dare to question her decision, even by shuffling or the clearing of a throat, but there were no takers. 'He has to go back and behave as normal because if he alerts Irina Akis, or the punters, sorry, paedophiles, who enjoy destroying young children's lives, we'll lose the lot.

'Yes,' she said, in answer to concerned looks around the room, 'there will be several young children at the house this afternoon, hence the need to for caution. After what happened to DCI Gould last night, I want this op to be quick and clean.'

Garrett took over. 'Most important is the safety of the children.' He included a nod towards the Child Protaction team. 'We intend to get there and be in place by five forty pm, well before it kicks off at seven pm and we plan to go in about thirty minutes after that. Pelakais says that the children will be there by six. He expects there to be an older child who recruits the younger ones bringing them, he's assuming, by bus or taxi. Usually, Jed Abrams picks the children up and drops them off, but obviously he can't do that today. The filming is over quite quickly, no second takes. DS Yelland?'

'Yes sir. We will wait until you have secured the building and then bring the children out. We'll wait in the farmhouse yard until you give the go signal.'

Sally Ellis slipped into the room and beckoned to Dan. He moved across and she whispered in his ear. A brief frown flittered across his face before he spoke.

'Ma'am, you may have to start without me and Sally – Jamie May is talking and he wants to tell me what happened to Carly Braithwaite. I think we're getting somewhere.'

'That's tough, but you need to see that through. Join us later if you can.' She gave a wry smile. 'I think we can just about manage without you. Getting a confession for Carly Braithwaite's murder is still top of our list.'

The flowerpot men, who had been silent until that point, stood up. 'Ma'am,' said Bennett, 'can we take DI Hellier and Sergeant Ellis's places?'

Oliver didn't answer straightaway.

Larcombe spoke, 'DCI Gould was our friend and colleague. We want to do this. We want to be part of the attack team.' Oliver stared at the floor. She had already lost one close colleague, and these two were like her uncles.

'I know how you feel,' she said, 'we all want to avenge Ian's death, but it could be dangerous and I don't know if...'

Dan came to her rescue. 'I think it would be a great idea if we had an extra body in two of the patrol cars, ready to give chase if the targets run. Still got your Advanced Driving certs up to date, lads?'

Oliver nodded in relief. That would do. They would be there, part of the action, but safe. With a bit of luck, the gang wouldn't be running anywhere.

'Okay, sort out which patrol cars you're going in and position yourselves near the farm entrance.'

The sergeants grinned and nodded their thanks at Dan.

'Dan and Sally, off you go. If you do come along later, let me know and follow protocol. Okay?'

They left in a rush, heads down to hide their disappointment.

'Right, ladies and gentlemen, body and head protection is ready. Sort yourselves out, we're leaving in one hour. And remember, no noise, no blue lights, and no heroics. We've got DCI Garrett's team for that kind of back up if we need it. Good luck. See you back here afterwards for a de-brief.'

The little interview room was stuffy and warm. The only sound as Dan and Sally entered was the quiet snuffling of Sandra May and the shuffling of the solicitor's papers.

'Sergeant Ellis told me that you would now like to tell us how Carly Braithwaite died, Jamie,' said Dan. 'Why don't you begin with the party on Saturday night?'

Jamie's voice shook in time with the rhythm his hands were beating on his knees. 'When Carly won the competition it was great, we were all dead excited, because she said that we would still be her band and everything, even if she got famous. She made Mr Westlake let us have a party at his house, because his wife's left him.'

He glanced up at Sally. 'It's really hard to say no to Carly when she wants something. She just goes ahead and does it anyway, doesn't matter what anyone else thinks. So me and the band and Carly and a few of her mates went over on Saturday night.' He hesitated.

'Go on, Jamie, you're doing fine,' said Sally.

'You're gonna think this is really stupid, but I … I bought her a ring. To show, well, to show she was my girl, but … but she laughed at me.' He screwed his eyes shut to stop tears escaping. 'She said I was just a friend. A friend.' He scrubbed his arm across his face and wiped the tears onto his hoody sleeve. 'I knew that wasn't right, we'd been more than friends since way before Christmas.' He shook his head from side to side, as if trying to shake out the feelings of betrayal that had found him again. 'I walked off round the back garden. I was really mad. It was a right kick-back.' He turned to his mother. 'I loved her, Mum.' Sandra May took his hand and squeezed it.

Dan held his breath. Please let the kid keep on talking he prayed, to any god that might be listening. Don't let him stop now.

'Go on, Jamie,' murmured Sally. 'You're doing really well. Tell us what happened then.'

He stared at the wall, not blinking, lost in the memory.

'Then I saw her with sir, Mr Westlake, through the kitchen window. It was obvious, then. She was hanging round his neck and kissing him, and he was kissing her, too. It was disgusting. He's a teacher!'

Eyes closed and face screwed up in pain he said, 'I think I was the last one to know.'

Dan allowed a moment's quiet while Jamie's breathing calmed. 'What did you do next, Jamie? Did you argue, or fight with Carly?

Did you do anything to show them how upset you were?' Dan aimed to match the quiet, restrained tone of the other adults in the room as it seemed to calm the boy, and his previous technique had been a spectacular failure.

'Do anything? No, I didn't do anything.' The boy's voice rose in frustration. 'How can I compete with a teacher, a grown man? Who'd have believed me anyway? I'm just a kid with a bad attitude, aren't I? A trouble causer.' His hands balled into fists, which he banged down hard on the table. 'Who'd believe me against a fucking teacher?' He stared around the room, daring them to disagree with him. The lack of response took the bite from his voice.

'No, I just got pissed and slept in the baby's room. I went home on Sunday morning. But the more I thought about it, the more angry I got. He's married, he's got a kid and he's messing about with my girl.'

'So, what did you do on Sunday?' Sally asked.

'I was supposed to be at Carly's house for four o'clock to help her get ready and have a quick practice before we went into town for the recording session. I said I'd be there because she wanted to have a word with Jenna about something before we went out. But I was really angry with her, so I didn't go.'

'Where did you go?' Dan tried for eye contact but the boy's eyes swerved around him to look at the floor.

'I went to the graveyard for a walk round. I like it there. Mum was on shift, so I went home and got something to eat. And I suppose I calmed down a bit. Then I thought like, I was letting her down, on her big day, so I went to her house later.'

Dan watched Jamie's eyes jump from him to Sally. Was that a calculating glance, or a frightened one?

'What time later?'

'I dunno. Maybe five o'clock? Does it matter? I could hear a real screaming row coming from upstairs. Carly and Jenna were shouting and chucking things - I could hear it from outside on the street.'

'What were they arguing about, Jamie?' Dan asked.

Jamie flushed a deep, punishing crimson and stared down at the gnarled table-top. 'I can't…' He cast a desperate look at Sally. 'I can't say. Not in front of my mum. It's totally embarrassing. Can I just talk to you? Please?'

Sally hesitated and looked to Dan.

'Jamie, I can ask your mum to step outside but you are in a formal interview, so both of us and your solicitor have to stay.'

'It'll be alright, Jamie,' said Sandra May, squeezing his hand. 'I'd rather hear it from your mouth, and I won't be embarrassed, I promise. Just tell us what happened, love.'

'And I promise you I have heard it all before, Jamie,' sighed Vanessa Redmond. 'There are very few things that surprise me anymore.'

Jamie shrugged and sagged back into the chair. 'Okay. I knocked on the door but they couldn't hear me so I went in. I didn't think their dad would be there or he'd have stopped them fighting. I could hear what they were arguing about as I went in.' He glanced at his mother. 'Jenna's been doing porn.'

His mother barked out a laugh. 'Porn? Young Jenna? Are you sure, love?'

Jamie pulled his hand away from her grasp. 'I'm not stupid, mum. Of course I'm sure. D'you want to hear this or not?'

'Go on,' urged Dan. 'Tell us what happened. Take your time.'

Jamie grunted his assent. 'The arguing stopped, just like that. So I ran upstairs to Carly's room first, but they weren't in there. They were in Jenna's room and when I got through the door she was kneeling on top of Carly. Carly was on the bed, flat out. She wasn't fighting back or anything.'

'What did you do, then?'

'I was shouting at Jenna to let go. Jenna had her arms round Carly's neck and was strangling her. Carly was going purple. I had to drag Jenna off her. She was like a mad bitch - screaming and crying and laughing. It was horrible.'

The self-control he had been working hard to maintain was lost. Jamie sobbed like a small boy. 'I was too late. Too late. Carly was just lying there. All still.' He took a gulping sob of air. 'If I'd got there earlier, I could have saved her. I could have saved her.' He dropped his head onto his arms, and they watched his shoulders shake as he released the pain.

Sandra May sobbed once with relief and rubbed her son's shoulders. 'I knew he didn't do it. That girl has got everybody feeling sorry for her but look, look what she did. I'll be able to take my boy home now, won't I?'

'Let's not be hasty, Mrs May,' said Dan. 'We still have many questions for Jamie.'

Sally could control her disbelief no longer. 'Jenna? You're saying that Jenna killed her sister?' She shook her head. 'Are you telling us the truth, Jamie? Because if you're lying to cover up for whoever did kill her…'

'Don't threaten my client, Sergeant Ellis.' Vanessa Redmond interrupted and glared at Sally over her glasses.

Sally glared back. 'Just trying to get to the truth. It's what we're here for.' She turned and stared at the boy. 'Well, Jamie?'

Jamie flinched under her attack, but held her gaze. 'I'm not lying. It really did happen like that. It was horrible.'

'Are you sure it wasn't her dad, making her cover it up for him?' asked Sally, still unwilling to accept the boy's version.

Jamie looked confused. 'No. He wasn't even in the house.'

'So what happened then, Jamie?' Dan stayed calm, flashing a warning glance at his sergeant to back off and let the boy tell it.

'I had to scream at Jenna to shut her up. Then she realised what she'd done. We tried to give Carly mouth-to-mouth but she didn't breathe. We were both panicking.'

'Why didn't you ring the police? Or find Mr Braithwaite? You must have known he was in the pub. That's what normal people do,' said Sally.

Jamie stared at her and shook his head. 'You don't know what her dad's like. He'd have killed Jenna if he'd found out. And me, too. He's insane.' He turned back to Dan. 'We didn't know what to do, or how to hide her. I wrapped her in the duvet at first but you could see it was her and I couldn't keep it rolled up. And Jenna was no use, she was in a right state. So in the end, I rang Jed Abrams and asked him to help us because he's got a van.'

'What?' interrupted Sally. 'Why on earth would you ring this bloke, who you hardly know, and expect him to help you move a dead body? The body of a girl who should have been at his studio at that very minute?'

'I hardly know him, yeah. But Jenna probably knows him from Youth Matters. Alright?'

'Probably knows him? Probably isn't going to make someone break the law and put themselves in the frame for a murder.'

She raised her voice, and Dan noticed that the softness had disappeared. 'Tell us the truth, Jamie. Why did Jed Abrams agree to help you? What is your relationship with Jed Abrams?'

'I haven't got a relationship with him.' The boy looked horrified. 'I don't know what you mean. What you trying to say? I'm not gay.' He looked to Dan again, fellow male in a room full of women, trying to find a shared disgust at what she was implying. 'I just met him at the competition. I didn't have a relationship with him. I'm not gay.' He looked at the solicitor. 'Is she trying to say I'm gay?' He swung back to Sally. 'I've had enough of this. I'm supposed to be helping you and you have a go?'

'Calm down, Jamie,' Dan said, 'Sergeant Ellis is just doing her job. We need to be sure we have all the facts before we do anything else. You're doing really well, just hang in there.'

'Hold on,' said Sally, shuffling papers on her knee. 'There are no calls to Abrams on your phone log.'

'There won't be,' Jamie replied, voice twisted by sarcasm, 'because I used Jenna's.'

'So Jenna has Abram's phone number on her phone? Why? And where is Carly's phone?'

'I don't know, alright? I don't know all the answers to all your effing questions. I'm doing my best, alright?' He furrowed his eyebrows. 'Yeah, I think Carly's phone got broken when they were fighting. There was glass on the floor. But I don't know where it is.'

Vanessa Redmond cleared her throat. 'I doubt that this mode of aggressive questioning is going to help engender trust between the two of you, sergeant. You can hardly expect my client to remember tiny details after such a traumatic incident. Why don't you just listen to what he has to say and then we can go back over anything that you don't like, later?'

Sally subsided with a sniff. She cast a sidelong glance at Dan. He could see she was quite enjoying playing nasty cop. He hoped she'd shut up though, and let the boy tell it.

'And then,' Dan asked, 'what did you do?'

'Yeah, well, we had to wait 'til it got dark. Jed came over with his van about nine o'clock. He helped me to take her to the woods at the top of school in his van. It was the only place I could think of. We were going to go back on Monday night and take her somewhere and bury her properly.' The boy's shoulders began to shake and he faltered. He looked at the black ballet shoe, still on the table in its evidence bag.

'I don't even remember taking the shoe. I must have just put it in my pocket.'

'What? You were just going to stick her in the ground somewhere and forget about her? Didn't you think her dad might notice she was gone?' Sally's face was picture of disgust. 'Not very convincing so far, Jamie.'

'I'm telling the truth. Why don't you believe me?'

'I know when someone's lying, Jamie.' She glanced at him, and looked back down at her notes.

Jamie threw up his hands and flopped back into his chair, arms folded tightly over his chest.

Dan intervened, 'Tell us about Jenna. What did you mean about Jenna being involved in porn?'

'That's what I was trying to tell you,' Jamie answered, frustration making his voice even more gruff. 'Carly had seen Jed's number on Jenna's phone and told me she was going to find out why. Jenna was pretty jealous of Carly. But Carly found other stuff on the phone as well. She showed it to me when Jenna was in the bath on Friday. But she didn't want to say anything then because her dad was in.'

'What sort of stuff?'

'There were pictures of Jenna with blokes on her phone.'

'What kind of pictures?'

'You know, sex pictures, with no clothes on. Oh yeah, and kids, too.'

Sandra May gasped, 'No! But she's a child herself, a little kid!'

Vanessa Redmond reached across and placed her hand on Sandra's damp fist.

Jamie didn't look at his mother, but focussed on Dan's face. 'That's what they were arguing about when I got there on Sunday. Carly had hold of Jenna's phone and said she was going to tell her Dad what Jenna was up to and she'd get put into a home for prostitutes or end up dead from drugs.' He paused. 'She was saying bad stuff. And then Jenna must have lost it and killed her.' Jamie lifted his white face towards Sally, as if waiting for her to find fault with his story.

'Thanks, Jamie. Good job. So let me re-cap,' said Dan. 'Jenna happens to know Jed Abrams. Jenna has pictures on her phone of herself and other children having sex with men. When her sister finds out about this, Jenna kills her in a fit of rage rather than let her father find out. You and Jed Abrams then hide Carly's body at the school.'

Jamie nodded, relief lifting his features. 'Yeah, that's how it happened. I didn't mean to do anything bad. I was just trying to help Jenna.'

Sandra May blew her nose and made an effort to sound calm. 'Can I take him home now?'

'Not yet, Mrs May, we still need Jamie, I'm afraid.' Dan felt for her. She'd come into the room thinking her child might be a murderer, but there was a now at least a chance she would leave in a different frame of mind.

'I want you think hard, now, Jamie. When Carly showed you the pictures on Friday night, did you recognise any of the people in them? Besides Jenna, of course.'

'No. Just some old geezers. They were disgusting old paedos.'

'Did you recognise any children besides Jenna?' asked Sally.

He thought for a moment. 'I didn't, but Carly said Jenna's friend was in one picture. I think she was going to tell the girl's mum, too. She was so angry at Jenna.'

Having finished his confession, Jamie looked lighter, and sounded lighter. 'I don't think Jenna meant to kill Carly. It was a fight gone wrong. Will she have to go to prison?'

Sally, who had understood the meaning of Dan's raised eyebrows, and kept quiet during the latter exchange, responded, 'Oh, we're a long way from that point, Jamie. We don't usually lock people up just on one person's say-so. That wouldn't exactly be fair, would it? No, we have lots of investigations to carry out yet.' She tapped her pen on her notes. 'We have to check out your story, for example, make sure we have all our facts straight.'

Dan watched Jamie's brows knit together and headed off an explosion.

'Thanks for everything so far. Let's take a break. I'll send in a PC to take you to the toilet or get you a drink. Back in a couple of minutes.'

Dan caught Sally's eye and beckoned her out of the room. He swung to face her in the corridor, excitement and adrenaline making his movements jerky.

'I reckon he's telling the truth, Sally. He's got most of the details correct, and he couldn't make up the bit about moving her body, or about what position she was in when she died, could he?'

'No, I suppose not,' she replied slowly, 'but ...'

'But, what? I know you don't trust him, and I understand why - he's a bit of a time bomb, especially the way he attacked Claire Quick.'

'Yes, about that. Claire isn't keen to press charges. She doesn't want to go to court, and she thinks Jamie was acting under extreme provocation and wouldn't do anything like that again. She'd rather drop it, I think, which is bonkers. He shouldn't get away with behaving like that towards anybody, let alone a nice person like

Claire Quick. Although, I might be able to persuade her to change her mind.'

She stopped and looked at him with her hands on her hips. 'Would you do me the courtesy of listening to me, please, boss?'

Dan was chewing a fingernail and staring at the wall. He re-focussed. 'Sorry. Just thinking. I know you don't like Jenna for this, but she had means, motive and someone to help her deal with the body. A pretty slick operator, if you ask me.'

'Exactly,' she responded, exasperation obvious. 'With all due respect, sir, you don't know the girl at all. I just don't think she's got it in her to be 'slick'. It has to be somebody else. I don't trust Jamie May as far as I could throw him. He could have been there, not because he was helping hide the body, but because he is the bloody murderer.'

'But we have the link, Sal, can't you see? Jed Abrams is the link. Jenna is the link. Carly is just the innocent victim.'

He grabbed her arm, using the other hand to smack the front of his forehead.

'Oh my God!'

'What?'

'What if Jenna is one of the kids due at Abrams tonight? What if that's why he agreed to help them hide Carly's body? Because he needs Jenna for tonight?'

Sally followed his line of thought. 'Yeah, that feels right. It would be typical of Abrams to want to protect his investment.' She took in Dan's flushed face and shining eyes. 'I assume that making that link will make you feel a bit better about Ian's death, too.'

'Yes, it will. Now I know Abrams really is up to no good, and it's not just wishful thinking. It feels like his death wasn't a total waste.'

'I still think we're missing a trick here. Would a thirteen-year-old have the gumption to kill her sister and arrange for removal of the body? Her grief seemed so genuine to me.'

Dan saw the appeal in her face, but his brain was working so intensely making the links that it was hard to talk it through and think at the same time. 'Oh, I don't think for a moment that she intended to kill her sister, Sal. But she didn't need to do anything once she thought about ringing Abrams, did she? He took over the problem and disposed of it. And, of course she's feeling sad. It's just that she was more frightened of her dad finding out what she was up to, than she was of Carly. She could scheme that far.'

'Okay, I see the way you're thinking, but I'm uneasy about Jamie. He's lying through his teeth. Watch his eyes, his body language. He's squirming all over the chair, trying to get sympathy from us all in turn. He's a tricky customer, and I don't trust him, and I'm worried that you do.'

Dan controlled a flash of anger. 'Sal, he's given us the best story yet of what happened to Carly Braithwaite. We don't have to like him to see that. We have Jenna in the frame for her sister's murder.' He gave a short laugh of disbelief. 'Who would have thought it?'

'But what would motivate a girl like that to turn to pornography?'

Dan sighed. 'Just the usual, Sally. Money, attention, all the things she wasn't getting at home, I guess.'

'That Jed Abrams.' Sally felt real anger burn her insides. 'He just picked her off the discard pile and used her, didn't he? The other sister, the one with no talent. Easy meat. Bastard!' She felt her fingernails cutting into the soft skin of her hands as she formed two fists.

'We have to nail him, boss, and we have to do it right. Trouble is, we haven't got any real evidence yet. Not even the phone with the pictures on it.'

'Don't worry about that. We might have more evidence than we want later on today, if my hunch is correct. We need to get Jenna Braithwaite in for questioning.'

He checked his watch. 'We'd better get back in there. See if we can wrap it up and get to Abrams' house before it's all over.' He caught her arm as she turned. 'You know we're not going to be able to keep Jamie in, if Claire doesn't press charges? Oliver won't give us the extra twenty-four hours. Redmond will know that, too.'

Sally glared at him. 'Bad move, boss. We need to keep him here. What if one of Abrams' Latvian friends finds out he's talked? He could be in danger. And I still don't trust him. I think you're going for the answer he wants you to accept.'

Dan stared at her. He wanted to snap, to ask what was the matter with her, to ask why she was spoiling a great moment, what was her problem? But she was a good officer, and still learning the job, so he softened his features. 'Point taken sergeant, but as we seem to have two thirds of the Latvian gang in custody, I can't see that you have any reason to worry on that score. I don't think Jamie's telling us everything either, but I won't know that until I've had Jenna under the microscope. Come on.'

Dan entered the interview room slowly, attempting to get his breathing under control and adopt his previously cool demeanour. But he couldn't stop one foot from tapping a fast rhythm on the table leg as he felt a nervous elation surge through his body. He switched on the recorder. 'Jamie, thank you for telling us what happened with Carly. It must be a great weight off your shoulders. It was too much to expect you to keep this all to yourself.' The boy shuddered out a great sigh.

'There are still some questions we need to ask you about Miles Westlake though, and we have to sort out the charges regarding Miss Quick, so we have to keep you here for another night, I'm afraid. Then we can let you go home on bail.'He could sense Vanessa Redmond rearing up even before she came into his line of vision.

'Inspector Hellier, I think it is perfectly clear that this young man is no longer a danger to anyone. He has been honest with you, even though some of what he has said will go against him in court. Miss Quick has said that she will not be pressing charges, so the serious charge of assault and kidnapping no longer stands.' She held her hand up to stop any potential interruption. 'I know he has aided and abetted the concealment of a body but that's not the sort of everyday criminal activity that warrants overnight detention . . . As you very well know.' She skewered him with her stare. 'So, are you intending to charge him?' She pointed the nib end of her pen at his face. 'If so, what are those charges? If not, please release him under the recognizance of his mother until tomorrow.'

'I'll have him back here in the morning,' offered Sandra May. 'He won't be going anywhere, I promise.'

Dan hesitated and looked to Sally who shook her head. She would argue black was white to keep him in. He was stuck. He either had to charge Jamie May with accessory to murder, and sort it out after he had interviewed Jenna Braithwaite, or charge him for the original assault and kidnap, which wouldn't stand if Claire had withdrawn her statement - or let him go home. He chewed the stub of a fingernail. He didn't believe Jamie had killed Carly, although he did accept that his sergeant's reading of the events on Sunday evening could possibly have a grain of truth in it. Was he simply accepting the boy's version? No, he was convinced the evidence was right. It pointed clearly at the sister and Jed Abrams. It was all happening so fast, and he was desperate to get to Abrams' house for the Latvian take-down.

He shrugged. A decision had to be made, and he hadn't got time for a fight with Vanessa Redmond. 'Alright. I'll let you go home for the night, Jamie. You must not leave your mother's home until you come into the Station tomorrow at nine o'clock, so that I can question you further. If you break these conditions, you will be kept under arrest and in custody for the duration of my investigation. Understood?'

Jamie and Sandra May nodded and smiled and thanked him. He chose to ignore the satisfied smirk of the solicitor as she strode from the room and led them to the front desk where Jamie was returned his few possessions. He also chose to ignore the angry frown creasing his sergeant's normally placid face.

As they watched the small group leave the building, Dan let out a breath that he felt he had been holding since Monday morning.

'Let's get a car sent round to the Braithwaite's in case Jenna is at home after all, and bring her in for questioning.' As Sally turned towards her desk, he added, 'and we need to update the Super. No, we'll do that on the way. Come on, let's get a move on, it's gone six.'

Colin White stopped them at the front door as they were leaving. He was holding the phone and talking to someone on it.

'DI Hellier, you need to take this, it's Alan Braithwaite.' Suppressing the need to look at his watch, and dreading telling Braithwaite about the allegation made against his daughter, Dan took the phone.

'DI Hellier?' Braithwaite sounded strained and was breathing hard. When Dan answered, he shouted,

'I'm sitting on that bloody idiot teacher. He came in through the front door as I got in from shopping. He's raving, something about Jenna and Carly. Can you send an officer to get him out of my house, quick, before I smack him one?'

Dan felt a smile twitch on his lips. 'You do whatever it takes to keep him quiet, Mr Braithwaite, it will be in self-defence as he broke into your property and violated your right to privacy. I'll get a patrol car over there as soon as possible.'

He looked over at Sergeant White, who turned his hands up and shrugged in the way of all humans faced with an insurmountable problem. 'What car?' he said. 'Oliver's got them all. I'll have to radio Traffic and borrow one of their vehicles to send round.' He gave a hard-done-by sigh and lifted the radio receiver.

Dan told Braithwaite a car was on its way, and then, as he'd got him on the phone asked him if Jenna was at home.

'No, she's left me a note to say she's going to her friend's house for tea.'

Dan looked at Sally and shook his head. 'Ok. Will you be home later, only one of us would like to pop round and see you?'

'If you must,' said Braithwaite, and then stopped. 'Why are you coming? Have you found something out? Do you know who did it?'

'We just need to ask you a few more questions. It will be late, I'm afraid. Bit busy at the moment.'

'Well, I'm watching the match anyway so it doesn't matter what time you get here. And bloody hurry up getting a car here, he's looking a bit dodgy now and he's gone all quiet.' He was silent for a second.

'Fuck, he's not breathing. Ring for an ambulance.' He dropped the phone.

Dan handed the phone back to Colin White. 'It's an emergency now, Colin - ambulance needed, not patrol car - can you see it gets there quickly? It seems Braithwaite has captured Miles Westlake, and he's collapsed, so get him under guard in hospital again, please. Let's try not to lose him this time.'

He took Sally's arm and led her at a fast walk towards his car before anybody else could interrupt them.'Jenna's "at a friend's for tea", Sal. Now I'm convinced she'll be at Abrams' house. She is the connection between Abrams and her sister. I knew it.' He paused, a vertical wrinkle appearing between his eyebrows. 'I don't want to tell her father yet though, he's got enough on his plate, especially as Westlake seems to have taken a turn for the worse on his hall floor. Thing is, Westlake obviously knows that Jenna killed Carly. I reckon he's arrived at Braithwaite's looking to hurt Jenna.'

'Balance of his mind is somewhat disturbed after all the pills and alcohol he took,' said Sally. 'Probably hasn't a clue what he's doing.'

'True, and I'd say our little friend Jamie has been torturing Miles Westlake over these last couple of days, telling him all sorts of stuff to get him wound up. Exacting his revenge.'

'So do you reckon that's what he was doing at the house on Monday? Making Westlake pay for the affair with Carly? He's a right little angel, our Jamie, isn't he?'

'He'll be disappointed that Westlake's suicide attempt failed. That would solve the problem for him without him having to do anything illegal.'

'That's why I know he's bad, boss. He's bad.' Sally waited by the passenger side of the car for Dan to find his key, aware of the frown on his face. 'He's not the only one who'd like someone else to do his dirty work for him,' she said. 'Was I hearing things or did you give Braithwaite carte blanche to give Westlake a good going over?'

Dan laughed and broke the stiffness between them, 'Sergeant Ellis, how could you possibly think that? A valued member of the community is merely defending his property.' He paused. 'Shit, I hope he doesn't really harm him. We need Westlake's testimony. Ah well, can't worry about that at the moment. Come on, it'll take us ages to get to Poltimore in rush hour traffic and I don't want to miss all the action.'

He took a moment before settling himself into the seat, feeling the evening sun on his face. 'We're close, Sally, aren't we? Close to sorting it all out?'

Sally didn't answer. She flung herself into her seat, slamming the door closed. The more she thought about it, the more angry at herself she became for not having picked up on the clues two days ago at the Braithwaite's house. Jenna hiding her phone under the pillow when Sally had walked into her room. Whose phone? Jamie's need to see Jenna once he knew the body had been recovered. Was he threatening her? Blackmailing her? The fact that Jenna had said she didn't get on all that well with her sister. The fact that no one could say when Carly had left the house on the Sunday. Because, she never did leave. Well not alive, anyway. Her own insistence that Miles Westlake or Jed Abrams had to be the guilty party - all distracting her from spotting the real culprit.

She took stock. If Jenna *was* the real culprit. Jamie had been convincing, but there was something cold about that boy that didn't ring true to her. Like the way he had taken to goading Westlake to the point of suicide, and the way he seemed to go into a rage whenever the questioning got too difficult for him. She slumped back, fuming at herself and the world as they waited to filter out into the evening traffic.

'Sally,' Dan said glancing across at her, 'I can see what you're doing, so stop it. There were six of us investigating this case and none of us suspected Jenna Braithwaite. In fact, if she hadn't involved Jamie May in disposing of the body, we still would never have suspected her. So, get over it and concentrate on what we're doing now. Okay?'

Sally gave a tight smile. 'Ok, boss, enough with the pep talk. It just makes me so angry when I miss things.'

'And it's what makes you a good copper. So, get on your phone and tell her ladyship what we now know, and tell her we'll be there as soon as possible.' With that, he negotiated his way into the traffic queue and headed east out of the city.

Chapter 36

Date: Wednesday 25th April Time: 17:54 Poltimore, near Exeter

The black Mercedes van was still in place in the car park at the hospital where Grigor Pelakais had left it several hours before. Stuck to the front windscreen was a parking ticket. Pelakais tore it off and threw it onto the floor. In the van, he changed back into his wool and silk mix jacket and his soft leather loafers, binning the clogs. He knew that the success of this mission, and his survival, depended on what he did next. Although every cell in his body was screaming at him to run, he started the engine and headed out of the city towards Poltimore.

As he reached the lane that turned off the main road, he saw the children. He recognised the older girls, but they had two new ones with them. They were chatting and teasing each other as they walked along, not a care in the world. He resisted the urge to stop and tell them to run, too. This would be their last time, and, just maybe, the two little ones would have nothing to remember but a bit of excitement at the end of the day. He drove slowly past them and wound his way along a lane bursting with green shoots and signs that spring had arrived. Grigor wondered if this would be the last spring he would see for many years. He didn't care. Escape from Irina and her father was worth whatever price he had to pay.

Grigor drew into the drive and followed the gravel path around to the rear of the house. He parked close to the back door, leaving room for the other cars that would arrive soon. He didn't know the men that were coming, only that there would be five of them. He stared at his eyes in the mirror. How low he had fallen.

Just possibly, he could do something good now. He switched off the engine, left the keys in, and prepared to face Irina.

He entered through the kitchen, leaving the door on the latch, as promised. There was music coming from the living room and the usual smell of scented candles. These days, the smell of vanilla raised bile in his throat. He walked down the hall towards the living room just as she opened the door and stepped through.

'You are late.' She didn't say anything else. That was bad. She stood, arms folded, framed by the doorway.

'The children are on their way up the lane,' he muttered, 'I just passed them. I need to get the camera set up.' She grabbed his arm as he made to walk past her.

'What have you been doing, Grigor? Have you been to the hospital?' She searched his face. 'Yes, I can see that you have seen Filip.' She sneered. 'Yet, he is not here with you, so you failed in your heroic rescue attempt. When will you understand that you are nothing without me? That I made you, and that I own you? When will you learn to do as you are told?'

She raked a nail across the delicate skin under his eye, leaving a roughened red scratch that wept blood as soon as she took her finger away. She rubbed the blood on her fingertip onto his lips.

Grigor stood still, heart pounding. Better to wait until she had finished, than to anger her further.

The sound of childish laughter came trilling on the early evening air. Irina took her hand away.

'Go, get ready. We will talk about this later.'

She turned from him and opened the door to greet Jenna and her friends.

Albert Farmer had lived at Castle Farm for more than seventy years. His wife, Josephine, had been with him for the last fifty. Their children were all grown up and gone. None of them had wanted to follow them into dairy farming, and sadly, Albert had to agree that he had seen their point. So they had gradually reduced their livestock and sold land until their farm was less than thirty acres of the surrounding countryside, a size they could still manage. A procession of police cars and unmarked vans in the middle of afternoon milking had been the most exciting thing that had happened to them since Josie had won all the baking categories at the County show, ten years before.

Josie Farmer was waiting for them as Oliver gathered her team in the yard. She had a tray of fresh-baked scones with jam and cream, an industrial size teapot and a dozen china mugs. The milk was still warm, straight from the cow.

Julie Oliver stepped out of the first car and walked across the yard. What on earth was the woman thinking?

Before she got a word out, the men and women who would follow her every order, the men and women who represented the face of the law in East Devon, had dodged around her back. They were stuffing scones in their mouths and slurping tea, nodding their thanks to the rotund lady with the pink cheeks.

Bill Larcombe put a consoling hand on her shoulder. 'Never mind boss, we work better when we're fed,' He grabbed another scone as he headed for the patrol car that would be his base for the operation.

Oliver sighed and raised her eyebrows at DCI Garrett.

'You have to see the funny side,' he said. 'Only in Devon can a major operation be halted by a cream tea.'

Five minutes later, Josie Farmer had a clean plate and the officers had moved fluidly into position. The two senior officers climbed an oak staircase and found their way into a small room under the eaves that had once been a girl's bedroom. It was ideal as it had two small windows, one overlooking the side of the Abram's house and back yard, and the other overlooking the lane at the front of the property.

A communications specialist followed them up the stairs and speedily set up a field communications system that would allow them to contact their teams. She put on a pair of headphones and called in each team, one at a time, checking the equipment was working. Once satisfied, she called Oliver over.

'Ma'am, we have helmet cameras on all of the armed officers, so you can follow the action from here,' she indicated a laptop screen. 'They also have live microphones, so we can hear what is happening, too.'

Oliver nodded. The officer pressed one earphone to her head. 'Just heard back from sniper One and Two, in position.' She laughed briefly, 'Sniper One is complaining that if he moves more than foot to either side, he will fall into a cow's toilet.'

Julie Oliver breathed a noisy puff of air through her lips. All was in place. She said a quick prayer to a god she did not believe in and perched on the end of the pine dressing table so she had a good view through the small gable window.

Garrett picked up the binoculars and scanned the lane. Nothing yet, but Pelakais had returned as promised. Then they waited. It was six-twelve pm.

Jenna led her little gang up the lane. She was feeling sad. She hadn't expected to miss her sister so much. It seemed weird that she had spent much of the last year hating Carly, but now she was gone, she really missed her. She had put a picture of Carly in the same place as she kept her memories of her mum, a shoe-box under the bed, so she could think about them sometimes, but not all the time, otherwise she didn't know how she would carry on. And she couldn't even think about Jamie. She'd nearly had a fit when he came round to the house. At least her dad had chucked him out. But he might come back, and she was scared of what he might do.

And she was worried about Jed. Why wasn't he answering his phone? She had left texts, too, but nothing. Where was he? She'd been shocked when Irina rang her. She said Jed was away for the night and that she and the other kids should make their own way to a house in Poltimore, not the studio, and she had sent her the directions on her phone. She'd had to find the right bus stop and everything.

It was all a bit weird, and she needed to see Jed. He'd make sure it was alright. She liked Jed a lot, he was the only person she knew that made her feel special, and pretty. He let her smoke and drink in the studio and treated her like a grown-up. Not like her dad, who only had eyes for Carly, and treated Jenna like she was the maid.

Deep down, and only to her-self, Jenna admitted that she knew that what she was doing was wrong. Especially since she and Maddie had started finding the younger kids for Jed. But, oh, she liked the money, and the attention, even if the old blokes did make her feel sick. Irina had some good stuff that she let Jenna have, too. It made her sleepy and feel happy, it took away all her worries and made the whole filming business pass by in a flash.

She cast a quick glance at the two small ones. She would get a lot of money tonight, for bringing them. Then, maybe she could buy her own stuff from Jed and have it all the time, not just when Irina came. Then, she would feel better about Carly and not mind so much about her dad.

Jenna hurried them along and down the long drive of a yellow-brick house that glowed in the evening sun. Irina was waiting at the door with a smile. She was so beautiful.

The first sign of action was the arrival of the children. DCI Garrett spotted two older girls, he thought they might be about twelve or thirteen. They were accompanied by a girl of five or six, and a boy a little younger. He hoped the hothead from Vice was in position and stayed there, because he was finding it hard himself, at the moment, not to leap down the stairs and scoop them up and away to safety. He alerted the Child Protection officers, so they knew how many to expect.

Tom Garrett was a father of three, all teenagers now, but he couldn't even begin to imagine how he would feel if a police officer had knocked on his door with the news that one of his kids had been involved in this kind of abuse. It was going to be a long hard night for some families.

He nudged Oliver who followed the children's progress up the drive, and they got their first view of Irina Akis as she opened the front door.

'Sniper One, close up on the suspect's face, now.'

Garrett turned towards the seated comms officer and stared at the screen. A blurred picture was instantly relayed. She refined the picture and a coldly beautiful, Slavic blonde stared out at them, smiling for the children. As the woman ushered them in, she cast a quick glance around the garden, and shut the door behind them.

Within thirty minutes, he watched the men arrive who paid for the opportunity to abuse children. Three cars, five men. They drove around to the back of the house, parked and got out. They were carrying cans and bottles. Sniper Two, lying flat on top of the milking parlour got clear pictures of three of the men, which he sent back to headquarters so they could be checked against the Sex Offenders' Register. Garrett's heart thudded against his ribs. Got the bastards.

The voice of Carl Manley, the Vice squad officer, came over the speaker. 'I recognise one of the men, ma'am. Andrew Falkirk. I arrested him last June but he got off with a warning. Kid's family wouldn't go to court. Got the bastard now, though.'

Oliver sniffed, 'Yes, we have, Sergeant Manley, but don't go jumping in there too soon. We want all of them, preferably alive so they can face prosecution. I don't think they're going to wriggle out of this one.'

She glanced at Tom Garrett. She didn't know him very well, but she was just about to put her team's safety into his hands. She hoped his reputation was justified. Before she could speak, however, her phone rang. Garrett watched her face change from incredulity to horror as she listened to Sergeant Ellis. Her hand shook as she put the phone down.

'Are you alright, ma'am?' he asked.

'No, Tom, I'm not.' She looked over his shoulder at the farmhouse behind him. 'The taller, fair-haired girl who has just walked through that door is the sister of our murdered girl, Carly Braithwaite. And if that's not a sick enough coincidence for you, it looks like she might also be her sister's murderer.'

Oliver experienced a series of almost physical jolts as several pieces of this frustrating mess fell into place. Jed Abrams was the key to all of this. Dan's hunch was right. Abrams was the one who linked it all together. The one responsible for Ian's death. And he must have recruited Jenna. When or how, she would work out later. For now, she was glad they had him safely in custody.

She focussed on the hands of her watch, willing the agreed fifteen minutes to pass, breathing deeply and taking herself into a state of calm.

Then, 'Go, Tom. Go now. Get them.' Eyes clear now, breathing under control, she moved to the window and stared through her binoculars as her colleague assumed command.

The sun had retreated behind the trees at the front of the house, throwing the backyard into shadow. Team One, led by Duncan Lake, rolled over the hedge and scrambled in silence towards the back door. Lake pushed at the door and it fell open an inch.

Team Two followed Carl Manley at a low run along the nearside of the stone wall separating the two farmhouses, and waited for the signal to cross the wall and enter at the front door.

Team Three moved into position at the rear of the house, ready to capture anybody trying to escape.

On the 'go' signal, Lake pushed the door wide, swept a glance round the kitchen and slipped into the hallway. Pelakais was waiting in the hall as instructed. Lake gestured at him to get down on the floor, left one of his team to cuff him and opened the front door to admit Team Two. They could hear laughing and the noise of a television coming from the living room to their right.

Team Two positioned themselves at the door and waited for the signal to go in. Lake could hear at least four voices. They were watching the football.

Manley flexed his fingers around the gun, and wiped sweat from his top lip with his free hand. Lake nodded to him, raised his hand in a "wait until I give the order" motion, and waved his own team onward.

Team One ascended the stairs. As Lake paused to work out which bedroom the others were in, the bedroom door to his left opened, and out walked a little boy. He stood at the top of the stairs and looked down. He didn't seem to know what to do about a group of armed men pressing themselves to the wall. Lake smiled and made a 'shushing' motion, placing a finger to his lips. The little boy smiled back, and waved. Calmly, he wandered back inside the room where he let out a huge wail, and called for his mum.

Lake whispered a command and Manley and his team burst into the living room. Two of the men were up and out of their chairs in seconds, scrabbling to get away from the machine guns and the copper with the mad glint in his eye. The other two couldn't move, rooted to the sofa, mouths slack with fear.

Manley dragged them to the middle of the room, cuffed them with relish and laughed as the men began their protests. He laughed again when he realised that Andrew Falkirk must be upstairs, being filmed.

'Got you now, Falkirk,' he yelled at the ceiling, spinning the last one around and pushing him to the end of the line. 'You won't get a clever barrister to overturn this conviction.' He grinned. 'You won't terrify the witness into withdrawing their statement this time, you sick shit.' He stopped and eyed all four men, now standing silent in a terrified row. He realised that the other members of his team were uncomfortable with his outburst, but he didn't care. He felt jubilant. 'You couldn't pick this lot out in a paedo parade, could you?' He looked at the PC guarding the door. 'They look so normal. Makes it worse, somehow, that they could be someone's dad or husband. Let's get the bastards locked up. Collect all their belongings.'

He turned to the other officer. 'PC Salter,' he said, 'call for one of the vans. It'll be a long night in the cells for this lot, and then a nice stretch at Her Majesty's pleasure.'

In the upstairs bedroom, the situation was different. Lake peered through the narrow gap the boy had left. A little girl was on the bed with a large, jowly man whom they took to be Andrew Falkirk. The blonde woman, Irina Akis, was leaning over the side of the bed, holding the naked child still. A film camera was balanced on a tripod next to her. He could just see the bare leg of one of the older girls, perched on a tapestry cushion, and in front of her, the wailing boy. Irina shouted over her shoulder for Grigor, but her voice died in her throat as the door slammed open and the barrel of a gun came through it. The man on the bed cowered away, covering his nakedness and shrivelling erection with a lace cushion.

Irina acted instantly, and in her own interest. She dropped the little girl, picked up the movie camera and threw it as hard as she could at the door, crashing it shut onto Lake's hand. Then she slipped into the bathroom and out through the casement window onto the eaves. Pressing herself flat, she slid down through the shadows at the rear of the house.

In the yard, DC Sam Knowles had jumped into the Mercedes driver's seat and started the engine, intending to drive it to the station for forensic examination. He was trying to put it into reverse when his door was wrenched open and he was dragged by his hair from the seat. Irina was in the car and had slammed the door shut before he could even raise a shout.

Sam scrambled to his feet and ran to stand in front of the van, waving his arms and yelling to attract attention. 'Stop!' he yelled at Irina. Then, wildly, 'Someone stop her. She can't get away!'

Up in the attic bedroom, Garrett barked orders at Team Three.

Officers ran from the fields towards the revving Mercedes.

'What the hell is she trying to do?' Sam screamed.

What Akis was doing was taking the initiative, thought Garrett, as he saw her make a tight reversing left turn that took the front side panel off the Mercedes on the rear bumper of a parked car. She drove straight through the hedge, scattering Team Three and forcing the van into a sharp left as she bumped her way over the ploughed field towards the lane. Sam could hear the DVDs sliding around in the back of the van and slamming against the sides.

'She's getting away,' he wailed, his anguish clear in his voice.

Garrett barked at sniper Two, 'Suspect escaping in black van. Take out her tyres. I repeat, disable the vehicle. DC Knowles, get a grip, man. You're not helping by stating the obvious.'

Irina judged the low stone wall in front of her. If she could smash her way through it, she could be gone before they were even in their cars. She accelerated towards the wall and was thrown hard against the steering wheel as the front of the van buckled against the ancient granite. She reversed and went again, and again. After the third ramming, enough wall collapsed to let her roll over the top of the rubble, engine roaring. She turned a crazily sharp left and felt the back tyre blow as she straightened up. She fought to control the steering as the DVDs and the loose recorders smashed against the van wall. She wasn't stopping for anybody. This was her last trip. She was going to Sweden to be with her child. She renewed her efforts to control the veering van and get out onto the lane.

Stuck in the small attic bedroom, Oliver remembered that Dan and Sally were on their way.

She rang Sally.

'Yes Ma'am?' came the calm voice.

'Where are you?' Oliver shook. She could see the Merc breaking through the wall and turning onto the lane.

'Almost there, I can see the Farmer's place. What's happening?'

'Sally,' Oliver shouted. 'Get out of the car, now!' Sally stared at the phone and up the lane. Dan looked over at her.

'What?'

'Oliver says we have to...'

At that moment the battered van came barrelling towards them, swerving across the lane on blown tyres and smacking into the hedges like a drunk in a pub toilet. Dan reacted on impulse. He braked, slapped the seatbelt holders and pushed Sally out of her door. Then, he slewed the car sideways across the lane and threw himself out of the passenger door as the Mercedes ploughed into the driver's side of the Audi.

Oliver watched from the window. She screamed a helpless 'No!' as she saw what Hellier had done.

Garrett didn't react. He was still watching the van. He saw the door open and a slight figure stagger out and limp off across the field. 'She's still alive, ma'am. She's going to try to run for it. Just give the order.'

Oliver didn't hesitate. How could this foreign bitch come into her city and hurt children and hurt her people?

'Shoot her, Tom.'

Sniper One took two shots to bring her down as she was weaving all over the field. One to the thigh, and one to the shoulder. She limped another six feet before her knees buckled and she dropped.

Garrett yelled. 'Get out there and arrest her, Team 3. Don't hang about for Christ's sake!'

Bennett and Larcombe were first out onto the lane. When they reached the crash site there was nowhere to pass, so they abandoned their patrol cars and ran. The wreckage of the van and the destroyed Audi filled the entire lane. Bennett picked up a piece of the Mercedes' offside panel and used it to break open a hole in the hedge large enough to let them squeeze through. The scene on the other side was a disaster.

Bill Larcombe would say later he felt his heart stop when he saw Sally Ellis lying on the ground a few metres away.

He groaned, 'No, not Sally. Not her as well.'

He knelt beside her and felt for a pulse. To his relief it was strong, but she was bleeding from a wound on the back of her head. Had probably knocked herself out. He took off his jacket and used it to cradle her head. Sally opened her eyes slowly.

'I've been having such a weird dream,' she said to him, her voice high and shaky. 'Why am I lying on the ground?'

'You've just had a little car accident. Don't worry, soon get you sorted out.' He rang Oliver and gave her the good news before he rang for an ambulance. Then he stood and looked round for Ben. And where was the boss?

The force of the Mercedes hitting the Audi had not been so very great. The van was hardly under control and could not have accelerated much. However, it had been moving fast enough to destroy the driver's side of the car and shunt it into the hedge.

Dan was lying at the side of the road, his legs trapped under the passenger-side door. He hadn't quite made it. He was stroking what was left of the bonnet. His beautiful car, ruined. Ben Bennett was standing next to him, watching the tears slip down his boss's face.

'I think you might have a bit of concussion, boss,' he was saying, 'it's only a car.'

Chapter 37

Date: Wednesday 25th April Time: 22.13 Exeter Road Police Station

DC Sam Knowles sat on a chair in the corner, watching the night sergeant processing the men arrested at the scene. Superintendent Oliver had asked him to oversee the process, and to come back up to the main office once they were all safely locked up for the night. It was too late to do anything other than charge them and put them in a cell, but Sam was happy with that.

Colin White had agreed to take an extra shift to charge the men and sent one of the night-shift boys to the hospital to guard the woman, Akis, who was injured but alive.

'How you doing, Sam?' he asked.

Sam winced. He was in quite a lot of pain where the Latvian mad woman had yanked out a lump of hair and some of his scalp, but he was bearing his injuries stoically.

'I'm alright, Sarge, thanks for asking.'

'Only you're looking a bit peaky, lad. Were you okay out there?'

Sam nodded. 'Yeah, it was quite exciting, actually. 'Specially when the snipers took out the foreign woman - hoo wee!'

He'd been out in the field and done well, apart from the embarrassing bit where he may have got a bit upset.

Lizzie popped down with a mug of tea and smiled at him. 'You'll need to be de-briefed before you go home, Sam,' she said. That felt good, too.

'And how was the new boss out in the field?' asked Colin.

Sam contemplated Inspector Hellier's heroics and shook his head in wonderment. The man was a maniac. 'You know, Sarge, he looks a bit wimpy, but there are balls of steel under that smooth exterior. He was brilliant, saved the day.'

And a shooting, too. What a night.

The area car dropped Dan off at the front entrance to the station. He had sent Sally home once they had escaped from the hospital. She had concussion and wasn't making much sense. He touched the plaster on the front of his forehead as he limped his way to the main office on throbbing stockinged feet. He figured he would live. He was thankful that it was very late and there were few people around. He couldn't have explained the depth of his tiredness if he'd tried.

He could hear raised voices as he drew near the interview rooms. The angry tones of Alan Braithwaite were easy to identify through the walls. Dan looked through the window. Jenna was sitting hunched on a chair, turned away from the table, playing with a lock of hair and humming to herself. Stoned, he guessed.

Alan Braithwaite was arguing with Bill Larcombe and Lizzie Singh. The other person in the room was, Dan supposed, a social worker. He sighed. He'd wanted a few minutes to gather himself before this confrontation.

Braithwaite swung round as Dan entered the room and lurched towards him.

'Been drinking, Mr Braithwaite?' Dan asked and dodged round him, making for a chair on the other side of the table. The guy was intimidating enough when he was sober, There was no way Dan was going to stand up to him in a confined space, when he was drunk. And with feet that resembled tenderised steak, he wasn't getting into a fight with anybody. 'Why don't you sit down and tell me what's happening?'

He nodded to the other officers. Larcombe moved to stand next to the door, and Lizzie took the other empty seat next to Jenna. Braithwaite didn't move. He swayed backwards and forwards as if he was on a ship.

The social worker attempted to speak but Braithwaite went straight over her. 'Why is my daughter here? Why won't you tell me what's going on? Why can't I take her home with me?'

Larcombe looked over at Dan and shrugged.

'Okay, this is what we do,' Dan said. 'Lizzie, take Jenna and the social worker next door and make them a drink. Jenna may want a snack or something, too. Then Mr Braithwaite and I can have a proper chat.'

As Dan spoke, Braithwaite moved towards the table and leaned on it, glowering over him.

'Would you like a coffee, too?' Dan asked, and looked up into Braithwaite's face. 'Have a seat, Mr Braithwaite. I'll explain what has happened to your daughter, I promise. No messing about.' He gestured towards a chair and waited for Braithwaite to sit.

The girl left the room with her head down, led by Lizzie Singh and the social worker.

Dan allowed Braithwaite time to sort himself out while he tried to find a way to tell this bereaved father what he suspected his youngest daughter had done. He wished Sally hadn't been injured, she was so good at this stuff.

Braithwaite leant back in his chair. He'd folded his arms across his chest and crossed one leg over the other thigh. His foot banged a regular angry rhythm against the metal leg of the chair.

'First, can you tell me how Jed Abrams came to know your two girls?'

Braithwaite looked up under his black fringe. 'Youth group they go to.'

'Not the singing competition?'

'Nah, that was done at Christmas. They've been going since last September on a Thursday night.' He paused. 'Jenna's been going on a Wednesday, too, sometimes.' He put his head in his hands. 'This is to do with Jed Abrams, isn't it? I should have got the slimy bastard when I had the chance. I always knew there was something wrong about him.'

Dan watched the colour rise in the man's cheeks as his voice got louder and harsher. He realised he was too tired to do this diplomatically.

'Mr Braithwaite, I wish I could make this easier, but I can't. Jenna has been the victim of child abuse. Possibly not Abrams himself, but men he knew.'

Alan Braithwaite stopped in confusion. He didn't see the mug of coffee placed beside him, or register that Bill Larcombe had taken up his position once more near the door. He stared at Dan, his eyes angry and shocked.

'What do you mean? How?' He shook his head in disbelief. 'No. I'd know. I'm her father. I'd know if something was wrong.' He looked across at Dan again. 'It's not true. You've got the wrong girl.' He stood. 'You've made a terrible mistake, mate. I'll just collect Jenna and we'll go. It's late and she needs to get to bed.' He turned and made for the door.

'Mr Braithwaite, you have to listen to me.' Dan rose, too. 'We have just brought Jenna back from a house where my officers witnessed a younger child being abused. Jenna was in the room, too, Mr Braithwaite. Jenna had taken three other children with her to that house. She wasn't at Maddie's for tea. She went to Jed Abram's house, knowing what would happen there.' He raised his voice. 'Please sit down. There is more I have to tell you.'

Braithwaite looked longingly at the door. 'I don't want to hear any more crap talked about Jenna.'

'There is another reason why I can't let you take your daughter home tonight.' Braithwaite turned and stared. 'What? What's worse than this?'

Dan took a breath and blew it out through his lips. He couldn't think how to make this one easier either, 'This afternoon, an eye witness said they saw Jenna strangle Carly on Sunday at your house.'

Braithwaite coughed out an incredulous moan. 'What? What? Who said it?'

Dan ignored the question. 'We have to investigate that allegation. We have to keep Jenna in custody tonight. But she won't be here in the station. We'll take her to a secure children's home. She'll be quite safe, I assure you.'

Braithwaite had buckled back onto the chair at the mention of Carly's murder. He fixed on a spot above Dan's head and didn't move. The room fell silent.

Dan glanced across at Bill Larcombe. The sergeant shrugged. This kind of news took people in different ways.

'It is just an allegation Mr Braithwaite, but we have to investigate. You do understand that?'

'Can I get someone to give you a lift home?' Dan suggested. Braithwaite didn't move. 'Maybe you would like to see Jenna before you go? You can spend some more time with her tomorrow. We all need to get some sleep.' Still no response. Dan pushed on. 'Sergeant Larcombe will get one of the patrol cars to pop back to the station and give you a lift home.'

Larcombe rose and took Braithwaite's arm to lift him out of the chair. 'Come on, chum,' he said, 'no point in you hanging round here. We'll make sure Jenna is safe tonight.'

'Can you get the victim support woman on the phone and ask her to go round first thing tomorrow? She can bring him in.' Larcombe nodded and guided Braithwaite out.

Dan stood for a few minutes in the empty room, and swallowed two painkillers with the neglected mug of lukewarm coffee. His head hurt. The whole of his left side hurt. His feet and ankles hurt where he'd been pulled out from under the crushed wreck of his car. He was beyond exhausted. He didn't know how a person was supposed to react to the kind of news Braithwaite had just received, but what amounted to a catatonic trance seemed appropriate in the circumstances.

Forcing his body to respond, he limped to the adjoining room for his last task of the night. He smiled wearily at the duty solicitor as he followed him into the room.

There was no defiance left in Jenna Braithwaite's eyes. She looked like a thirteen year-old kid who had been caught doing something wrong, knees up to her chest, arms wrapped protectively around them, eyes huge in the pale face, holding onto Lizzie Singh's hand.

She looked behind him, 'Where's my dad?'

'I got a police officer to take him home, Jenna. He wasn't well.'

'Who's that?' She stared at the duty solicitor.

'He's a solicitor, here to make sure we all do this interview properly. He'll help you if you get stuck or don't know how to say something. He's called Paul Fowles.'

He indicated the social worker. 'This lady is …?' he shot an enquiring look at her.

'Kate Spicer.'

'Kate,' he nodded his thanks, 'will take you to a safe place for tonight, and you can see your dad tomorrow. He needs a bit of space at the moment.'

'Yeah, right,' said Jenna, 'space away from me, you mean.'

'Well, Jenna, you have to admit, tonight came as a shock to all of us.' He paused and scrutinised her face. Jenna looked away from him and shuffled her feet on the chair, knuckles white round her calves. The duty solicitor opened a legal pad and nodded.

'I want you to give me a statement regarding your involvement with Jed Abrams and the foreign woman. We need to know how you started going to see Jed Abrams, and why you kept on going. Okay?' There was no response.

'Is that okay, Jenna?' There was a reluctant nod of the head.

'Is Jed in trouble?' she asked.

Dan let out a reflexive snort of disbelief. 'What do you think?'

'He didn't make me do it. I wanted to.'

The social worker interrupted, 'Did Jed give you booze and ciggies?' Jenna looked at the floor. She nodded.

'Did he give you money, too?'

Jenna nodded again.

Lizzie Singh reached across and took the girl's hand. 'I bet he made you feel really grown up and special, didn't he?'

Jenna looked up at her, grateful to have someone there who could understand. 'Yeah, he did. I'm not clever or pretty like Carly, and I can't sing or anything, but he made me feel like I was…' she struggled for the word, 'beautiful.' She stopped, and looked at the floor again, blushing, conscious that she had said something so unbelievably stupid they would all laugh at her. But there was silence in the room, and they looked kind and were smiling at her. Maybe they did like her.

Kate Spicer started to gather her things.

'There is one more thing I have to talk to you about, Jenna,' Dan said, and the social worker sat down again. 'It's about the murder of your sister.'

The expression on Jenna's face was hard to read. Hunted rabbit was the closest he could get.

'Jenna, we spoke to Jamie May earlier today.'

Jenna stared at him but said nothing.

'He said that he was at your house on Sunday, and that he saw you and Carly arguing.'

'I already said that we argued. I said that to Sally.' Panic made her voice rise. The solicitor ruffled the legal pad as he turned a page.

'I know you did. But Jamie said it went a bit differently. He said that when he came into your bedroom, it was you who was strangling your sister. He said you did it, and he and Jed helped to hide the body.'

The girl's face went white. 'Jamie said that?'

He nodded, focussing on the girl and ignoring the glances being exchanged on the other side of the table.

Jenna's face showed utter betrayal. She thought for a few seconds, fighting some kind of internal battle, and then her head came up and she wailed through tears, 'I didn't kill her, Jamie did. He told me he'd kill me, too, if I said anything.' She looked round the table, hanging onto Lizzie's hand, tears pouring down her face. 'I didn't do it, I didn't do it. I want my dad.'

Dan took a minute while the two women did their best to calm the girl down. She subsided, sobbing into Kate Spicer's arms while

Lizzie brought more tissues. He glanced across at the solicitor who met his eyes with weary resignation.

'So, if Jamie's lying, can you tell us what actually happened, Jenna?'

'I did have a fight with Carly.' She sniffed and lifted her sleeves to show a long scratch mark on her arm, and bruises round both wrists. 'I ran off when Jamie got there because she let me go. I went for a walk but I was really mad and I wanted my phone back. I had to stop her showing Dad the... the pictures.' She swallowed. 'When I came back upstairs, Jamie was white as a sheet. He was on the landing. He said I had to help him get rid of her body. He killed her, not me. When I went in, she was just lying there, on the bed, not breathing or anything.' Jenna curled herself into the smallest ball she could on the cold metal chair and clung onto Kate Spicer, tears bleeding from her tightly squeezed eyes.

'What did you do then?'

Jenna shook her head from side to side, keening despair making her voice cracked and ragged. 'I didn't want to do it, but I had to. Jamie tried to wrap her up in my duvet and tie it up with my scarf, but he couldn't do it. And he was so angry. Shouting at me to do something. He said he would blame me and no one would believe me, and I'd have to go to prison. He said my mum left because I was so bad.'

Dan sat back in his chair, his earlier blithe acceptance of Jamie's story gnawing at him, acid in his stomach.

'So, what did you do?'

'I didn't know what to do.' She blew her nose hard on a tissue. 'Then, then I thought of Jed. He's got a van. I let Jamie ring Jed, and then he told me to go out and he would sort it out. He said I owed him, and he would be back. So I ran out, round to Maddie's. I was so scared. And when I came back, Carly'd gone. Like my mum. Just gone.'

The wracking sobs took over her whole body. Dan gave her a few minutes to calm down, guessing that the drugs in her system were beginning to wear off.

'Why was Jamie at your house yesterday, Jenna?'

She spoke through snot and tears, reluctance making her whisper. 'When he came on Sunday, me and Carly were arguing. She looked at my phone and saw…' She stopped.

'We know what was on there. Just tell us in your own words.'

'Pictures of me and Maddie. With some blokes. She said she'd tell dad

and I'd get put in a Home. She was always telling me what to do. I'd had enough of it.'

'What happened to your sister's phone?'

Jenna pulled out a phone from her jeans back pocket and placed it on the table, lining the edge of the phone up with the edge of the Formica. She kept her eyes down. 'This is her phone. It was mine that got broken in the fight. I chucked that one in the bin on Monday morning.'

'So, what did Jamie want?'

Her top lip curled. 'Money. He wanted my money. That I've earned.He saw it on the bed on Sunday. I think he would have killed me to get it, if dad hadn't walked in.' Jenna looked at the social worker. 'I was so scared. If he could kill Carly, he could kill me too.'

'Are you telling us everything, Jenna? It's really important that you do, otherwise, it's just your word against Jamie's.'

The girl nodded and dropped her head, and Dan watched the tears dripping off her nose onto the table-top.

Dan had pretty much believed Jamie May earlier in the day. It had fit his own understanding of the story so well, had fit into the pattern he had made. But now he saw holes in the boy's story, and feared that Jenna may well be telling the truth, and he could see that he had fallen into a basic, trainee's trap. He hadn't followed the evidence. He hadn't questioned Jamie closely enough. The stupid solicitor had got him on edge with all the objections to keeping him in custody. No, he amended, he couldn't blame her, it was his own fault. He'd rushed it, wanting confirmation of what he already thought, and that's when he'd made mistakes.

Sally had tried to warn him, she knew something was wrong, but he'd ridden straight over her.

He'd also let the boy go home without putting up a decent fight against the scary Vanessa Redmond, because he had so desperately wanted to get to Abrams' house and be involved in the action. The place where he thought it was all happening, when in reality it was all happening right under his nose. And all he'd gained from rushing to Abrams' house, was an injured sergeant, bruising to his feet and a destroyed car. He bit the tide of self-criticism off before it became a torrent, and brought the interview to a close.

'Jenna, thank you for telling us what happened.' He caught the girl's desperate gaze and tried a smile. 'You've done the right thing. Jamie would have let you take the blame, so don't feel bad. We'll protect you, and get you home as soon as we can.'

He glanced at the social worker over the girl's head. 'Why don't you take Jenna with you now, Kate? She looks like she needs some sleep.

'I'll see you in the morning, Jenna. Your dad will be here, too.' He touched her arm, not a gesture that came naturally to him, and helped her up from her chair. The poor kid looked wrecked.

'Don't worry. If you have told us the truth, you have nothing to worry about at all. Do you understand?'

Jenna didn't seem to register what he said. She'd gone past the stage of being able to respond. She noticed that Dan had no shoes on and stared at his feet as Kate Spicer and the solicitor walked her out into the corridor. Dan shuffled them back under his chair. They were still throbbing. He let his head drop into his hands and blew out a long breath.

'Are you alright, sir?' Dan had forgotten Lizzie was still there. He shook his head.

'No, Lizzie, I'm not alright. I'm a total bloody pillock, that's what I am.' He almost smiled to see the shock on her face. 'Don't worry, I'll be fine. I think I've finally got it. See Ms Spicer and Jenna out of the building, will you? And then go home. I need you here in the morning.'

Dan made his painful way up the stairs to Oliver's office. It was close to midnight but he knew she'd still be there, writing up the shooting and arrests at Abrams' house. He was just about to add another little twist to the tale of his incompetence that wouldn't cheer her up at all.

The main corridor was dark, lit only by the red emergency lighting. There were sounds of a vacuum cleaner from one of the offices and he could hear the cleaners singing and chatting as they dusted the conference suite. Light spilled from Oliver's room. The door was half open. Dan knocked and went in. Oliver was leaning back in her chair with her legs crossed at the ankle resting on top of the desk. She was on the phone. She waved as Dan entered and pointed to the corner of the room, where the blessed Stella had left two sandwiches in plastic containers and a thermos of coffee. He realised he hadn't eaten for hours. Funny, how cheese and chutney on brown could make a totally crap day more bearable. He chomped on the sandwich and swigged it down with strong coffee, feeling the light-headedness recede a little.

Oliver finished her call.

'Dan, you've done a fantastic job.' She smiled one of her rare smiles. 'We've got the Latvians, broken up a porn ring and you're now going to tell me that Jenna Braithwaite has confessed to her sister's murder.'

The last bit of sandwich stuck in Dan's throat and he had to take a slurp of coffee to get it down before he could speak. He felt the heat of blood rushing into his face. A dead giveaway, as usual.

'The thing is, ma'am, I have spoken to Jenna, and I now don't think she did it. She says it was Jamie, and that he threatened to kill her too if she told anyone what had happened. Having spent time with Jenna , I believe her. I don't believe she can lie as convincingly as he did. Sergeant Ellis was right. I reckon he could lie for Britain, though, the little shit. He fooled me with all his bluster, and it was a good story. Just not the right one.'

He risked a glance at Oliver, who sat staring at him open-mouthed. 'It makes more sense, ma'am. She's such a skinny little thing, I can't see her having the strength to hold her bigger sister down long enough to kill her. It points back to our original hypothesis, that the motive was jealousy.' He put both hands palm down onto the desk top. 'I should have thought it through before acting, ma'am. It's obvious now.'

Oliver sat very still while she thought this revelation through.

'Tell me Jamie is still in custody.'

Dan took a deep breath. Here it comes. 'No, ma'am, I agreed to let him go home for the night with his mother.'

She gave him a look of such incredulity he almost winced.

'I'm so sorry. I wanted to get out to the Abrams' place and I wasn't thinking straight. I couldn't think what to charge him with under the pressure of the moment. It was a bad judgement call.'

'You can say that again, Tonto.' She thought for a moment longer. He could see her working out, yet again, how to rescue his cock-up. 'Well, as the boy probably thinks he's in the clear, we just have to hope he's at home in bed. Give me the phone number.'

He shuffled through his notebook and read it out. They in silence as Oliver pressed the speakerphone button.

'*Hello?*

'Mrs May? DCS Oliver here. Sorry to disturb you so late but I just need to check that Jamie is safely tucked up in bed. Would you be an angel and just pop in to see for me?'

'Why can't you leave us alone? He hasn't done anything, has he?' Sandra replied, but they could hear her walking the phone upstairs and opening a door.

'Jamie? Jamie, love?' There were grunts, and the sound of Sandra walking the phone back downstairs. *'He's fast asleep, alright?'*

'Thanks so much, Mrs May. See you in the morning.' She put the phone down and mimed wiping her brow. 'Phew! I'll get the first day shift to pick him up at six and have him ready for us when we get in. What about Jenna?'

'She's gone to Willow House for the night. I haven't told her dad that she didn't do it, yet. He was almost catatonic when he left and I…' He faltered, 'I don't want to tell him anything else in case it changes again, poor bastard.' He could feel exhaustion pricking at his eyes. 'Ma'am, I'm so sorry. I messed up, again. I should have taken more notice of what Jamie May was doing. Why he was so keen to get to Westlake's place, why he hurt Claire Quick.'

'And?'

'I think he told Westlake that he had killed Carly to hurt the guy. He taunted him just for revenge. But when he heard Westlake talking to Claire Quick, he panicked and assumed he would tell her his story. Thing is, I doubt Westlake would have told anybody, because he was by then implicated in under-age sex.'

He thought for a bit longer, sorting the facts, linking the gut feelings. Oliver poured herself a coffee and stood by the window, staring out into the darkness.

'Or,' he struggled to order his thoughts, 'maybe he told Westlake that Jenna had done it? Setting up his cover story. And that was why Westlake escaped from hospital and went round to the Braithwaite's earlier today. He wanted to hurt Jenna.' He paused and looked up at his boss. 'It makes sense, doesn't it?'

'And it was Jenna who arranged for Jed Abrams to move the body?'

'Yes. Well, she set it up. Jamie arranged it. Abrams has a van. No wonder he was so scared when we started nosing round. He needed to do something so that Jenna was available for the filming tonight. He was just protecting his investment. Oh, and Jenna said Jamie was at her house because he wanted the money she made from the films. She was scared half to death that he was going to kill her too.' Dan paused, checking his phone for texts. 'Sam located Abrams' van, by the way, it's in the multi-storey under the cinema. Reckon it will give us the evidence we're looking for.'

'Right.' Her face cleared as she turned to face him. 'So stop moping. We're almost there. We've just got to arrest Jamie May and get him into custody in the morning. We've got everybody else where we want them, long as you're sure about Jenna.' She gave him a half smile. 'You have been a bloody idiot at times but things aren't always neat and tidy, Dan, however much I'd like them to be. We deal with real people in all their muck and filth and weirdness, but if we get the right murderer, or robber or rapist, then we're earning our keep. So cheer up, you've done a great job, and sod off home.'

Dan pushed himself out of the chair and hobbled to the door.

Oliver watched him trying to walk with no shoes on.

'Actually,' she said, 'I'll give you a lift home, if you like. I hear you trashed your car earlier?'

Chapter 38

Date: Thursday 27th April Time: 06:15 Jamie May's home

A flock of squabbling sparrows outside the bedroom window had woken Sandra May at five thirty. She lay on her side with the pillow clamped over her head, contemplating cutting the tree down, and trying not to listen to the row. She then tried not to listen to the squeal of brakes, the running up the path and the banging on her front door. Nobody needed to tell Sandra who was banging. They were shouting it at her through her letterbox.

There was no sound from Jamie's room as she tottered past and made for the stairs. He must have been exhausted last night.

The officer at the door did not smile. Sandra couldn't understand what he wanted. 'I'm going to bring Jamie into the station myself, later,' she protested. 'It's not even six thirty yet. You'll wake the neighbours.'

'There's been a change of plan, love. I'll just go and get Jamie out of bed. Why don't you get some clothes on and you can come with us?'

'What d'you mean, a change of plan?' She clutched the stair post for support. 'What's happened?'

The officer pushed past her towards the stairs. 'New evidence, Mrs May. We need to ask young Jamie a few more questions.' He opened the only closed door on the landing and shook the lump on the bed. The lump of rolled up clothes, which were definitely not Jamie, fell apart under his hand.

Sandra May stood in the doorway. She could not work out what was happening. 'Where is he?' she cried, looking wildly about her as if her son was playing some sort of practical joke. 'Jamie?'

The ringing was a distant thrum that settled into the same beat as the banging in his head. His body felt like a struck bell, reverberating with pain. Dan reached across the bed for the phone and answered,

'Mmmm?' He knew words were probably in there somewhere, if he could just have another couple of days to find them in the mush that had once been his brain.

As he listened to the duty sergeant speak, Dan sat up and swung his legs off the bed. He ended the call with a request for someone to pick him up. Looking at the livid bruises and swelling round his feet and ankles, he reckoned driving was out of the question for a while. Which was good, as he hadn't got anything to drive.

The news that Jamie May had run away did not come as a surprise. He'd known he'd made a mistake in letting the boy go as soon as he'd agreed to it, but he'd pushed the intuition away, and he'd had the same sinking feeling in the gut when he'd had to tell Oliver what he'd done the night before. They had all underestimated the guile of Jamie May. Sixteen years old, clever enough to pull the wool over all their eyes, and amoral enough to allow another child to take the blame for his own crime. He guessed he might have to resign if they didn't find the boy soon.

'Great career, so far, Daniel. Great, but short,' he muttered as he limped towards the bathroom.

A shave, a shower, two paracetamol followed by two ibuprofen, a mug of coffee and four slices of toast later, he was ready to be picked up. Whether or not he was ready to face the day was a different matter. He'd not been able to get his shoes back onto his swollen feet, and one of them was ripped anyway, so he was in an open-necked shirt, jeans and trainers. Felt liberating, like "dress-down Friday" must feel for normal people.

The buzzer rang.

Sally waited for him at the foot of the stairs. Dan examined her as he descended, clutching the rail. She looked alright if you ignored the bandage round her head. And if her sides were feeling like his, after rolling out of a moving car, then she was covering it well. You never saw this on the telly, he thought. Of course, they were real men, just bounced back, never felt pain, never got bruised... He greeted Sally with a wry smile.

'How you doing?'

'You know, boss,' she said squinting up at him, 'when you made me liaison for the Braithwaites at the start of this op, I was so miffed. I wanted to be part of the main action. Now, chatting to people on a sofa is becoming a very attractive option…' She grinned. 'No, I'll be fine. After all, we've caught them, haven't we?' Her smile slipped when she saw Dan's face fall.

She sat with him in the back of the area car so he could explain the changed situation to her on the brief journey to the station. She nodded and listened and looked relieved. He was grateful that she didn't say "I told you so".

Everybody was gathered in the incident room by eight am. Oliver sat at the head of the table and indicated that Dan should sit to her left. He hobbled to the chair and sank into it, smiling at the sympathetic winces from around the table.

'We'll keep this short and sweet. We have two members of the Latvian paedophile ring in custody and they are co-operating fully. The third member and alleged leader of the gang was shot down yesterday and is under armed guard in hospital. We will be liaising with the Latvian police through Interpol concerning her future. Jed Abrams is also in custody and will be prosecuted for his role in this sordid mess.

'We have Jenna Braithwaite in secure accommodation. Yesterday, the girl said that she did not kill her sister, and named Jamie May as the murderer, and he certainly looks a better fit for the murder than she does. She will undergo a formal interview this morning.'

She glanced down the table at Hellier. 'Unfortunately we allowed Jamie May to leave the station last night under the care of his mother. He duped his mother into believing he was sleeping in bed, but has disappeared. I have all patrol cars out looking for him.

'Ben,' she turned to the sergeant. 'Drop evidence collection for now and co-ordinate the uniforms. Sam and Bill, I need you on the phones too, and pinch a couple of people from Team One, their investigation is nearly wrapped up. Check the bus station, train station, on-ramp for the motorway, and the motorway services. First priority is to catch this boy and bring him in.'

She caught Adam Foster's eye. 'Adam, go back to the school and see if he has any friends where he could be hiding out. Check if any of his friends are absent today.

'Lastly, thanks to Mr Braithwaite, we have re-captured Miles Westlake, who is in a weakened state in hospital. He was apparently mumbling something about Jamie and Jenna, but he collapsed on Braithwaite's floor. Inspector Hellier and I will go over to the hospital now and take his statement. If Jamie May did confess to Carly's murder at some point over the weekend, then Miles Westlake is a key witness and must be protected. It may well be that he is still in danger from May.'

Having finished her summary, Oliver cracked a smile which transformed the sharp planes and angles of her face into something that almost made her pretty. 'We are so very nearly there, folks. You have done a fantastic job so far and we have a two-case puzzle almost solved and put to bed in four days. Must be a record.'

She indicated the Mind Map on the wall. 'Look how close we were. We all knew the poor lass had to know her killer, and that jealousy was a motive. We just needed to work out who killed her. And, although I still have an open mind, the fact that Jamie May has scarpered pushes me towards fancying him as the guilty party.'

She took in the assembled team, one at a time. 'Last night was handled cleanly and went as well as we could have hoped. All the children are safe. It was nice to see some of the oldies back on active duty, too!' She grinned over at the flowerpot men. 'So, focus and get cracking. The sooner we catch Jamie May, the sooner we should be able to wrap this one up. Drinks tomorrow night are on Dan.'

Dan had the grace to smile, but he was painfully aware that Oliver had stepped in and taken over his investigation properly this time. Couldn't blame her. The team broke into pairs and began their day's work, but he just sat there, not sure what his role was going to be for the rest of the investigation.

'Come on, Hopalong,' Oliver said. 'Let's find out what Westlake knows a.s.a.p. and get back here to watch the formal interview with Jenna Braithwaite.'

'Are you going to let her dad in with her?'

'Still your case, Dan. What do you think?'

Dan felt a little surge of hope. 'No, I think he should be outside. He can watch, but he's bound to be an emotional wreck and he would upset everybody. We need Jenna calm and co-operative.'

'Exactly, which is why Sally is leading the interview and we are staying outside.' She sighed. 'It's a difficult one. Jenna did groom those other kids and persuade them to take part. And she did hide Carly's phone. And she did help to arrange the removal of her sister's body.'

'She also withheld information which could have led to the arrest of Jamie May on the day of the murder.'

'Dear God,' muttered Oliver, 'she's thirteen years old. What kind of future will there be for a messed up kid like that?'

Jamie had spent an uncomfortable three hours under the dripping tree at the bottom of Jenna's garden. He'd left his house at four am, carrying only the things he needed in a rucksack. He had been sitting in one place since then. He had tried throwing stones at her window and texting her, but he'd had no response from either tactic. He knew that running away was risky, but he couldn't think of what else to do. And to run, he needed money. The one person he knew who had money was Jenna. He'd seen rolls of it in the box on the bed. The one in which she had a picture of her mum and other stupid little things that were precious to her. He'd never keep a picture of his dad in a box under the bed. Might be tempted to keep his dad in a box though, if he knew where he was.

Jamie tossed the back door key in his hand. He'd found it under a stone near the back gate. People are so dumb, he thought. The trouble was he was too scared to enter the house without Jenna. He had a feeling her dad would kill him if he saw him in there again. He didn't think Jenna was stupid enough to squeal, but her dad was already suspicious, and coming across him in the house would be pretty bad.

Jamie decided on the same tactic he had used at his own house. He moved as close to the back door as he could, sank behind an overgrown gooseberry bush and watched for movement.

Minutes later, Alan Braithwaite rolled into the kitchen, yawning and scratching his stomach. He drank tea and fried bacon and eggs. Jamie could neither hear, taste nor smell the food cooking, but all his senses were as alert as if he was standing next to the man.

Jamie noticed he was salivating and realised he hadn't eaten since yesterday. Where *was* Jenna?

He really needed that money. London was looking favourite. Kids got lost there all the time. And the roll of cash would give him enough to get a place to live and, with a bit of luck, a job. Although, he could always busk. He thought of his guitar, stuck at Westlake's house because of that bloody Ninja policewoman. Maybe he could pick it up too if he was quick about it, then over to the motorway services and hitch a ride.

Alan Braithwaite finished his breakfast and disappeared from view. Ten minutes later, Jamie saw him open the bathroom window to let out steam. He was tempted to have a go then - just slip in through the back door, into the bedroom and out. Only take a couple of minutes. No, too risky. Braithwaite could come out at any time. Better to wait. He was obviously getting ready to go out somewhere, which would be even better.

Jamie dumped his rucksack under the shrub and padded over towards the back corner of the house, waiting for the front door to slam. After another interminable wait, it did.

Braithwaite wasn't driving his own car, though. He climbed into a small hatchback driven by a woman Jamie had never seen before. It didn't matter. It was time to move.

He unlocked the back door and slipped into the kitchen, leaving the door ajar, and ran up the stairs to Jenna's room. He had her keepsake box on the bed and the money in his pocket when he heard a noise, a key in the lock of the front door. Jamie froze. He heard Braithwaite's voice in the hall, shouting back to the woman in the car outside.

'A blue folder? Can't see it. What the..?' He'd seen the open back door. Jamie stared around him in panic. There was no way out except to force his way past Braithwaite, and he didn't fancy his chances there.

He made a dash for Carly's room as it faced the back of the house. He could jump out of the window and still get away. He was bound to be faster than the old geezer. He got no further than two steps outside the bedroom door when he heard heavy boots pounding up the stairs two at a time.

Braithwaite leapt at the boy and brought him to his knees, pulling the legs from under him and squatting on his back. Then, as if Jamie were just a plastic kid's toy, Braithwaite flipped him over and punched him in the head, shouting and screaming his rage and grief at the boy until Jamie stopped trying to fight and lay still, eyes huge in his terrified, bloodied face.

The Victim Support worker organised the police car to pick up Jamie May. She helped Alan Braithwaite to wash his hands and dry his tears, and guided him out of the house and into her little car. He was calmer by the time they reached the station.

Whatever the police or the clever lawyers might say about Jenna, Braithwaite knew he had caught the killer of his daughter.

Chapter 39

Date: Thursday 27th April Time: 08:43 Royal Devon & Exeter Hospital

Dan felt tricked. Oliver had driven him straight to A and E and made him sit in the queue to have his feet looked at again while she interviewed Westlake on her own. He had to admit, though, that just a short while later he was walking better because the tight bandages supported his feet and ankles, and were helping to reduce the swelling.

He knew that most officers would be relaxing and having a week off after injuring themselves on a job, but that he just had to be there. It was his first case, and he couldn't let it go, even if he had made a total bollocks of it.

And Oliver had understood. That was why she had insisted on him going with her this morning. She knew he wouldn't argue when she made him get his feet sorted out. They had given him some decent painkillers, too, which were also helping.

He had a reflective moment when he thought about how his boss back at the Met would have reacted to his gross stupidity, and was suddenly thankful that he had moved home.

Oliver had put her trust in him twice now, when all the evidence had pointed the other way. As they walked back to the car, he promised himself he would be a better policeman. He would learn from this.

'My interview with Miles Westlake was frustrating and, ultimately, sad,' Oliver said as they walked back to her car. 'Jamie May had indeed told Westlake that he had killed Carly. He also added, just to twist the knife, that Carly was sickened by Westlake and had decided to tell her father.'

'Nice,' said Dan, still amazed at his own gullibility, but unsurprised that Westlake had fallen for Jamie's lies.

'That isn't all. Jamie told him Carly had posted stories about their affair on Facebook, and that she and her friends were laughing at him behind his back. Then, after he heard Westlake and Claire Quick talking, and he had hit her to stop her going to the police, he had completely changed his story and told Westlake that actually, it was Jenna who had killed her sister out of jealousy.' She shook her head in disbelief. 'It's all potential rubbish that any sensible person would have checked out and laughed off, or investigated further. But, of course, Westlake was devastated at Carly's death and not thinking straight at all.'

Dan interrupted, 'Hence the suicide attempt?'

'Yes, and a weird belief that God had spared him to kill Jenna so that then he could join Carly in heaven. Poor sod's a basket case. I don't think he'll see daylight for some time.'

'Hard to feel sorry for him, though.'

Oliver looked thoughtful. 'Hmm, maybe.'

Her phone rang while she was driving back to the station. She answered it, nodded, and made a few 'Hmms' and 'Uh-huhs'.

Dan was trying to get his own phone out of his jeans pocket when she pulled over into a layby, turned to him and flashed that rare, brilliant smile once again.

'We've got Jamie May, Dan. We've got him. Well, rather Alan Braithwaite got him trying to nick money from Jenna's bedroom. Apparently he had hundreds of pounds on him.'

Dan struggled to process the information for a second, and then he felt the warm glow that, for a day or two, he had thought would never be his again. He smiled back at his boss, 'Thank Christ for that,' he said and he laughed, and banged on the dashboard in a little fanfare.

Chapter 40

Date: Thursday 27th April Time: 09:57 Exeter Road Police Station

Jamie had been put in and left in the same interview room he had been in the day before. There was a uniformed cop standing just outside the door. Jamie couldn't see the point of setting a guard. He was hardly likely to get through a whole police station full of fuzz, without getting caught.

He felt his nose. It was squashy and there was dried blood inside that was itching. He'd had enough nosebleeds as a kid to know that he mustn't mess with the clotting, but the temptation was overwhelming, especially as his eyes wouldn't stop leaking everywhere, and he needed to blow his nose. He took a huge, juddering breath.

Alone in the stuffy room, Jamie picked away at his feelings for Carly as he picked away at the scab she had caused on his arm. He'd had to bury those feelings deep when he took her to the woods, but they rose up now, like the monsters that had haunted his childish dreams. He shuddered to think of Sunday night. A worm of horror writhing through his body set him squirming on the chair. The feel of her. The weight of her. The lolling head. The beautiful black hair dragging in the mud. That disgusting paedo's hairy hands picking her up, touching her, looking at her with his filthy pervert eyes.

And he, what did he do? Left her alone with the dead birds in the dirt for anybody to find. Another huge breath juddered out of him.

He'd had to have it out with her on Sunday; he hadn't been able to let it go. Couldn't let it go after she had shown him up on

Saturday night, and thrown his love back in his face like that. It hammered in his brain and wouldn't give him any peace. Why? Why would she make him feel so small? It wasn't right to treat him like that. She really was sleeping with Westlake, and that hurt, that really hurt. He'd had to go round and sort it out with her.

Carly had been in Jenna's room when he'd arrived. He could hear the shouting from outside the house. Carly had been screaming, 'What have you done Jenna? Where did the money come from? Oh my God, look at these pictures. He's a dirty pervert! I knew he was. I'm telling dad.'

Going mad at her, saying over and over she had to stop or she would tell her dad. He had run upstairs, but they were going at it, shouting and scratching, like girls do. That's when he saw all the money lying on the bed. Whose money? Where from? He was staring at the money when Jenna let go of Carly's arms, and legged it past him, leaving him stupidly staring in the doorway. When he looked up at Carly, she was using the phone. Ringing him. Ringing Westlake. And that was it. The final insult.

Hit her then, he did. Smacked her head - bang, bang, bang against the door. She made him do it. Making him feel small. Too small for her. Made her drop the fucking phone - no ringing him. Smashed the phone - glass all over. Crackling onto the floor. He could still feel his arm round her throat - squeezing and squeezing. I'm strong now, strong now, Carly. Squeezing and squeezing, kneeling on her back, bending her head back - give in, give in, give in. Bitch! Bitch! Until she had stopped fighting. One slow dragging breath and she just lay there, still.

He hadn't meant to kill her. A boy wouldn't have died so easily.

He choked back snot, blood and tears and focussed his lost eyes onto the red weal of the scratch on his arm. He bit down where the scratch burned, sucking at the blood. She was in the scratch, taunting him, and he had to rub, to rub, scrub at it until she was gone ... until she left him alone ... until the pain stopped.

Through the window, Hellier watched the slow disintegration of the boy's fragile poise as he waited for the solicitor to arrive.

No sneaking in for a quick chat now, everything had to be done by the book. Hard to believe that the sobbing wreck behind the window, was a vicious, conniving little killer.

Vanessa Redmond bustled down the corridor. She seemed subdued this morning, lacking her usual peremptory bluster. 'It seems you were right, Inspector, you should have kept him in overnight. Still, no harm done, eh?'

Dan glanced sideways at her. 'No harm if you don't count him being beaten up by the girl's father as harm.'

He saw her frown. 'Don't worry, Miss Redmond,' he said before she got going, 'I don't blame you. You were just doing your job. It was my fault. I should never have allowed him out of the building. That won't happen again on my watch, I can assure you.'

Her raised eyebrow suggested he had made an enemy, but, frankly, he didn't care.

'Where's Mrs May?' she asked.

'She doesn't want to be in the interview, so she's in the little ante-room with a cup of tea. Shall we go in?'

When they opened the door, the boy was slumped over the table, sobbing like a child. He lifted his head when he saw Vanessa Redmond.

'I never meant to kill her, Miss. I loved her. She fought so hard and I didn't know...I didn't know she couldn't breathe.'

Jed Abrams sat in the Interview Room. He leant his elbows on the table and joined his palms as if in prayer.

Dan observed Abrams through the window. Left it a bit late to ask for divine guidance, mate, he thought. Oliver arrived in the wake of the same duty solicitor that had appeared for Jenna the night before. Dan nodded at him, 'Busy couple of days for you, Paul.'

'Yeah, but got a feeling this one's going to be a damn sight more fun than that poor kid last night.' They shared a chuckle.

Oliver sniffed at them. 'Appropriate responses, please gentlemen. Fix your faces before we go in.'

Abrams spun round as the door opened, relief at seeing his brief, mixed with loathing for the police officers.

Dan smiled once more as he settled himself at the table and began the recording. 'So, Mr Abrams, shall we start all over again? And, shall we have the truth this time? Because if you try to pull the wool over our eyes this time, well, I guess it will go very badly for you, indeed.'

Abrams licked his lips and tried to catch the solicitor's eye. 'Maybe we could do a deal, if I agree to co-operate?'

'Oooh, no. Too late for deals. We've got the lot, DVD's, recorders, the Latvians, the children, the paedophiles… What kind of deal could you offer us?' Dan grinned and shook his head.

'Mr Abrams,' said DCS Oliver, 'What we want from you is a full and frank confession, and then we will place you in the hands of the legal system, which has the reputation as being the best in the world for offering a fair trial to anybody, regardless of what they may have done.' Then she smiled, too. 'Let's make a start, shall we?'

The buzz in the station seemed to be pouring out of the walls. The gossip machine had got cracking as soon as Dan had charged Jamie May, and he and Oliver had promised the gathered news teams a conference before the day was out. They had stoutly refused to be bullied into giving anything away except that they had the murderer, and all those involved, under arrest.

There was cheering and whooping as they walked back into the incident room. The whole team seemed to be back from their jobs, wherever they had been sent earlier in the day.

Oliver took Dan by the elbow and walked him towards a corner.

'Enjoy this feeling, Dan. Tell them how brilliant they were and make sure you buy them all a drink. You don't get many double results in this job. I'll get started on your disciplinary interview, it should go better for you after such a good result.'

She looked at his stricken face. 'Trust me, it'll be fine. Oh, and take a week or so off, so your feet get better, to give me time to sort things out. I'll call you in as soon as I can fix a date. I'd better get this confession processed.'

She gave him a smile, gave the assembled team a thumbs-up, and headed alone up to her office, back held straight as usual.

Dan looked around the room, crowded now with files and paper and people and waited for a semblance of quiet. He perched in his usual place on the edge of the table. Slowly, the team put down their papers, looked up from their computers and focussed on him.

'You were fantastic,' he said. 'I could not have done this without you. I feel lucky and proud to have you all in my team, especially when I act like an arrogant twat.' He nodded towards Sally Ellis. 'Luckily, I've got Sally to put me straight, and I will listen in future, Sal, or you have permission to beat me over the head with the Code of Conduct.'

Cheers rounded the room.

'Drinks are on me tomorrow night. Not tonight, because I don't know about you, but for some reason, I'm a little knackered. Oh,' he added, 'and get a late night pass – we need to give Ian a proper send off and no-one escapes sober.' He swivelled his eyes towards the corner desk. 'Yes, PC Singh, I am looking at you.'

'I don't drink, sir,' she replied, and looked up at him under her eyebrows, brown eyes giving nothing away. 'Just kidding- a large vodka tonic will do nicely. I can almost taste it now,' she sighed. 'And can we go for a curry first, just so you blokes don't get bladdered too early in the evening and have to be driven home by your long-suffering wives?'

Dan laughed. 'You'll do, Lizzie. You'll do very well. Lizzie is in charge of Friday night, folks. Get the kitty started.

'Right, do your reports first, then bugger off home. I'm off with the Super to talk to the press.'

'At least you didn't sustain damage to your face in the carrying out of your duties, boss,' said Bill Larcombe. 'Couldn't have you on the telly not looking your best.'

He and Ben Bennett, sitting next to each other as usual, shook their heads in unison. 'Wouldn't do.' They clanked their mugs and saluted him. Everybody else cheered and wolf-whistled.

Dan felt a flush begin to rise up from his neck. 'Alright, leave it out,' he said. But inside he glowed. 'Let's put this to bed before we put ourselves there, eh? Sally, I want the results of the Jenna Braithwaite interview ready on my desk for when I get back. Half an hour, okay?' And with that he escaped to the relatively normal world of the press conference.

Sally had wound up the interview with Jenna Braithwaite as soon as she heard about the arrest and charging of Jamie May. Regarding the murder of her sister, she had gathered enough from the weeping girl to make a witness statement that would stand up in court.

She would leave it to the Child Exploitation and Online Protection team to get the statement they needed for the prosecution of the paedophile ring. That would be a much longer process. Jenna had a strong sense of loyalty towards those who had abused her, and as yet, little understanding of why what they had done to her, and to many other children, was so wrong.

Time and counselling would help, she supposed. Although, she was not very hopeful for Jenna as she had seen too many young girls get a taste for the life before drug addiction and disease finished them off.

Sally left Jenna with her father and the social worker. A lot of talking would need to be done to heal some old wounds in that family.

Quietly, before she left the room, Sally had handed the girl her mother's phone number. It was up to Jenna now.

She turned to her computer and opened a fresh page.

Bill Larcombe caught Dan as he entered the Incident Room half an hour later.

'Pelakais and Sarkov are going to co-operate fully with the police enquiry, in return for asylum for them and their families, and the Latvian police are sending a senior officer to help process the case against Akis, who looks like she will survive.' He chuckled. 'The Latvian officer was dead chuffed when I mentioned that we'd captured Irina Akis. They've wanted to close down her father for years, and now they might have the opportunity. Seems like Pavels Akis has police and ministers in his pocket, and runs his business like the Mafia - drugs, money-laundering, child and Internet porn you name it. If it's filthy, he's got his hand in it.' Bill shuffled the notes in his hands and looked down at them. 'Good job, boss.'

Dan nodded his thanks as Bill added the report to the Mind Map. At least one part of this investigation had gone well, and everybody who mattered was safe. Part of him wished they had killed Irina Akis. He knew she would cause trouble when they tried to deport her.

He surveyed the map on the whiteboard. All the links had been there from the start, but it was pulling together the strands that made him love this job, even when he was hating it.

He headed for Sally's desk. She'd finished her report and had left it for him with a KitKat balanced on top. He unwrapped the chocolate bar and ate it two fingers at a time while he scanned the transcript of the interview with Jenna Braithwaite. Maybe his next case might give him time to eat a proper meal every now and then. They can't all be so frantic, he thought. Can they?

Reluctantly, he drew his phone from his pocket and perched on the edge of Sally's desk. No time like the present, he thought, and thumbed through to his mum's number. At least I can give her some good news with the bad.

Chapter 41

Date: Saturday May 6th Time: 11.00 St Michael and All Angels, Church Street, Heavitree, Exeter

The funeral of Detective Chief Inspector Ian Gould took place in St Michael and All Angels Church, close to where he and Marilyn had lived for over thirty years. Dan arrived early and stood under the old yew tree that legend said was where the last witches were hanged in Exeter. He didn't believe it. The tree was too small to be that old. He stood back as dignitaries and the press trampled over old graves and crushed spring flowers as they made their sombre way inside. He liked the solid stone and square tower. He hoped Marilyn found some comfort in its cool stillness.

The funeral car came last of all. Dan put his head down and slipped inside as the hearse drew up to the doors of the church. He found a space towards the back of the church, and listened to the organist playing something that sounded modern. Although not a believer, nor a churchgoer, Dan liked being in churches. The faintly musty smell and the stripes of dusty light through the long, ornate windows evoked something in him that he didn't really have words for. It was the same with church music. He'd loved going to concerts in churches with his parents when he was young. Choral music gave him shivers in a way that the blues and rock he favoured nowadays never could.

An honour guard of uniformed officers from the Exeter Police Service stood at the end of each pew and saluted as the coffin passed, followed by the family and the vicar. Dan felt his emotions, so carefully battened down, begin to break free.

He wanted forgiveness, but it wasn't on offer from anyone in that building. He scrubbed at his eyes and examined the stained glass panel to his right until his breathing settled down.

He spotted Julie Oliver at the front near the family, looking serious and commanding in her black uniform. She stood to give the eulogy and managed to raise several laughs and many tears with stories of Ian's long career in the force.

Marilyn Gould was flanked by her pregnant daughter and son-in-law. Dan had still not been able to speak to Marilyn. The hatred in her eyes was unrelenting, and he didn't know what he could say to her to make it better. In her eyes, the death of her husband would always be his fault, and he would have to live with that.

Assistant Chief Constable Pallister was there. In the front row, of course, standing next to the local MP. He'd obviously spotted a photo opp. Bill and Ben were to his right, with their wives. Lizzie Singh was standing with Sam Knowles and Adam Foster a couple of rows in front of Dan, their crisp and still-new dress uniforms shining black and silver in the barred light seeping into the shadowy side of the church.

He craned his head to the right, looking for Sally, and registered a wheelchair parked in the aisle before he realised it was Chas Lloyd, there with her parents. Mr Lloyd, a lay preacher, sang all the hymns with a lusty verve and prayed as loudly as the vicar. Chas flicked Dan a swift glance, but dropped her head before he could acknowledge her. He didn't mind her being there. It was good that she wanted to pay her respects. She would have her whole life to atone, poor kid.

Campbell Fox stood at least a head above everyone else in the church. He dabbed his eyes and blew his nose at each hymn and prayer, and Dan felt the clutch of shame round his heart once more. He would be a better policeman from now on. He would.

From behind him, he heard the sound of a small child arguing with its sibling, and the urgent, quiet shushing of a parent. He realised that Sally had brought her family, but had positioned herself for a quick exit near the rear door if they became troublesome. For a moment, he felt a pang of envy for her normal family life.

Finally, his gaze came to rest on the shining gold head in the row in front of him. Claire Quick sensed that he was staring at her and looked round, giving him a small smile of sympathy. He had no idea why she had wanted to come to the funeral, but he was glad she had. He thought that maybe, if he was lucky and didn't make a total tit of himself, she might agree to go out for a drink with him sometime. That thought carried him through the rest of the service.

The service continued until at last the coffin was slowly wheeled down the aisle towards the waiting hearse.

A ripple of soft sobs echoed around the church as the congregation stood to see Ian Gould pass with his family trailing behind.

The wake was to be held in Ian's favourite pub, The Barn Owl, but Dan wasn't intending to go, he knew he wouldn't be welcome.

With quiet insistence, Dan's phone vibrated in his pocket. He lifted it out and put it to his ear as unobtrusively as he could. It was Sergeant White.

'Sir?'

Dan watched Claire leaving the church. She turned, waved and gave him a little questioning smile.

'Sir? Are you there?'

Dan waved back and, indicating the phone, shook his head and smiled, shoulders lifting into a shrug. Claire made a 'call me' gesture and his heart sang as she walked out alone into the sunlight.

'Yes, I'm here, Colin. What can I do for you?'

White sounded relieved. 'Some idiot teenager is shooting at passers-by with an air rifle. Refusing to put down the weapon. Has your sick leave finished yet, and if so, could you come back to the station straightaway, as there doesn't seem to be any bugger about?'

Acknowledgments

Thanks to my lovely husband, who supplied me with enough biscuits, tea and gin to complete this novel. Thanks also to the bunch of dear friends who read the early drafts and made such useful comments and recommendations, I couldn't have done it without you. Thanks to Andrew Vernon, who checked out the police procedure, and agreed that a bit of poetic licence was entirely necessary. Finally, thanks to the team at Bloodhound Books for taking me on – here's to many more!

Printed in Poland
by Amazon Fulfillment
Poland Sp. z o.o., Wrocław